The Everett Exorcism

World of Shadows

Book I

By

Lincoln Cole

Published by Lincoln Cole, Columbus, 2017
Lincoln@LincolnCole.net
www.LincolnCole.net

Cover Design by M.N. Arzu
http://www.mnarzuauthor.com

Table of Contents

"Submit yourselves therefore to God. Resist the devil, and he will flee from you."

James 4:7

Prologue

"Come out, come out, wherever you are!"

Father Paladina knelt in his uncomfortable position beneath the staircase, eyes closed and struggling to control his breathing. Each gasp sounded like the cracking of a tree branch, and he couldn't fight down an occasional sob of terror. His heart beat in his ears, and his veins seemed about to burst open.

"I can smell you, Priest. I know you didn't run far. Where are you?"

The voice came from upstairs in the local priest's office. Niccolo couldn't remember a time in his life when he had been so on edge and afraid. It felt like a sickness in his stomach, as all of his muscles tensed simultaneously. It made his body shake, and he worried that he might throw up at any moment.

"We both know how this will end. If you come out now, I'll do it quick. If you make me come and find you, though ..."

Niccolo struggled to control his breathing as hot tears ran down his cheeks. He reached into his front-right pocket for the single item he kept there. His rosary, which he held between his fingers and pressed against his lips, praying as hard as he could for the strength to deal with whatever was happening to him.

Not to overcome it, though. Part of him—if he were honest, a *large* part—knew he was about to die alone in this church, and the only thing he prayed for was the strength to die well.

After all, right now, not only his life hung in the balance: so did his everlasting soul.

"This basement has no exits. I know this church. This is *my* church. Not yours," the man—if still a man—said from just upstairs. "I never thought I would actually get to kill a priest here. This is delightful!"

What is he waiting for? Niccolo wondered, in fear. Tim Spencer—or whatever controlled him—seemed to enjoy taking his time. Every muscle in Niccolo's body ached, and he had to fight to keep from sobbing. *Why is he doing this? Why is he waiting up there?*

It felt like he'd been hiding under the stairs forever, but it had probably lasted for less than a minute.

"We're having fun, aren't we, Priest?" Tim asked.

Niccolo couldn't contain a shudder, and the movement caused his shoulder to bump against one of the boxes behind him. The noise it made wasn't that loud, but to Niccolo, it rumbled like an explosion in the stillness of the basement.

If his pursuer heard, though, he didn't let on. Tim hummed to himself as he took his first step down the staircase. It creaked heavily underfoot, and Father Paladina winced when dust fell on his head.

Another step; the sound of the boot on the stairs sounded like a nail in the priest's coffin. Tim kept on coming, humming a tuneless tone, until the father could see muddy boots in front of his face.

"Priest? You know I'll find you. You can't hide from me."

Niccolo's whole body trembled, and the man had called it true. His hiding place seemed weak and pathetic now. As soon as Tim reached the bottom of the staircase, he would spy Niccolo. The priest had backed himself into a corner and had nowhere to go.

He shouldn't have stayed here at Saint Joseph's Cathedral alone. Should have gone with Father Reynolds to his home; splitting up had turned into a terrible idea, and one that might well cost him his life.

Father Reynolds's life, too, Niccolo realized. Jackson had gone home, but no doubt, whoever had sent this creature after Niccolo had gone after him as well. Father Paladina hadn't warned his friend of the danger. He regretted that, now. Jackson had no way of defending himself and knew nothing of the danger. Niccolo had led him like a lamb to the slaughter.

Tim Spencer reached the bottom step, and Niccolo could see his back through the gap in the risers. He had nowhere to run and no possible way to get out of this. It was over. He was about to die.

He should at least face his death head on.

As a servant of God.

Easier said than done, however. His body struggled against him. The priest forced his wobbly legs to move and rose from his crouched position, stepping out from beneath the stairs to confront his pursuer. Tim heard him and turned.

"Well, then. There you are." The man grinned and bared his teeth. He looked more feral than anything. "Well done, Priest. Found a little courage after all. Are you ready to meet your maker?"

Father Paladina opened his mouth to speak, to pray, but no sounds would come. His voice had abandoned him, and the words he'd studied and practiced for years caught in his throat.

"What? Cat got your tongue?" The man stepped closer to him and continued to grin that insane grin. "Let me get you started: Our Father, who art in heaven ..."

"Vile abomination, you don't belong here," Niccolo muttered.

"By the power of Christ, I compel you." He held up his rosary, hand still shaking. "In the name of the Father, the Son, and the Holy Spirit, I order you to leave this place."

The man stopped moving forward, his grin fading. "You think that will work? You, of all people, think that a prayer could compel *me* to just drop everything and leave?"

Father Paladina grew emboldened, feeling momentary strength while the words poured out of him. The demon was lying, and the words did have some impact. They gave Niccolo courage and knowledge that, despite everything, he did not stand alone. It had an effect, the power, the prayers, and his faith. They held the man at bay.

Maybe he *could* get out of this alive. If his faith held up.

"You do not belong here, creature. Return from whence you came. Through the power of Christ, I demand that you leave this holy place."

A long moment passed, the only sound Niccolo and the man's breathing. The priest held his rosary forth, hand unwavering and back tall. They stared at each other, locked in place, as the seconds ticked by.

"Silly priest," the man said, finally, his grin returning. "Don't you know you have no power here?"

The man reached up and grabbed the rosary in Father Paladina's hand. A sizzling sound filled the basement, as though flesh burned, and the priest could feel the metal heating in his hand.

Niccolo watched in horror when Tim stepped closer to him, pressing the cross against his forehead. The metal burned Tim's skin where it touched, and he burst into a wild and maniacal laugh.

Father Paladina released his grip on the rosary and jerked back in disgust. The man let it fall to the floor, a sizzling chunk of metal, and there it lay.

"How does it feel?" The man took another step closer to Father Paladina. Still grinning that sick and toothy grin. "How does it feel to know you are truly alone?"

He reached forward, grabbing the priest around the throat and squeezing. His grip felt like iron, crushing down on Niccolo's windpipe.

"How does it feel to know that God has abandoned you?"

Chapter 1

Two Days Earlier

Father Niccolo Paladina stepped off a bus and into the chilly Everett air in the middle of the small city. Though early in the afternoon, with the heavy cloud cover it proved difficult to determine an exact time of day.

To ward off a sudden burst of cold air that washed over him, he clutched his coat tight to his chest and felt his teeth chattering. He'd grown used to winter weather and unfavorable climes but certainly not a fan of them.

He picked up his suitcase and watched as the Greyhound shuttle pulled away from the curb, leaving him on the street alone. Then he felt thankful he hadn't packed a lot of luggage for this foray because it looked as though it would rain soon, and he didn't want to spend a lot of energy lugging too much around the city with him.

With any luck, he wouldn't have to stay here in the state of Washington for too long before making the trip back to his home in Italy. He hadn't been in favor of making this trip at all, but when orders were orders, and when his superior gave him a directive, he didn't dare refuse.

This made for only his second time coming to the States at all, and he wasn't much of a fan. From his education and studies, the priest knew that the States spread out across vast geographical zones and climates, but so far, he had visited Maine and Washington, and even though both looked beautiful and pristine in their own ways, he doubted he would willingly make a return trip. Maine felt too cold, and Washington had quickly turned out too wet.

With a sigh, he began his trek down the road in the direction he hoped led to his hotel. The bus stop stood only half a mile from the place, but he hadn't brought a map with him and didn't know exactly where to go. It was dark and dreary and the streets poorly lit, a fact which further frustrated him.

Niccolo had gotten sent here on behalf of the Vatican to meet with the local priest about Church business, and not the kind of business they wanted locals to know about, which meant it stayed only between himself and the priest, Father Jackson Reynolds.

Reynolds, a young man, had charge of a new parish—'new' to Niccolo meant anything built within the last hundred years—and had impressed a number of higher-ups during his education and training in Rome. Jackson went to the Pontifical Gregorian University in Rome and had excelled.

Supposedly, he'd made a brilliant student with a bright future ahead of him, but he had committed a critical mistake in the last few weeks. An error that had brought Niccolo here to this god-forsaken town when he could have been eating in a street market near his home: Jackson had gone over the local bishop's head and contacted the Vatican to request help. Such a mistake should cost the priest his position and livelihood, considering the transgressions committed.

At least, that made for Niccolo's opinion on the matter; not that anyone asked for his opinion.

To go over the bishop's head exhibited unacceptable behavior, much less requesting an exorcist get sent to the town. The requesting of an exorcist, or even an evaluation of demonic activity like this, meant a big deal: an order of events existed for situations like this, and a chain of command through which communications went. And attempting to bypass links in that chain eroded the fabric on which the Church's trust had formed, and the fact that Jackson's insolence had ended up rewarded by Niccolo getting sent to talk to him irked Paladina quite a bit.

Not enough to transgress on his own, however. Niccolo intended to investigate the situation that had brought him here to the best of his abilities, of course, but he also intended to straighten the priest out about how situations like this should work. By all accounts, Bishop Glasser was a reasonable man overseeing a few Parishes in the area, and if he didn't believe that the situation warranted Vatican attention, then it probably didn't.

Which meant Niccolo doubted he would find anything untoward within Father Reynolds's claims about demonic possession in Everett.

He walked past a two-story building with a sign on the front that read: Labor Temple, and then made a right-hand turn at the next corner. He was beginning to fear that he had gone in the opposite direction from the bus stop but didn't see anyone he might ask for help. No choice but to continue forward.

The worst part about his trip here? When he reported such news back to the Vatican, they would, no doubt, give the young priest a slap on the wrists and forget his transgression had ever occurred. In many similar cases, such a wayward priest would get significantly more than a slap on the wrist, but his powerful friends merely wanted him to get chastised for his mistake rather than dealt with harshly.

It bothered Niccolo but, to be honest, it remained none of his concern. The only reason it bothered him right now was that he felt exhausted, hungry, and cranky. Small droplets of rain pattered against his skin, and it concerned him that his jacket would get soaked before he made it to the hotel. Half a mile hadn't seemed so far to walk, but just now, he wished he'd simply paid for a cab. The only thing he cared about at this moment was checking into his room, finding food, and warming up for the evening.

He stopped walking and stepped under an awning when the rain suddenly came down in earnest, certain now that he had made a wrong turn at some point. Niccolo had glanced at his map on the bus, but he wouldn't consider himself familiar with the city by any means. Fairly sprawling, many of the streets looked alike. He set down his luggage and dug the map out of his pocket.

The wind whipped by every few seconds, flushing his long strands of black hair into his face and obscuring his vision. A frown creased his features as he brushed away his tangled mane. The cold rain ran down the back of his coat, wetting his skin. He had an umbrella packed in his bags, but the thought of digging it free only to be blown about by the wind didn't appeal much to him.

Focused on the map, he traced his finger across the streets and realized his mistake. He had turned too soon and gone a few blocks off-course. The good news was that he now stood only a short distance from his hotel and just needed to backtrack a little.

Carefully, he folded the map and slipped it back in his pocket before walking once more. He nodded politely at a passerby, who happened to be out, but the man refused even to spare a glance his way. He stared at the ground with a blank expression on his face, hurrying and leaning against the wind. This man, like Niccolo, just wanted to get out of the rain.

A few minutes later, he arrived at his hotel. A two-story brick building with faded red paint and a tired looking welcome sign out front. It looked old and worn and not at all aesthetically pleasing. He despised the exterior but found himself warming up to the place when he stepped inside the antechamber. It felt toasty and comfortable and appeared quite clean. For a moment, he stood just basking in the warm air, letting the water drip off him.

A red-haired woman sat on a stool behind the check-in counter with a magazine open in front of her. She stood when he approached, folding her hands in front of her on the counter, and smiled at him. She had long hair and dimples and looked just over five-feet tall.

"Yes? May I help you?"

"I have a reservation," he said, setting his bag on the carpet and pulling out his wallet. He removed his ID.

"Name?"

"Last name, Paladina. First name, Niccolo."

She looked at the book in front of her. "I don't have any reservations under that name. Are you sure you have the right place?"

He bit back his annoyance, reminding himself that he just felt tired and hungry. "Father Jackson Reynolds prepared the reservation, so it might be under his name."

She scanned again, taking an inordinate amount of time to look over two pages of names, and then nodded. "Yes. I have a room under Father Reynolds. Looks like it is reserved for three days with a note that it might need longer. Is it just you tonight?"

"Yes," he said. Three days would give more than enough time to handle his business, he hoped. In fact, he hoped to get done in a day.

The woman turned around and pulled a key from a wall of hooks. She handed it to him.

"You'll find your room on the second floor. Two-oh-nine. Do you need any help getting your luggage up the stairs? We don't have an elevator, unfortunately."

"Not unfortunate," he said, accepting the offered keys. "Quite fortunate, actually."

She tilted her head to the side, confused. "Sorry, what?"

Niccolo doubted she'd ever heard anyone show happiness at the idea of a hotel not having an elevator, but in his estimation, the idea of putting something so wasteful in a two-story building seemed a travesty. Exercise and health had gotten lost with the new age of innovation.

He clarified, "I have no issue with your hotel's lack of modern privileges."

"Ah. We sort of have a reputation in the area for being old-fashioned, and it's not usually considered a good thing. Would you like help moving your bags up to your room?"

"No," he said. "I have just the one bag. Thank you, though."

"Of course."

"Would it be too much trouble to ask that you set an alarm for me?"

"Of course not. What time in the morning would you like for me to set it?"

"This evening, actually. I've had quite a long flight and would like to take a nap, but I have a scheduled engagement I would rather not miss. Would seven-thirty be acceptable?"

"Of course," she said. "I'll set it in the system, and you will receive a call."

"Pre-recorded?"

She hesitated. "Yes."

"Would it be possible if a human calls me instead? I'd rather get woken by a person than a machine. I, myself, am considered rather old fashioned as well."

She pursed her lips, visibly annoyed and trying in vain to hide it. "No trouble at all. It will be after my shift ends, but I'll leave a note to have Donald call you."

"Thank you. I'm sorry to be such a bother."

She smiled her most pleasant customer-service smile, one which Niccolo could tell wasn't genuine. "No trouble. Will there be anything else?"

"I don't believe so."

"Very well, Mr. Reynolds. Please, enjoy your stay."

He thought to correct her that Father Reynolds was the man who'd made the booking, and that he was Father Paladina, but then elected not to. He was a precise man, but rarely petty.

Niccolo carried his suitcase up the stairs and down the hall to his room. The décor of the hallway appeared plain with a maroon color palette on the walls and carpeting that simultaneously attention grabbed and disgusted. The lights glowed soft and dim and very yellow.

His room seemed better, but not by much. The walls still sported an off-shade of red, and the carpet layered too thick, but at least it looked less ostentatious. On a cursory inspection, the bed appeared lumpy, and he found mildew in the bathroom. His only consolation came from the fact that he wouldn't stay here for long.

He set his luggage on an armchair by the window, checked the thermostat to make sure it was set appropriately, and then turned his attention to the bed. It looked old and worn out, and he couldn't help but imagine the thousands of previous guests who might have slept here. He wouldn't dare to sleep underneath the sheets, but perhaps on top of the blanket would prove acceptable.

Niccolo took off his shoes but left the rest of his clothes on before lying on top of the comforter. The bed felt softer than he would have liked, but in his present state of exhausted jet-lag, he didn't much care.

Paladina closed his eyes and laid his head back on the pillow. Rather quickly, he fell asleep.

A ringing sound from the bedside table next to him awoke Niccolo sometime later. The hotel room had grown considerably darker than when he'd first laid down, and it took him a few moments to gather his bearings.

Outside, rain pattered against the window, coming down in thick sheets and blanketing him in a constant lull of sound. He rubbed his face, pushing himself into a seated position, and then he rolled his body toward the sound.

It came from the room's telephone, which meant it was probably his wake-up call. He could hardly believe it had reached that time already, considering it felt like he'd only laid down minutes ago. He fumbled for it, missing the handle a few times in the darkness, before finally knocking it loose and onto the table. Then he picked up the handle, groggy, and held it to his ear.

"Hello?"

"Uh ... Mr. Paladina?"

"Father Paladina," he replied before he could stop himself.

"I was ... uh ... supposed to call you?"

"Was that a question?" He rubbed his face again.

"I had a note on my desk." The young man on the other end of the line sounded like a teenager. "It said to call you and wake you at this time. And, uh ... well, wake up, I guess?"

"And I have," Niccolo said. "Thank you."

Then he dropped the phone back onto the stand and collapsed back onto the bed. If anything, he felt worse from his short nap and wanted nothing more than to roll over and fall back into the comfort of sleep. The rain sounded gentle and relaxing, and the warmth of his lumpy bed seemed rather pleasant just now.

However, he had an engagement with Bishop Leopold Glasser that he couldn't afford to miss. Niccolo had called the bishop prior to his flight to Everett, hoping to get his take on the situation at hand and to explain his purpose for coming here. It would be improper to work behind the bishop's back, even if it were his duty on behalf of the Vatican, and he owed him at least the courtesy of explaining the situation in person.

Bishop Glasser had insisted they meet at his house, though Niccolo had remained unwilling to divulge the nature of his visit over the phone. He wouldn't speak of something so important over such a long distance, especially when he couldn't smooth things over in person. Paladina had no doubt that his business here would infuriate the bishop and undermine his authority; exactly what Niccolo didn't want to do.

Niccolo had, graciously, accepted the bishop's invitation to visit his home. So, he couldn't let himself fall back into blissful sleep on his lumpy bed and would need to get moving so that he wouldn't arrive late.

With a heavy sigh, the priest forced his legs over the side of the bed and stood, stretching out his tired body. He stumbled to the restroom, flicking on the light switch as he went, and splashed cold water onto his face. It helped a little, and he took a moment to study his reflection in the mirror. Tired bags hung under his eyes, and his hair looked wild and tangled, but otherwise, he looked acceptable.

Niccolo liked to think himself a handsome man, in his early thirties and dignified with a long face and striking black eyes. He kept his mustache trimmed and thin, wore his hair long, and spent a lot of time and effort maintaining his cultivated appearance, and knew he suffered from a modest amount of vanity, but it translated into confidence.

He enjoyed standing out in a crowd.

Finished using the facilities, he turned off the light and headed out into the main room to gather his shoes and dig his umbrella out of the luggage. He had, of course, packed one for this sojourn, much the same as if he had been heading to England or somewhere else where it often rained, and he would have felt surprised if he hadn't found occasion to use it on this trip. The priest hadn't dreamed he would need it earlier, though, and didn't intend to get caught off-guard a second time.

A few minutes later, he found himself back out in the rain in front of the hotel. A car sat waiting next to the curb for him, a black limousine, and the driver stood next to the passenger door with his arms folded. He wore a poncho, but he looked soaked nevertheless. No doubt he had stood waiting there for some time for Niccolo to show.

The man had the practiced and blank expression of someone long used to serving important men without letting his emotions through. He didn't speak, but instead, opened the door and allowed Father Paladina to slide in to the backseat.

A moment later, they wove their way through the city of Everett, Washington, and beyond, heading for the private residence of Bishop Leopold Glasser. The bishop lived a few miles outside the city, and by all accounts, he had an impressive home.

Chapter 2

The trip to Leopold Glasser's countryside estate took longer than Niccolo expected. The bishop lived far outside the city in a thickly wooded area. Trees surrounded them in all directions and flanked the roadway like a tunnel. The estate backed up against a Federal park that extended for dozens of miles.

Father Paladina felt certain the drive would have looked beautiful in the day with the sun out to light their way, but traveling through the forest at night turned out quite eerie and made him uncomfortable. The trees seemed to close in around them, tall and spindly without their leaves.

Bishop Leopold Glasser's estate outside of Everett appeared ostentatious and expensive; two floors and many thousands of square feet. The sight of it made him cautious about the bishop. Niccolo disliked such wasteful spending, yet many clergy leadership participated in the activity. Such men spent more effort propping up their station and creating an image than they did on solving problems in their communities.

They did, however, work as servants of their communities. The more distance they put between themselves and the people they served, the more difficult it became to understand what such people needed.

An unfortunate, yet forgivable, offense.

The rain stopped at some point during the drive; something of a relief. The air had a pleasant and earthy taste to it when he stepped out of the town car and onto the gravel driveway. He breathed deeply, enjoying the scents of nature, before heading up the steps toward the front entrance.

The door opened as he approached, and a butler met him. A tall and well-dressed man with hard eyes and an emotionless demeanor.

Wordlessly, he led Niccolo through the foyer of the home and upstairs. Leopold met him in an office on the second floor, but the first thing that greeted Niccolo was the smell of cigarette smoke pouring from the room.

The chamber appeared rich in its decor with soft cream-colored walls and gray carpeting. A fireplace spilled heat into the room, and an overhead fan sucked up a cloud of smoke as it wafted lazily across the ceiling.

Rich and ornate tapestries decorated one wall. They depicted historical events throughout the past millennia that had importance for the Church, including the Last Supper and a rather immodest representation of Joan of Arc that Niccolo disregarded immediately as tasteless.

Finally, Niccolo turned his attention to the bishop. Leopold Glasser seemed a short man with a trimmed black beard, and he had a bald spot at the top of his head. He held a cigarette between stained fingers, and a crumpled pack rested on the desk beside him. In his late forties, he'd started to turn gray, but not in a dignified way. Time had not been kind to him.

A young man sat in a nearby chair, reading a book. He was maybe fourteen years old with curly black hair and angular features. He looked up when Niccolo entered but didn't say anything. He frowned at Niccolo and then returned to his book.

Father Niccolo had heard a lot about Washington's Bishop, and very little of it flattering. Much of it, he assumed, came down to pure gossip—a favorite pastime at the Vatican.

In practice, Niccolo disregarded such rumors. He didn't like to cast judgment upon people he'd never met and preferred forming opinions of his own about people; however, he also acknowledged that rumors and prejudice, on occasion, held nuggets of truth. After surveying Leopold for only a few seconds, his first impression indicated that he wouldn't much like the man. He seriously doubted that the bishop could do much to change his opinion.

"Welcome," Leopold said when Niccolo walked into the room. He leaned heavily against his expensive wooden desk with a small smile on his face. "It is a pleasure to meet you in person finally, Father Paladina."

"Likewise," Niccolo said, striding over and shaking the smaller man's hand.

The bishop gestured his hand toward the young man. "This is Jeremy. He's been staying in my home for the past few weeks. Jeremy, please say hello to Father Paladina."

Jeremy didn't look up from his book. "Hello."

"Hello, Jeremy," Niccolo said.

"Run along now, Jeremy. I have much to discuss with Father Paladina, and I believe you have lessons to attend to anyway."

Jeremy flashed Niccolo a look of annoyance, but he did nod. He closed the book and walked out of the room, brushing rudely past Niccolo and into the hall. A few moments later and a door slammed shut.

Bishop Glasser turned his attention back to Niccolo. "I apologize. The child has been through much. He recently lost his family."

"No apology needed."

"I trust you had a pleasant journey?"

"Not exactly pleasant, but acceptable."

"I must confess, your presence here intrigues me more than a bit. On the phone, you told me little about why you planned to make this trip. It seems a long way to come just to have dinner at home; so, might I ask why you came all this way?"

Niccolo couldn't suppress his frown at the man's demeanor. Leopold got right to the point and in a mildly aggressive way, which gave another strike against him. Civility and pleasant conversation provided an important cornerstone of modern civilization. He would have greatly preferred discussing issues like this with a full stomach.

"The silence about the issue was intentional," Niccolo replied. "This is a rather delicate matter that should get attended to in person. Not over the phone."

"Oh? I trust it isn't anything too serious?"

"It pertains to one of the priests whose Parish you oversee. Father Jackson Reynolds."

A look of something—dislike, maybe—flashed across the bishop's face when Niccolo spoke the young priest's name. It disappeared almost as soon as it had shown, however, and the man's small and demeaning smile returned.

The bishop shifted to the side, dropped the butt of his cigarette into an ashtray on his desk, and then drew another one out of the pack with his teeth. He lit it, took a deep draw, and then, finally, turned his attention back to Father Paladina. He lowered himself into a seat across from Niccolo and pursed his lips.

"Ah, Father Reynolds. He is a dear friend."

"I was told he came to you a few weeks ago about a member of his congregation. An elderly woman, behaving erratically, and who he believed needed help."

The bishop frowned and waved his hand in dismissal. "He spoke of this in our last meeting. He believed the woman had experienced a possession and wanted me to request an exorcist from the Vatican to help her."

"Yet, you did not send his request along?"

"I went through my due diligence and looked into the matter personally. I gave his request all of the attention it deserved and met with the woman myself."

"Did Jackson go with you?"

"No, I went alone. I wanted to meet with Ms. Rose Gallagher without any preconceived notions or biases. After meeting with her, I did not agree with his conjecture."

"You didn't believe she was possessed?"

"Rose lives by herself and suffers from loneliness. She sees her family only rarely, and I admit, she seemed quite troubled when I met with her. Troubled but not possessed. I denied Jackson's request to pass the information to the Vatican and asked him to speak no further of the issue."

Niccolo nodded, pursing his lips. "The issue did not end there."

"I can see that."

"I've come here to present a full report on the situation and determine if Jackson's concerns should get looked into further."

"You're an exorcist?"

Niccolo squirmed a little in his chair. "I am. But, should I determine that the Church will get involved in this situation, they will send someone else to handle the exorcism itself."

"I see. I feared something like this might happen," Bishop Glasser said. "Jackson is a rather … persistent young man."

Niccolo could tell that the word 'persistent' hadn't come to the bishop's mind first. He also couldn't fault the man for his edge of anger—he would have felt furious, too, if one of the priests under his charge went over his head and attempted to supersede him on so important an issue.

"My duty is to search for evidence and report back without biased input from either of you," Niccolo said. "However, I thought it only dutiful to notify you that I will speak with Father Reynolds in the morning about these matters on behalf of the Church."

"It's a waste of time."

"Of that, I have no doubt. Nevertheless, I must oblige the young priest and investigate this issue. I intend to report everything I find to the Vatican as accurately as possible. As I am sure you can imagine, this puts me in a rather tricky position."

"One I don't envy." The bishop nodded. "Naturally, Jackson will ask you to speak with the old woman, and you will come to the same conclusion I did. She is a lonely woman who needs help, but not the kind of help that the Church can offer."

"My superiors believe that as well."

Bishop Glasser rose from behind his desk and walked over to a counter. It had various decanters on it filled with amber and brown liquids.

"Would you like a drink?"

"No, thank you." Niccolo stood too. "I don't partake."

The bishop poured himself a glass and took a long sip before turning back to face Niccolo. The expression on his face seemed one of poorly disguised frustration, tinged with something darker.

He held up the glass to the light, swirling the liquid.

"So, the Church sends an exorcist to dismiss the rumors of a wayward priest?"

"I didn't come here as an exorcist."

"Come now. Your reputation precedes you, Father Paladina. I know those whom you serve."

"I have been trained, but I have not sat in upon a true exorcism."

"Never called upon to serve God in that capacity?"

Niccolo frowned. "No."

"And why do you think that is?"

A moment passed in silence. Niccolo struggled to ascertain whether the bishop meant to insult him or not. He hoped that the bishop simply spoke out of ignorance. "An occasion has never arisen in which the Church has asked me ..."

He trailed off when a mocking smile spread on the bishop's face.

"No. It has nothing to do with *occasion* or *circumstance*. It is because demons *are not* real," the bishop said. "A fact which every priest worth his salt knows but none feel willing to admit. You know it. I know it. The Church knows it. Demons are an invention to scare lay people into giving larger donations to their parish."

Niccolo didn't respond immediately, but his blood seethed at the words. The bishop might be correct in his beliefs—Niccolo tended to feel torn on the issue—but it wasn't Bishop Glasser's place to speak openly about something like this. Certainly not to a practicing exorcist.

However, attempting to refute the ignorant man would prove a waste of time. A growing sect of the Church shared the bishop's opinion. It made for a sensitive topic, and one not often brought up in gatherings. The people who felt passionately one way or another about the existence of demons never got swayed easily.

Niccolo's opinion on the matter came down on the side that demons represented a darker part of humanity, much like the idea of heaven and hell. Demons represented a loss of control. Such a loss, even if only a perceived loss, could become devastating.

To personify them came down to design. Demons were human creations to help build symbolistic connections between the mundane and religious aspects of life. They inspired understanding and faith, and even if purely abstract, they also proved very real.

He didn't believe that *actual* demons existed in the world, which lived in hell, like many in the Church maintained. Niccolo did allow that demons served as a representation of the inner darkness within humanity itself. He had taken courses at the Vatican on exorcism and demonology and had come to realize that much of the teaching and process was about offering forgiveness to people who believed themselves unworthy of it.

That provided the job of an exorcist—to form an anchor for people lost at sea. He could offer forgiveness to the unforgivable and help people regain control of their lives.

Forgiveness, Father Paladina had learned, proved something difficult to come by. Some people believed they weren't worthy of it, and that they had no right to ask for such. His duty in his capacity as an exorcist was—or would be, considering that the Church had never asked it of him—to offer that unquestionable forgiveness and salvation.

In any case, they hadn't sent Father Paladina here to help lead this bishop out of ignorance. He had more important matters to attend to, and this visit only offered a courtesy.

A wasted one, but a courtesy nonetheless.

"Father Reynolds called upon the Church to ask for help with a sensitive situation, and whether or not you agree with his request, it remains our duty to support him in any capacity we might. I came here so that I can offer him assistance."

"For now," the bishop said, sipping his drink.

Niccolo tilted his head. "I'm sorry?"

"This isn't the first time Father Reynolds has acted outside the best interest of the Church, and I don't believe it will make for his last. At a certain point, his mistakes will surmount the power of his friends, and the Church will have no choice except to take action against our young friend."

"You believe he will end up excommunicated?"

"It seems a distinct possibility. The Church follows a certain set of rules and expectations. Continually stepping around those systems can result in negative repercussions."

Niccolo had assumed a small possibility that the bishop might take his visit personally, but now his concern became fully validated. If the bishop felt willing to go through the arduous process of having Father Reynolds removed from the Church simply because the priest had spoken up, then he must dislike the man seriously.

That, however, was none of his concern. It presented an issue—and a fight—for another day. He took a steadying breath and asked about dinner. From the expression on the bishop's face, it became clear that he had overstayed his welcome. Dinner seemed like a distant prospect now.

That didn't bother Niccolo much, though. In speaking with

the bishop, he found that he'd lost his appetite.

"Thank you very much for your time," he said, shaking the bishop's hand once more.

"No, thank you," Bishop Glasser said. "I truly appreciate your honesty in this matter."

"I merely wanted to ensure that we would have no hard feelings regarding the tenuous situation we both face."

"Of course," the bishop said, "and I would like to assure you that there are absolutely none."

His expression, however, made it clear that there would be hard feelings. Niccolo didn't much care. He hadn't come here to make friends, and he wouldn't shirk his duty to make Bishop Glasser happy. His task at hand ordained that he analyze the situation and make a determination for the Church about whether an actual exorcism would prove necessary.

If, in his dealings, he reported back that it would, then no doubt they would send someone else to deal with it. Someone more appropriate to handle a situation like this. That seemed perfectly fine for him.

In either case, his only goal tonight had been to warn the bishop about the investigation before it began so that the man didn't get blind-sided by his showing up in the city. Niccolo considered it a courtesy both necessary and polite, and now that he had taken care of it, he could move on to the rest of his concern.

"Then, if our business is concluded, I would like to get back to my hotel to rest for the night. I have grown exhausted from the trip."

"You won't stay for dinner?"

"I would rather not infringe upon your hospitality, and I am afraid I would not make for good company. I am simply too tired."

"I understand. My driver will, of course, drive you back to the city."

After saying this, Bishop Glasser rose from his chair and leafed through miscellaneous papers on his desk. The dismissal seemed clear, and Father Paladina wasted no time in heading out of the room and back down the staircase to the front entrance.

The butler led him outside and gestured his hand toward a waiting car. The cool night air washed over the priest, chilling him, and he wanted nothing more than to get away from the bishop's estate and back to his hotel.

✳✳✳

By the time Niccolo made it back to his room, he felt bone-weary and could barely stay on his feet. He'd thought he felt tired earlier, but this seemed something else altogether. The jetlag had gotten to him, and he felt as though he could sleep for a few days, if not weeks.

However, when he laid on the lumpy mattress and shut his eyes, he found that sleep wouldn't come. His mind spun, replaying the conversation with the bishop and pondering the circumstances that had brought him to this city.

The meeting hadn't gone at all how he'd expected. He didn't like the bishop, nor did he respect the man. The man's demeanor held something unsettling. An unpleasantness that seemed to permeate the entire estate, and the more Father Paladina ruminated on it, the more pervasive that feeling of unease became.

But that reflected his personal feeling about the man, not a professional one. He simply didn't like the bishop; however, that didn't make Leopold any less capable of performing his duties for the Church. Father Paladina couldn't let his personal feelings influence his investigation.

In either case, the time had come to meet with the man who had summoned him to Everett, Washington. He would meet with Father Jackson Reynolds in the morning at his church downtown. Then he could get the younger priest's perspective on the issue and start making some headway.

This initial meeting would give him the chance to discuss the matter at hand and introduce himself, and he hoped it would go better than his dinner engagement tonight had. He still felt hungry.

It would be important, he reminded himself, to stay neutral in the matter and examine the facts. He couldn't allow his dislike of the bishop to sway these dealings in any way.

Mostly because the bishop probably had it right. To be honest, he agreed with the bishop that, likely, there would be nothing here in Everett to find; certainly not a demonic possession. Father Reynolds, young and ambitious, had risked a lot to get him here, but the likelihood that any need existed for an exorcist in this town remained incredibly slim.

Maybe Niccolo would manage to convince Jackson to help Rose Gallagher seek more mundane assistance, perhaps through a therapist or other healthcare professional. That would provide the best outcome for everyone involved, including the woman. Then Niccolo's duty would shift from determining the need for an exorcism to smoothing over the rift between the bishop and the young priest.

That, however, didn't seem like an easy job either.

Satisfied that he would find an equitable resolution to the situation and get on a flight back to his home in Rome in only a few days, Father Niccolo Paladina finally found sleep.

Chapter 3

When Niccolo woke up the next morning, he decided to go for a walk to reach Saint Joseph's Cathedral and get a better sense of his surroundings. Everett seemed a small and quaint little city, comfortable and old-fashioned in a way Niccolo found appealing aesthetically.

The best part came from how quiet and remote it felt. The area reminded him of his neighborhood in Rome, and the more he saw of Everett, the more he liked.

It had dawned a beautiful morning, the veritable antithesis to the previous evening when he'd first arrived, and he felt well rested. The gloom and lethargy he'd experienced had washed away. The lumpy hotel mattress had turned out more comfortable than expected, or perhaps he had simply grown too tired to care. Either way, he felt great.

And ravenous, considering he hadn't eaten dinner the previous night with Bishop Glasser. His hunger would have to wait a while before getting sated, however, because he didn't want to arrive late. He'd woken later than intended and hadn't managed to sit and eat anything before heading to the church to meet with Father Reynolds. Niccolo considered the young priest a punctual man and dared not keep him waiting.

He strolled through the city, enjoying the sights and solitude of it all. Most of the locals appeared already hard at work or going about their daily lives, and so the streets seemed barren. The air tasted fresh after the night's rain, and everything struck him as relaxed and peaceful.

Saint Joseph's Cathedral, a small church, had barely enough seating to handle thirty guests during a sermon, but in the small town of Everett, Washington, it seemed rather large compared to the surrounding buildings. The front door, made of thick and heavy oak, had ornate patterning. It seemed a pleasant little parish with a lot of character and charm, similar to ones Niccolo had visited many times in his life.

The door stood cracked open, and Niccolo eased it aside and went in. He took a moment to survey his surroundings—he could learn a lot about a priest from the way he kept his church: clean or dirty, cluttered or neat, welcoming or foreboding? This church appeared clean but cluttered and had a warm and welcoming feel to it; all good signs of a priest whose door always stayed open to his congregation.

He found the young priest in the main hall of Saint Joseph's

Cathedral near the main entrance. Jackson looked up when Niccolo strode in, a smile widening on his face.

"Good morning," Father Reynolds said, standing up and dusting off his hands.

"Good morning to you as well," Niccolo said.

They shook hands, and then Jackson gestured for him to follow. The young priest, busy cleaning the hardwood floor of the cathedral with a mop and bucket, immediately pushed it aside.

Jackson Reynolds, a striking man, had dark skin and eyes and soft facial features. He stood a full head above Niccolo and would have looked intimidating, but the shy and reserved way in which he carried himself made him seem the exact opposite.

He wore his head shaved, and the only facial hair he sported formed a goatee around his mouth. He looked barely into his twenties, though with a maturity that greatly belied his age. Niccolo didn't know his exact age but guessed him at least a decade younger than himself. Just seeing the priest standing there made Niccolo feel old.

Within seconds, Niccolo could understand why Jackson had become so popular at the Vatican. He had an affable demeanor, unlike Bishop Glasser, and appeared strikingly handsome.

"How was your trip?"

"Quite long, but not unpleasant."

"I'm glad to hear it. I've made the trip to and from the Vatican, and it is no small feat."

"It isn't the worst trip I've made," Niccolo said.

"Traveled much? I should like to hear some stories later. Please, have a seat."

"No, thank you," Niccolo said. "I've sat enough these past few days and would like to spend some time on my feet. I saw you mopping the floor a moment ago. Don't you pay someone to clean the church?"

"I do. A woman named Amanda Lockett comes by a few nights a week to take care of the place and should arrive sometime tomorrow."

"Then, why are you mopping?"

Jackson frowned. "I detest having someone else clean up after me. I hired Amanda because she could use the help and is fantastic company, but I'm not opposed to cleaning up my messes. I always clean in the mornings before she arrives. At least to the best of my abilities."

"Doesn't that defeat the purpose of hiring someone else to clean?"

He shrugged. "She is a single mother and takes care of three children at home. I consider myself privileged to give her this opportunity to make a little extra income.”

Niccolo acquiesced. “It’s your parish.”

Jackson seemed rather embarrassed just by the comment, as though Niccolo had insulted him. That hadn’t been his intention, but he didn’t know how to say so without making the situation even more awkward. He chocked it up to Jackson simply being a timid man.

In any case, Jackson seemed like a sincere person. Niccolo had met many priests like him, the kind who took their jobs seriously but didn’t have large ambitions.

Not that it made for a bad thing. Niccolo didn’t have big ambitions either. He used to when a young man, but as he got older, his world-changing ideas had slipped away.

Life had a way of stealing one’s plans.

“I can sympathize,” Niccolo said. “Have you nearly finished with cleaning? Would you like some assistance? I’ve been known to use a broom a time or two in my life.”

“No, I believe it is quite all right. Everything seems clean enough now that I won’t feel embarrassed when Amanda arrives. I merely occupied myself until you got here.”

“I apologize. If I had known you would have to wait, I would have come early.”

“No, no. Think nothing of it. I couldn’t sleep and decided to come in early. In truth, I haven’t slept well in general lately. Not since ...”

He trailed off, showing himself unable or unwilling to voice aloud his thoughts about the possible possession.

“I understand,” Niccolo said.

“Would you prefer that we go into the back rooms to talk, or is this acceptable? I rarely have visitors during the week, but if you would prefer more privacy?”

Niccolo’s stomach emitted a low rumbling sound. “Ah, please excuse me. I haven’t eaten anything yet this morning and had hoped that you might know of a place where we could talk over breakfast.”

“Of course. The town has a diner close by that serves an excellent brunch. It only takes a short walk from here.”

“That sounds excellent.”

“Give me a moment to put the mop away, and I will be ready to go.”

Niccolo nodded, and Father Reynolds returned to his bucket. He pushed it across the floor and into one of the back rooms. Niccolo turned and glanced over the rest of the church. It had a tall ceiling and appeared well lit with natural lighting, but he found that he didn't much care for it. The pews seemed too tightly packed, and it didn't feel open enough for him. He liked spacious buildings, and this one struck him as too cluttered.

Niccolo had never had a parish of his own. His life hadn't gone that way—not in the cards, so to speak. A few opportunities had arisen over the years, but he had turned them down. In many ways, he regretted it as another offer seemed unlikely to come along. His life of service at the Vatican felt fulfilling and complete, and he had become an important member of the clergy, but a selfish part of him would have liked to head a church like this with a small parish of his own.

He couldn't bite back all of his envy for the young and well-respected priest.

A few moments later, Jackson returned, wiping his hands on a towel. He had grabbed an overcoat and umbrella, and with a nod, the two priests headed toward the door.

They walked out of the church and down the sidewalk to the west. The sun had peeked its way through the clouds and felt warm on his skin. Niccolo enjoyed the weather and remained grateful that they didn't have to use their umbrellas.

"It rains quite a bit, I've heard."

"That it does," Jackson said. "You came at exactly the wrong time. It's supposed to rain on and off for the next two weeks."

"Better than snow," Niccolo said.

"That'll come in about a month. We've had unseasonable warmth. Of course, this is also better than spring. That's when we *really* get the rainfall. This is more like light showers."

The diner that Jackson had spoken of turned out to lay only a few blocks away; a small building that looked like it had gotten dragged forth from the fifties. A bell tinkled overhead when they entered, and swing music played from speakers set around the ceiling. Niccolo recognized the tune as *In the Mood*. The music played loud enough to hear in the background but not too loud to interfere with anyone's conversation.

They arrived after breakfast and before lunch. The diner seemed mostly empty, with only a quarter of the tables and booths occupied. Most of the current patrons looked of the older generation and sat alone with newspapers, sipping on coffee.

A server came out from behind the counter and greeted them, a middle-aged woman, slightly overweight, and with ruddy cheeks and shaking jowls. She had dirty-blonde hair pulled back into a haphazard ponytail with loose strands going everywhere.

"Welcome to Patty's," she said to Niccolo as they walked

further inside. She nodded at Jackson. "Hello, Father Reynolds."

"Hello, Patty," he said, smiling at her.

"Who's your friend?"

"Father Niccolo Paladina, from Italy. He's visiting for the next few days."

"Oh? Vacation? Seeing the sights and sounds of our pretty little backwater town?"

"Just business," Jackson said, attempting—and failing—to sound nonchalant.

She tilted her head to the side but didn't pursue the issue. Instead, she offered her hand to Niccolo, and he shook it. It felt a dainty handshake, and he didn't dare squeeze her hand too hard.

"A pleasure to meet you," he said.

"How are you enjoying Everett?"

"I love it," he said. "It reminds me of all the best parts of home."

She smiled and turned back toward Jackson. "Just the two of you today?"

"Yes."

She picked up two plastic menus from a nearby counter and waved them in the air to beckon the priests forward.

"Right this way, gentlemen."

The waitress led them over to a booth by the window and set down the menus, prattling on to Father Reynolds about her patrons and how nice the weather was and how much she'd enjoyed his last sermon on Sunday. She spoke quickly and never seemed to stop for air.

Jackson listened to her politely, offering input where necessary. It seemed clear from Jackson's expression that they made for longtime friends and that this proved normal behavior for Patty.

The two priests slid into the booth, and Patty handed them each a menu. "I'll bring you boys some coffee," she said, and then disappeared toward the kitchen area.

Niccolo didn't drink a lot of coffee, but the waitress hadn't given him the opportunity to object. When he gave it some thought, it didn't sound like a bad choice. He still felt jetlagged, and it might help him get his bearings a little easier. Besides, Patty had gone already. Niccolo chuckled, and then opened up the menu, glancing over it at Father Reynolds.

"Quite the presence," Niccolo said.

"You do like coffee, right?"

He lied, "Of course."

"I could ask her for some tea instead."

Niccolo held up his hand. "Coffee is quite all right."

Father Reynolds nodded. "This restaurant has been here for thirty years. She knows everyone in town, and everyone knows her. She always informs me about what people think of my parish and the gossip around town."

"Seems useful."

Jackson shrugged. "Depends on the day. I don't need to know the personal business of the people who come to my church unless they step into the confessional booth or ask for my help."

Patty returned a moment later, setting down the drinks and taking their orders. Ravished, Niccolo ordered the largest breakfast on the menu, adding to it an extra serving of sausage. Personal experience told him that his eyes proved much larger than his stomach, but right now, his eyes made the decisions.

Jackson had eaten breakfast earlier, and so ordered only a strawberry yogurt. Niccolo assumed that he'd ordered even that tiny item only for politeness so that he wouldn't have to eat alone. A kind gesture, and one the visiting priest greatly appreciated.

They talked about pleasantries for the next several minutes until their food arrived. Nothing of substance, only light details about their lives and histories. Once the food got there, Niccolo tucked into his breakfast. The coffee tasted slightly burnt, and the eggs overcooked, but otherwise, it seemed a delicious meal. To be honest, though, the food might have been terrible, but he felt much too hungry to care.

Jackson took tiny swallows of his yogurt, waiting patiently for Niccolo to finish eating before speaking about anything of substance. They sat in a comfortable silence until the food had gone and the dishes got bussed away. Sated, Niccolo leaned back in his seat and tapped on his stomach.

"Delicious," he said, realizing that he had eaten far too much. He blamed it on his jetlag and the fact that he hadn't eaten dinner. "Just what I needed after the previous day's travel."

"You won't find a better breakfast in town," Jackson said.

Patty came back, refilled their coffees, and then disappeared once more. Jackson watched her go, and then turned to face the older priest once more. His mood changed visibly. He grew much more somber and focused before leaning in close to Niccolo and frowning.

"I assume the Church informed you about why I asked for someone to come."

"Naturally. I have full awareness of the circumstances."

Jackson paused, then said, "I meant no offense."

"I took none. They also informed me that you brought this to the Vatican in disregard of Bishop Glasser's express forbiddance."

Jackson hesitated, then said, "I brought it to the bishop's attention, but he refused to acknowledge the possibility that something diabolical might be happening in Everett."

"He feels that no issue exists here that needs examination, and that you have exaggerated the situation or possibly fabricated this in your mind."

"Why would I do that?"

"I don't know," Niccolo said. "Nor do I agree with his feelings on the matter. I came here to ascertain the truth and nothing more."

"I didn't lie about anything when I spoke to the Vatican officials."

"And I believe you. However, when two people come forward with differing opinions about what they believe to be the truth, it becomes my duty to determine the reality."

"This woman needs help."

"I don't dispute that, and even Bishop Glasser agreed that she needed help. However, I see a difference between needing help and needing an exorcism, and just bringing up the idea to the Church can prove dangerous. With any luck, we will manage to determine what form of help this woman needs, mundane or otherwise, and assist her in locating it."

Jackson frowned. "Did you see the movie I made?"

"No. What movie?"

"I handed it over to Bishop Glasser on VHS. He claimed that he'd passed it along to the Church for viewing."

"I neither saw nor heard of any such movie."

"I assumed as much. Please, follow me."

They stood, and Jackson put some money on the table to settle their bill. The walk back to Saint Joseph's Cathedral felt considerably longer than the outward trip. Niccolo, completely full, wanted nothing more than to climb back into bed and take a long nap.

Jackson led him into a back room of his church, an office of sorts with a desk and old furniture. Like the church itself, it seemed cluttered. A television bracket hung on one of the walls, and Jackson walked over to it and fiddled with the dials and cords. Niccolo watched him working for a moment, and then settled onto a brown leather couch along the opposite wall and yawned, folding his hands over his lap.

"I kept a copy," Jackson said, digging through a stack of VHS tapes on the ground beside the television. "Just in case. I didn't think I would need it, but now ..."

"You said you gave one to the bishop?"

"Yes. I showed it to him, and then gave him what he thought was the only copy. He said he would send it to the Vatican for follow-up analysis, but it seems he never did."

"What do you have on the tape?"

Jackson didn't respond. Instead, he slid one of the tapes into the VCR and turned on the television. The crackling noise of static filled the room.

"Three weeks ago, I spoke with Rose Gallagher at her home on Richmond Street. I managed to record this."

He pressed the play button and took a few steps back from the setup. Niccolo watched as the screen came to life. Low resolution, the picture proved grainy, and he found it difficult to make out details, and the screen shook. Wherever Jackson had recorded, it seemed dark, and the video kept cutting out.

On the screen, an elderly woman sat in an armchair in what looked like a living room, rocking back and forth. Her face remained in shadow, and her hands lay on the armrest. A wheezing noise sounded like breathing, but little else came over the audio until Jackson spoke.

"In the name of the Father, the Son, and the Holy Spirit, I compel you to come forth." Jackson's voice came through the tinny television speakers. His speech wavered and trembled, and his words seemed barely enunciated. Whenever he had recorded this, Jackson had felt terrified.

A moment passed, and nothing happened. The old woman kept rocking in her chair, making that wheezing sound as she breathed.

Niccolo stood and walked closer to the television, squinting and trying to make out what happened on the screen. It appeared so dark and out of focus that he could barely tell what the room looked like. That wheezing sound held his attention and filled him with both disgust and dread, though he couldn't explain why. A few feet away from the screen, he stopped, watching intently.

"I compel you forth, demon," Jackson said on the recording. "What is your name? Speak your true name. Through the love of Jesus and the Virgin Mother, I command you to speak your name."

The old woman laughed, a deep and throaty sound, guttural. The sound sent a shiver of fear up Niccolo's spine. It seemed inhuman, wrong, and horrible.

"You have no power here, Priest. This vessel is mine. Go back and play with your toys."

"Out, vile creature. Leave this woman in peace."

The woman leaned forward. Niccolo leaned toward the screen, trying to see her face, but it remained hidden in shadow. He could see her eyes, though, and they glowed red.

"This woman is mine. You will not take her from me. You are nothing more than a pest attempting to stand in our way."

The video showed the dim lights in the room flicker. Father Reynolds chanted a litany, praying to God for strength, but the woman only laughed, leaning back in her chair.

"I will kill you, Priest. I will cut you open and spill your guts on the floor as you watch."

A moment later, the footage ended. Niccolo let out a breath of air he hadn't realized he'd held, shaken by the video more than he would have imagined.

"That was when I left. I ... I knew I shouldn't have gone there, but I didn't want to abandon her. I brought that video to Bishop Glasser to ask him to look at it," Jackson said, a touch of defeatism in his voice. "I could not help her, and I thought, maybe, the bishop could."

Niccolo frowned down at the frozen image on-screen. "This footage ..."

"I know," Jackson said. "It isn't terribly convincing but is all I have."

"It is dangerous."

"For the Church? I haven't shared it with anyone except the bishop. I wouldn't dare to release something like this publicly."

"Not the Church. For you," Niccolo said. "At best, this footage shows you harassing an elderly woman in her home."

"At worst?"

"It shows you attempting to interact with and exorcise a demon without Vatican permission. You have no training in such affairs, and you should be aware that such is not acceptable behavior from an untrained clergyman."

"I merely tried to—"

"What you *tried* to do is irrelevant," Niccolo said. "All you've achieved, quite possibly, is to get yourself excommunicated from the Church."

Chapter 4

A stunned silence followed Niccolo's words while Father Reynolds attempted to absorb what the older priest had said. Niccolo remained quiet, allowing the gravity of his words to sink in before continuing the conversation.

The young priest said, "I wasn't ... I didn't think ..."

"The bishop might have saved your career by not passing this tape on to the Vatican. Had this reached my superiors, I would, likely, have come here with an entirely different agenda."

Niccolo exaggerated; the tape itself looked unconvincing and made it difficult to draw any solid determinations. If it ever got brought before Church leadership, it would get dismissed as unreliable evidence and most likely a hoax. However, he didn't mind exaggerating the situation because it helped to drive home his point that Jackson had made a tremendous mistake.

He tried to make Father Reynolds understand the gravity of what he dealt with. Demon or not, an untrained priest shouldn't handle this situation alone. He didn't have the proper education on such matters, nor the authority; two mistakes that could cost him everything.

The real question came down to this—now that Father Paladina had seen the tape, did it change the circumstances of his visit here? His duty dictated that he report it with all due haste to his superiors, both because the bishop had withheld it and also that it showed Jackson disobeying their express orders. Father Reynolds had behaved carelessly in more ways than simply going over the head of his superior, and it could end up costing him dearly.

Niccolo decided, for now at least, to withhold judgment on the matter. He wouldn't report it—yet—he still had a job to do, and this transgression would need to wait.

"I *have* studied," Jackson said quietly.

"Unless you've studied exorcism and demonology at the Vatican under the tutelage of other exorcists, you should never attempt such action under *any* circumstances. It is dangerous and foolish and could cost you not only your career but your everlasting soul."

"I didn't think—"

"No, you clearly didn't," Niccolo said. Then he softened his expression and tone and continued, "You proved unable to compel any demon forth from the woman because there is *nothing* there to compel."

"What do you mean?"

"I mean that this woman is troubled, but not by a spirit or demon."

"You saw her."

Niccolo shook his head. "The Church receives thousands upon thousands of reported cases annually regarding demonic possession just like this. Incredibly few—and by some Church estimations, none at all—ever prove to be real cases needing the attention of an exorcist. Do you know what this involves in most cases?"

"What?"

"Mental illness. Almost every situation like this boils down to simple mental illness coupled with terrible circumstances or social anxieties. This woman needs help, but not the kind that the Church can offer."

"You heard her in the video," Jackson said, and a look of pleading settled on his face. "She spoke words in some language I don't understand."

Niccolo kept his face stoic, though he had to admit that some truth lay in what Jackson said. It had sounded like the woman had spoken another language, but it remained impossible to make out on the distorted tape. An old language, to be sure, but he couldn't take anything from the movie as evidence. Certainly, it didn't give enough to jump to any conclusions, and it would do no good to mention the possibility that Jackson might have it right and increase the young man's paranoia and fear.

"I will admit that she made strange noises, but it is difficult to tell what she tried to say, if anything. We cannot know the situation, nor the context, from this movie alone."

"I was there."

"Which only proves that you have a bias and a stake in the evidence," Father Paladina said. "And, you felt afraid and wouldn't have thought straight at the time. Thus, jumping to conclusions would prove both rash and dangerous."

Father Reynolds looked unhappy with what Niccolo told him. He appeared both annoyed and frustrated and, doubtless, he felt surprised that the tape had had this effect on Niccolo. It hadn't turned out the way he would have expected.

Jackson shook his head. He grew agitated. Niccolo would need to steer the young priest away from focusing on this tape for his own sake.

Jackson said, "I don't intend to jump to conclusions. I do want to help this woman through a terrible situation. Isn't that what we're supposed to do? The Church wants us to take care of the people in our congregation, doesn't it?"

"Of course. However, it remains important that we only give help when asked for and necessary."

"She needs my help."

"Yes, she does. You could have taken her to a mental hospital, and the Vatican would have paid her bill, had that been your request."

"She doesn't need a mental hospital. She needs an exorcist."

"You overstep," Niccolo said in a flat tone. "That is neither your call nor your judgment to make. This should have gone through the bishop."

"I did, and he shut me down."

"Then you try again."

"He never would have approved it, no matter how many times I asked. I waited for weeks, only to find out that he never even passed along my request."

"He has that prerogative. He is the bishop, not you. You said you showed him this tape. He watched it and refused to pass it along. That is for the best, but you seem to feel that there is something more to it."

"I am telling you that this is legit—"

Niccolo said, "I choose to believe that this tape is a fake. This was just a humorous thing you put together for my amusement, but one in which you never intended to show to anyone outside of this room. Is that correct?"

"But I didn't! It isn't—"

"Because," Father Paladina said in the same flat tone, "the alternative would amount to you attempting to communicate and deal with a demon, for which you have no training or authorization. If *that* were the case, I would have to report it to the Vatican, which would have you excommunicated."

He paused, staring pointedly at Jackson and pursing his lips.

"Luckily, that is not the case, correct? This just comes down to a humorous fake. Would this offer an accurate assessment of the situation?"

Jackson leaned back in his seat, frowning.

Niccolo waited patiently, giving him the opportunity to weigh his options and either accept or decline the olive branch. If Jackson stood his ground, he would go through with his threat, but he didn't want to end the young man's career over a mistake like this.

Finally, the young priest let out a sigh and nodded. He took a seat on the other end of the brown couch and waved his hand in dismissal. With great effort, Jackson managed to get himself back in check and calm down.

"Of course. I apologize that the tape didn't seem that *amusing,* but I did the best I could under the circumstances."

Niccolo nodded. "Think nothing of it."

"What happens next?" A note of resignation laced Jackson's voice. He looked down at the table and folded his hands in front of his face. "Is that the end of your visit here?"

"Not at all. That concludes my business dealings with you on behalf of the Vatican, but I also came here to speak with you and determine if we have a situation requiring an exorcist in this town. Next, I will go and speak with the woman, Rose Gallagher, and determine if anything exists here worth looking into in Everett, Washington."

Jackson looked up, surprise on his face. "You will?"

"Absolutely. I had hoped, in fact, that you might accompany me and serve as my guide while I remain here? You know the town better than most, and I would greatly appreciate your *unbiased* company."

Father Reynolds smiled in relief. "Of course. When do you want to leave?"

"Now, I believe. I would like to look into this issue as soon as possible so that I can report back accurately to the Vatican. That is, of course, if that works for you, and providing that we do, indeed, find Rose at home?"

"Most definitely. I have a few things to attend to, but it should only take an hour or two, and then I will be ready to go. Would you like for me to give you a ride?"

Niccolo smiled. "I'd hoped you would ask."

"Great. I'm going out, so I can drop you off somewhere. Would you like to wait here or at your hotel?"

"The hotel would be marvelous."

✳✳✳

Once he had made it back to his room, Niccolo took some time to pray. He knelt in the corner of his room—the cleanest one he could find—and beseeched the Lord for guidance.

The tape Jackson had shown him had bothered him quite a bit more than he had felt willing to let on while he talked with the young priest. He had seen many such videos in the past, mostly at the Vatican, but never quite like this. Jackson had faced off against a deranged woman, and something about her demeanor left Niccolo feeling anxious and scared.

A vast difference lay between a real situation and a Vatican tape. The tape had shown Jackson, a real person that Niccolo had met, speaking to a real member of his congregation, and something about that made it all the more visceral.

For definite, though, it didn't mean demonic possession. It just meant something had gone terribly and horribly wrong with the woman. Jackson had never studied to become an exorcist, which meant he had no idea how to deal with such a situation.

Niccolo had spent his entire life studying and learning about demonology and possession, but never once had he seen an exorcism in person. Everything came from a second-hand account, and if this were a demon, then Jackson already had more experience with the real thing than Niccolo.

That, however, seemed an unlikely situation. Demons, if they existed at all, proved incredibly rare and never showed up without a purpose. What purpose could one possibly have out here in the small town of Everett, Washington?

No, it seemed much more likely that the tape just showed a struggling woman dealing with a difficult situation in her life and nothing more.

At least, Niccolo chose to tell himself that as he knelt in his room and prayed for guidance. This just came down to a woman seeking help and guidance.

***

Father Reynolds called a short while later to say that he was running late and would come back to pick him up in another hour. Niccolo had grown hungry again and headed out in search of food. The part of town he stayed in seemed empty, though, and after some time walking, he found himself back at the corner diner to which Father Reynolds had taken him.

He didn't know the town well enough to search out any other options and felt too tired and hungry to continue exploring. The breakfast had proven acceptable, and he hoped for a repeat with his late lunch.

Patty remained on shift when he got there, and she remembered him from a few hours earlier. She smiled at him as she stepped out from behind the counter.

"Just you, Father?"

"Yes, thank you."

She seated him next to a window at a two-top table, and then disappeared back into the kitchen. He watched her go, and then turned to the menu she had dropped in front of him. This one looked different from the morning and had hundreds of options listed out. Only a few of them sounded appetizing. He stared at the menu, trying to decide what sounded good.

Or, if not good, then at the least, not disgusting.

He wished himself back home in Italy where he could have some simple street food with his friends. Oh, to have a nice bowl of soup and a salad, neither of which appeared on Patty's overloaded menu. Instead, everything looked deep fried.

In the end, he opted for a sandwich and cup of tea, careful to make sure she heard him this time, not wanting another cup of burnt coffee. He placed his order, and then settled back in his chair to look out the window and ponder his situation.

Part of him looked forward to meeting with Rose and resolving this situation, but another part felt leery about the entire thing and dreaded seeing her. The way her face had remained hidden in shadow, and her eyes. It felt like the images from the tape had burned into his mind, and whenever he closed his eyes, they became all he could see.

What if this situation did involve a demonic possession? He had met several exorcists over the years, and their time remained incredibly valuable to the Church. If he made the judgment call that they needed one of them out here in Everett—the first time he would make such a judgment in his career—then the situation would change dramatically.

When he reported back to the Vatican, he couldn't afford to get it wrong. Jackson believed that this was a demonic possession, but Niccolo would need to make his decision clearly and factually.

He would need to get a newspaper to see local stories and ask around town to see if any omens had occurred in the area. The demon—if one had turned up—would try to hide from him, so he would need to remain cautious and thorough in his investigation.

Jackson Reynolds's heart lay in the right place, and to be honest, Niccolo couldn't deny his slight feeling of concern regarding what he had seen on the tape. It had not necessarily convinced, yet certainly compelled.

He doubted the young priest would have dared to doctor the footage. It didn't seem like something Jackson might do, but it remained a possibility he couldn't discount. For that reason, evidence like this seemed so fickle. Still, even if Jackson hadn't tried to trick him, that didn't mean that it came down to a case of demonic possession. A whole host of other possibilities beckoned that could explain what had happened to this poor woman long before he got to demons.

The food arrived after only a few moments, and he found the sandwich greasy, cold, and entirely unappetizing. He swallowed a few bites and then settled back with his tea, taking small sips. He stared out the window, watching people flow past and absorbed in his thoughts. He still had twenty minutes or so to relax before he needed to get back to his hotel, and it only took a five-minute walk.

Lost in his thoughts, he didn't notice when Patty came back over to his table. She just stood there, staring at him without speaking. When he did notice her, she surprised him, and he shifted a little in his seat, causing him to blush.

Though she smiled, her expression looked blank. "Would you like another glass of tea?"

"No, thank you, I'm quite all right," Father Paladina said.

"How are you enjoying your time in Everett, Father?"

"Loving it," he said. "The whole city, at least what I've seen of it, feels rather ... quaint."

She nodded. "I love it here. It's so peaceful. Detached from the world, like our little corner of paradise."

For certain, he wouldn't have described it that way, but he didn't dare object. "How long have you lived here?"

"My entire life. I moved to Minnesota for a few years way back in my twenties, but I was born and raised up the road and found my way back."

He hesitated, deep in thought. Patty had lived here her entire life, so she would know a lot about the goings on. If anyone would have their finger on the pulse of a place like this, it would be her.

"Have you noticed anything ... strange happening in the last few weeks?"

She tilted her head to the side. "Strange? How so?"

He felt unsure how to explain demonic omens. Thousands of options offered themselves, and most of them obscure.

"Just something different. The weather, maybe, if it has been completely wrong for the season, or insects behaving erratically."

She laughed. "Insects?"

"Clustering or odd behavior. Maybe migratory birds started flying in the wrong direction recently, or odd smells showed up at different places around town. Just strange happenings."

"No, nothing like that."

He nodded. It had been a stretch, and he didn't feel at all surprised by her answer.

"Thank you."

"Why do you ask?"

"No reason in particular. Just some business I have, and I thought that maybe you might have heard things from your patrons."

"Church business?"

"Yes. Just some simple Church business on behalf of the Vatican. Would you mind bringing the bill?"

"Your money is no good here. A man of the cloth like yourself can eat for free anytime in my restaurant."

Father Reynolds hesitated, remembering that only a few hours earlier, Jackson had paid for their meal. He wondered if maybe her behavior came from prejudicial reasons and decided he didn't much appreciate her generosity.

"That's so kind of you, but I would much prefer to pay. I like to settle all my debts."

She shrugged. "Suit yourself. Father Reynolds said the same thing when I made him that offer, but he does get a discount. Would you prefer that?"

Niccolo hesitated, and then nodded. "That is acceptable."

"Call it an act of faith," she said. "I miss more Sunday sermons than I make, and this is my way of hedging my bets."

She pulled out a blank receipt slip, scribbled on it, and then handed it to him. It totaled far less than the meal should have cost, yet still more than he felt it worth. He pulled out his wallet and fished inside for a few bills.

"What's your opinion of Father Reynolds?"

"He's a good preacher. So kind."

"How does his congregation feel about him?"

"Most everyone loves him here. He's much better than the last priest we had, an old stuffy and gray bastard without a sense of humor. Plus, Jackson isn't too bad to look at."

"He's a man of God."

"I'm not."

Father Paladina only smiled. "That's good to hear. It's always nice when a priest fits so well with his congregation."

"There are some people who stopped going because he's ..." She looked uncomfortable.

"Black?" Father Paladina said.

She nodded. "But in the last few years, most of them came back. Skin color doesn't matter at all where God is concerned."

"So true."

"What about you? Where do you come from? Do you have a congregation in a town like this that you call home?"

"Alas, that never became a duty I had the privilege to undertake. My duty has always remained to the Vatican, and I never had the good fortune of looking after a parish of my own."

Patty nodded, smiling down at him. "Probably because of

your mother."

Father Paladina nodded his agreement, and then hesitated in confusion when the words sank in.

"Excuse me?"

"Your mother abandoned you and left you at the door of that Catholic orphanage in Italy, right? That filthy little place that never had any heat and always felt cold. Probably, you didn't get a congregation for yourself because your mother was a lying whore, and the apple never falls far from the tree. They wouldn't put the son of a whore like that in charge of a flock of people, now, would they?"

Father Paladina sat there, stunned and trying to process what Patty said. Flashes of his early life flitted unbidden through his mind; memories conjured up from a deep past that he never spoke of openly.

How could Patty possibly know about his mother?

The waitress nodded at him and left, walking away from the table and disappearing into the kitchen at the back of the restaurant. Father Paladina stood to follow her, thoroughly off-guard by her words as he tried to understand what had just happened. He wanted to follow her and question her and find out what she was talking about.

She had spoken correctly; he had gotten abandoned as a young child, but he'd never met his mother and didn't know her identity or why she'd left him. Moreover, how could she possibly know about his childhood and the years spent at the orphanage?

Why would she even care?

Maybe he had misheard her or jumped to conclusions about what got said. The words hung fresh in his mind, however, and powerful emotions he hadn't felt in a long time tainted them. She must have said something else than what he thought he had heard, and he could have simply misinterpreted it.

A long moment passed as he stood there leaning his hands on the table and trying to get back in control of his raging emotions. He'd known he'd gotten abandoned as a child at the door of Saint Francis's Church in Italy, but he hadn't known *who* had left him, mother or father. He had always wondered if maybe it was his mother, and he had prayed as a boy that she would come back to retrieve him.

Had his mother been the one to leave him?

It couldn't be. No way could Patty, a waitress out here in Everett, Washington, know something like that.

The more time that passed, the more Niccolo came to believe that his mind had played tricks on him. He had misheard, and his imagination had gotten the better of him. The conversation seemed impossible, and his brain must have exaggerated.

He forced himself to stand up tall and take a deep breath, pushing away the angst and worry of his childhood and regaining control.

Patty didn't return from the kitchen, and patrons sat and stared at him. With a sigh, Father Paladina dropped two bills on the table to cover his meal. He straightened out his coat, adjusted his collar, and then headed back out into the cold for the short walk to his hotel.

By the time he got there, he felt simultaneously more and less unsettled by the conversation in the restaurant. The memory of it had already grown fuzzy, but he couldn't deny that something strange had just happened. It didn't bring him anything that he could deal with just now, though, so he tucked the concern away to examine later.

Still, something strange had just happened.

Chapter 5

A short while later, Father Reynolds stopped by to pick him up at his hotel. The events from the restaurant with Patty had taken on a distant unreality that Niccolo found difficult to focus on. Part of him knew it had happened the way he remembered, but another part warned him that the memory was faulty and he should just ignore it. At first, he thought that he might bring it up with Father Reynolds, but then decided it wouldn't be prudent.

The beautiful morning, sunny and bright, further helped to distract him. He didn't much care for the extreme rain in the region but had to admit that, when not raining, the city and surrounding forests looked gorgeous.

When Niccolo climbed into the car, Father Reynolds offered him a sandwich wrapped in a plastic bag. It looked like tuna fish, though Niccolo couldn't be sure.

"I didn't know if you might feel hungry. I got stuck meeting with Brad Coley, and it ended up taking a lot longer than I thought."

"Ah," Niccolo said. "No, thank you. I ate already."

Jackson nodded, and then put the sandwich back into a cooler. "I'm sorry. I'd hoped to get back much sooner."

"Think nothing of it," Niccolo said. "I went for a walk and saw more of the city."

"Oh? See anything interesting?"

Once again, Niccolo lied, "No. Just got a bite to eat and enjoyed the fine weather."

Jackson nodded and put the car into gear. He drove them outside the city center and to a suburban housing district in a quiet little neighborhood called Lynwood. Though still sunny out, clouds gathered in the distance that might herald another storm later in the afternoon. Father Paladina didn't know the city well enough to make a general estimation about such things, but he had brought his umbrella with him just in case.

The house they'd driven to looked like a quiet little one-story affair with a quaint and tiny yard and a garden filled with tulips. It had a brick façade that appeared faded and worn with age. Many similar houses lined the street it ran along and seemed to form part of a larger retirement complex. They seemed cheap and old houses and had a faint air of death about them.

"Tell me the entire story," Niccolo said, pulling a notepad and pen from his pocket. He flipped about halfway through the book to a blank page. "From the beginning."

"You know most of it, I think."

"Humor me," Niccolo said. "I want accurate records of everything that's happened up to this point."

Jackson frowned but didn't object. "Her name is Rose Gallagher," Jackson said as he pulled the car into the driveway. "She never missed a sermon after I first arrived in Everett until about two months ago, and then she stopped showing up altogether. I reached out to her, but she wouldn't return my calls. We fell out of contact."

"Maybe it happened due to health reasons?"

"That was what I thought at first, but then one of her neighbors—Georgia ... she lives across the street—" Jackson pointed toward another house, this one with a maroon-colored roof. "—called me and asked if I would check in on her. She said Rose was acting strange. Erratic. She told me that Rose would come out of her house at all hours of the night and always muttered to herself. It seemed like she talked to someone not there ... that's how Georgia described it. Like Rose was never alone."

"And at that point, you went to check on her?"

The young priest nodded. "It had gone on for a few weeks, Georgia said, and she got to worrying. I didn't have any expectations of what I might find on that first visit, but I could tell that something seemed badly wrong. Her house looked a mess and smelled like rotten food."

The hairs prickled up on Niccolo's neck. "Rotten food? Like eggs?"

"Yeah. Rotten eggs. Why?"

"No reason," Niccolo said, scribbling away. "Please, continue."

"Anyway, when I showed up, Rose would barely even look at me, just kept rocking in her chair and whispering words I didn't recognize. I didn't stay long. I got too freaked out. When I went back a second time, I brought a video camera that I'd borrowed from a friend who used it to make home movies."

"You tried compelling the demon, too."

Jackson hesitated, and then nodded. "I read a few books about it before I went back. I thought ..."

When he didn't finish the sentiment, Niccolo dropped the issue. "It doesn't matter."

"You saw what I managed to capture while there. That happened a few days after my first visit, and I contacted Bishop Glasser about it to report what had happened. It felt ..."

"It felt what?" Niccolo caught the priest's gaze.

Jackson shrugged. "It *felt* like she had something inside her.

I don't know how to explain it. I didn't know what to do and felt worried about her. I thought the bishop would take me seriously and try to help."

"But Bishop Glasser rejected your claims," Niccolo said.

"He wouldn't meet with me for a whole week. When he finally did, he ignored all my evidence and forbade me from speaking with Rose or visiting her again. He said that it wasn't a matter for the Church to look into."

"And then you went over his head and contacted the Vatican."

"I waited another week before I reached out again. He said the Church would look into it, but when I called one of my friends at the Vatican, he said they hadn't even been informed."

"Who's your friend?"

Jackson hesitated again, and then said, "I would rather not say."

"Well, I apologize, but it is unlikely that your *friend* would know of such an investigation as this," Niccolo said. He raised his hand to cut off Jackson's objection. "However, in this case, he proved correct. We knew nothing of what you had said at that point. Still, you should have gone back to Bishop Glasser with your concern before getting in touch with us."

"I felt afraid for Rose, not my career, and I couldn't afford to wait any longer. It's taken too long already. When you meet her, you'll understand. I felt that I had no choice."

"Is that everything?" Niccolo asked, scribbling notes into his booklet.

"That covers everything until you arrived. I haven't gone back to see Rose since. I ... I felt afraid."

Niccolo flipped his notebook closed and slid it back into his pocket. "Well, then, let us go and meet with this woman you believe is possessed."

Niccolo climbed out of Jackson's small sedan and walked toward the front door of the woman's house. It had no doorbell, but an old and rusted out door-knocker hung in the middle of the wooden panel. Niccolo feared that it might break if he tried to use it, so instead, he pounded his knuckles against the hard edifice.

No immediate response came, but he could hear movement from inside. It took a full two minutes before the door finally opened, and a woman stood there, withered by age and just under five-feet tall.

She had a shawl pulled about her shoulders and held herself up with a silver walker resting on tennis balls. Most probably, she would have been beautiful at one point in her life. Now, she looked tired but smiled enormously when she saw the two priests standing on her doorstep.

"Father Reynolds!" she said, shifting her body around the walker to give the priest a hug. "It's so good to see you!"

Niccolo Paladina glanced over at the young priest, who looked taken off-guard at the way Rose appeared. The expression on his face showed how unsettled he'd grown at this engagement. This normal-seeming woman didn't present at all as he had expected.

Niccolo felt surprised as well. The old woman looked vaguely similar to the one from Jackson's home movie, yet also normal and nothing like she had seemed on the television in Jackson's office. In fact, there seemed nothing out of the ordinary about Rose at all.

"You as well," Jackson said, finally, gathering himself and hugging the woman. Jackson turned toward Niccolo, a helpless expression on his face. "Please, allow me to introduce a friend of mine. This is Father Niccolo Paladina. He is visiting from the Vatican."

They exchanged nods and greetings. Niccolo gave her hand a gentle shake, looking for any of the telltale signs of possession that he had learned about in his years of training. No sores, eye twitches, or anything else that might give her away. Just the pleasant smile of an elderly woman.

"Please, come in," she said, laboriously moving back from the door so that they could pass. The walker, as wide as the entry, made it difficult to maneuver. Father Reynolds walked in first, and Niccolo followed him into the woman's home. "I'm afraid I didn't know I would have guests today, or I would have baked some cookies or had snacks on hand."

"That's quite all right. I'm sorry to drop in on you unannounced like this," Jackson said.

"Think nothing of it. Would you gentlemen like some tea?"

"No, thank you," Niccolo said.

"None for me." Jackson gave her a smile.

She led them into her living room, off to the left, and beckoned for them to sit. Niccolo situated himself on an old blue couch close to a large bay window with pulled curtains, and Jackson sat on a wooden rocking chair resting near the left wall.

Everything in the house appeared old. A thin cloud of dust hung in the air, pushed around by an unseen fan somewhere deeper inside the house, and the air tasted musty and unpleasant. Dozens of picture frames decorated every surface, showing the multitudes of Rose's extended family, and a cabinet stood by the right wall next to a small television. Broken and faded porcelain dolls lined the shelves.

The home, though not clean, also wasn't the dirty and disgusting place from Jackson's video. If a demon was involved, then it remained unlikely that the effects of its possession would disappear over time. It certainly didn't look like the home of a woman battling a possession, but it did look like the quiet home of a retired lady living alone after her husband had passed away.

The television, though turned on, played at one of the lowest volume settings. Right now, the news showed, but Rose picked up a remote from the coffee table and flicked it off, casting them into complete silence. She sat in an armchair on the other side of the room, folded her hands in her lap, and smiled at the two priests.

A long while passed in awkward silence. Both men exchanged glances, and then Father Jackson cleared his throat.

"How ... uh ... how are your children?"

"Quite well, thank you."

"And your grandchildren?"

"Also fine. My youngest granddaughter, Eliza, just had a dance recital two days ago. It was at her school for Uptown Girl."

"That sounds wonderful. Were you able to attend?"

"Unfortunately, no. I didn't feel well at the time, but I would have loved to go. My son has done an amazing job at raising her."

"I know," Jackson said. "He's a tremendous father."

Rose joked, "I'll never know where he learned to be such a great parent."

"Doubtless Kevin learned it from his mother."

Rose laughed. "I couldn't possibly take credit for him or his children. I just feel proud that we managed to keep him alive into adulthood. It became touch-and-go there for a while."

Something about the way she said it sent a shiver up Niccolo's spine. The words seemed innocent enough and told in a self-deprecating fashion, but something about the way she said them made it almost feel like it wasn't a joke. It didn't give him anything he could put his finger on, just a feeling.

He studied the old woman's expressions as she sat there in her chair, searching for a twitch or an involuntary motion, something out of the ordinary that would give rise to Father Reynolds's concerns. He felt unsure what he expected to find, but something about the woman felt off.

Yet, she seemed normal and a little cheery. He could explain the cheerfulness at her receiving unexpected guests, but that didn't assuage his concerns. Also, he could explain the state of her home, quaint and well-cared for despite the inordinate amount of dust in the air. A distinct scent lingered, one shared by many such residences where older people lived that Niccolo attributed to old age.

Though, that didn't prove quite true—he couldn't attribute all of the smell to Rose's aging. The air also bore an undercurrent of some other smell, something far less pleasant, but he couldn't place it.

"To what do I owe the pleasure of hosting two such fine gentlemen of God?" Rose asked after a few more long moments of silence.

"We had hoped to talk to you about the ... uh ... situation from a few weeks ago," Father Reynolds said, awkwardly.

"What situation?"

Jackson fumbled over his words, "When I came to visit you, and you said you felt ... strange. Father Paladina has come a long way to visit and check in on you to make certain you are all right."

"Oh, *that* situation. I'm afraid that was just a simple misunderstanding. I had one of my spells. My son thinks I'm developing dementia, but I think it's the weather. I have good and bad days, and I'm afraid that visit happened at one of the worst in recent memory. I feel terribly sorry if I alarmed you."

Jackson shook his head, unsure of how to continue. "You said, the last time, that you thought you weren't alone in your body. You told me that the devil had possessed you, and you behaved erratically. I felt terrified."

"I apologize for frightening you, deary. I just wasn't myself and am so sorry if you've stayed worried about me all of this time."

"Rose, you don't need to lie simply because Father Paladina has come here. He's a friend."

She looked puzzled and a little offended. "I wouldn't dare to lie in the presence of a man of God, let alone *two*," she said. "I'm sorry for being a cause of concern, but I'm better now. I feel quite all right."

Niccolo could see that Father Reynolds had grown frustrated and belligerent from Rose's responses. It became clear this entire encounter hadn't unfolded the way he had expected, and that he felt backed into a corner.

However, for Niccolo, it didn't prove an encouraging situation at all. Quite the opposite, in fact. He'd prepared himself to see the same disturbed woman he had seen in the video, someone who might have a problem that would justify the young priest's fears. At least then it would be more likely to come down to an illness or mental issue and something they could deal with mundanely.

But Rose acted entirely too innocent and agreeable in their visit here. It seemed as though she hid something, and that gave enough to set off alarm bells in Niccolo's mind. It struck him that she attempted to convince them that everything remained fine, and if anything, she did too good a job.

It could be for many reasons. Maybe she felt embarrassed at how she'd acted when Father Reynolds came by on his last visit, or perhaps she felt intimidated at having two priests in her home talking to her.

Or, maybe, Father Reynolds had it right all along. Niccolo had learned in his years of study that demons had the willingness to go to great lengths to hide their presence when they felt threatened. Maybe the demon attempted to disguise its presence.

A lofty conclusion to jump to, however, and when Niccolo got down to it, he had nothing to support the theory. He needed a lot more evidence before giving rise to the idea of demonic possession. Which meant looking for involuntary actions or omens. There would have to be something to give him a clue about what, if anything, was going on.

Perhaps her home would give a clue. It had looked verily wrecked in the video from a few weeks earlier, and even if she had cleaned up to disguise the mess, there might remain some evidence left behind. He leaned forward on the couch to get their attention and interrupt the inane conversation.

"Might I use your restroom?"

"Of course," Rose said, pointing down the hall in the other direction. "It is just down that hallway and on the left-hand side."

"Thank you."

Niccolo stood and headed down the hall and away from the living room. He could still hear Father Reynolds and Rose conversing behind him, but otherwise, the house seemed empty and silent.

At the end of the hall stood a closed door, most likely leading to the woman's bedroom. To the right stood an open doorway leading into what looked like a guest room, though it didn't appear to have served that purpose for many years.

Instead, hundreds of dolls littered every surface, including all the countertops and the bed. Arranged facing toward the doorway, their large marble and porcelain eyes looked directly at him.

They all seemed to have gotten collected out of various historical eras throughout the last sixty years or so, depicting hundreds of different fashions and styles of doll making. Some of them wore dresses, while others sat naked; a few had broken or had missing eyes, and others remained in their original boxes and placed on shelves.

One doll, in particular, caught his attention. A red-haired

monstrosity with paint that looked faded with age. It had the left eye missing and sat turned sideways, facing toward the wall. The empty socket gave the doll an eerie expression. It had a sardonic smile painted on its face, but with missing paint, it looked more like a clown's face than a little girl.

Niccolo scanned the room, but his eyes continually drew back to that doll. Something about it both captivated and terrified. There had to be hundreds of dolls packed into this tiny room. It felt thoroughly unsettling, and he couldn't imagine anyone trying to sleep in this guest room with so many dolls surrounding them.

Creepy, but certainly not demonic. The oddities of some people. Just looking at those dolls filled him with dread and disgust. The way they sat arranged ... he couldn't imagine anyone gathering these up over the years. Why would someone want to keep such a collection?

He shook his head and turned in the other direction toward the restroom. It looked small and cramped and entirely uncomfortable. The shower curtain hung pulled back from an old porcelain bathtub, and a stool sat in the center. No doubt so that Rose could sit down while she bathed and avoid any accidents.

The smell he had noticed earlier when they first walked into the house seemed considerably stronger here, and it had a rotting and decaying quality to it that turned his stomach. It made him feel light-headed and nauseous, and he became afraid he might lose his greasy lunch if not careful.

He finished using the facilities as quickly as he could, barely allowing himself to breathe, and then hurried back out to the living room. The home felt uncomfortable, and the dolls creepy, but he saw nothing demonic about it.

Except ...

He paused as he passed by the guest room on his way out, taking a second glance at the bed.

The red-haired, one-eyed doll had moved.

He felt sure of it.

It sat a few feet from where he had first seen it, resting gently against a pillow. Though not sure, he also thought its clothing might have changed. Now, it had on a red dress that looked to have faded with age and had its arms extended as though to give a hug.

He blinked, wracking his mind to find some explanation. Maybe he recalled incorrectly. Maybe it had sat there the entire time, but he felt *sure* that it hadn't. He had seen it near the edge of the bed, next to a blonde doll still in its original position.

It kept staring at him with its one eye, unmoving and unblinking. He watched, almost expecting it to move, but it didn't.

Of course it didn't.

He must have imagined it because no one had come down the hallway while he used the restroom. He could still hear Jackson and Rose speaking in the living room, and otherwise the house stood empty.

Didn't it?

He blew out a breath of air, pushed down his discomfort, and headed down the hall toward the living room. He dealt in facts, he reminded himself. Not feelings.

Father Reynolds sat engaged in conversation with Rose Gallagher, and he seemed less bothered by the entire situation than he had a few minutes ago. More relaxed, like Rose had convinced him that she was all right, after all. Now, they sat talking like old friends.

They both glanced over when he strode back into the room. The time had come to ask some discourteous questions and attempt to figure out if anything untoward was going on. He found his way back to the couch, sat down, and turned his attention toward Rose.

"I don't wish to sound impolite," he said, "but I wanted to ask you about the smell. I don't have tremendous personal experience with this in particular, but I know enough to recognize the smell of death."

Rose frowned and nodded. "Yes. The raccoon."

"Raccoon?"

"I think it's a raccoon. It found its way into the crawl space underneath the house and got trapped. I think it died several days ago, and the smell has been terrible. This isn't the first time something like this has happened."

"It's happened before?"

"Not often. A few times over the years since I moved into this building. My husband used to clear them out until he passed away. My son is supposed to come by and get this one out of the crawlspace, but he's so busy, and I don't like to bother him. He has enough to worry about without adding my discomfort to the mix."

"I see."

"I barely smell it anymore, to be honest. I know that's a horrible thing to say, but it's the truth."

Father Reynolds turned to face Rose. "Would you like for me to get it for you?"

She perked up immediately at the suggestion. "Would you? That would be tremendous."

"Of course." He rose from the couch and dusted off his pants. "Do you know where the entrance is to the crawl space?"

"Around the side of the house to the left. You have to get in from the outside. It has a grate you can remove. I must warn you, though, that it's extremely cramped and won't make for an easy fit."

Jackson patted his stomach and smiled warmly. "I suppose I should cut down on my meals."

She chuckled. "I only meant because you're so tall."

"Do you have a flashlight I could borrow?"

"In the first kitchen drawer," she said, standing up. It seemed a laborious effort, and Father Reynolds moved to her side and helped her. "Been having trouble with my hip for weeks."

"Have you seen a doctor?"

"They want to do surgery and replace it. I'll wait until I don't have any other options, though."

They all filed into the kitchen, and Rose rummaged around in the drawers until she retrieved an old and long flashlight. It appeared unimpressive and looked to have been purchased at least twenty-five years ago.

"Will this do?"

"Yes, thanks," Father Reynolds said, accepting the flashlight.

"The batteries are old, but it should work."

"Do you have a trash bag as well? To put the deceased animal into."

Rose went to a cupboard and pulled a black bag loose. The thick material had a red drawstring to pull it closed.

Father Reynolds took it and then walked toward the front door. "I'll be back in a couple of minutes."

"I'll accompany you," Father Paladina said.

Jackson nodded at him, and together, they walked out into the yard and around the side of the house. He waited until they got out of earshot of Rose before turning his attention toward Jackson.

"Are you all right?" Niccolo asked.

"Quite," Jackson said. "I'm not a fan of dead things, even animals, but this sounds easy enough. I should have asked for gloves."

"I meant with Rose. You seemed rather agitated for a minute there when we first arrived."

"Frustrated would give a more apt description. This visit has turned out *nothing* like the last time I came here, but I suppose that's a blessing. Her home was in disarray, and she could barely focus for more than a few moments at a time. She seemed so out of sorts and kept muttering, incapable of conversing at all."

"She seems fine."

"Yes, this time she certainly does. Maybe whatever happened to her has ended? Is that possible? Would a demon just leave like that? Do you think she recovered on her own?"

Niccolo didn't respond. It seemed unlikely that a demon would vacate a host; not without a good reason. From everything he had heard, a demonic possession took a terrible toll on its host.

The damage that a demon inflicted proved highly subjective and depended on a lot of factors, including time. If the demon had only resided here for a few weeks, then little damage would have occurred. Usually, it took years to destroy a body beyond repair.

However, he didn't have any personal experience or expertise on the matter, so he had to admit that anything was possible.

After he'd sifted through all this, he said, "I don't know."

"What would a demon be like?"

"A demon is like a fire," Niccolo said. "They burn their hosts from the inside, gradually destroying them. If Rose *were* possessed, it would become nearly impossible for her or the demon to hide the damage it caused to her body."

"But it could?"

"Maybe," Niccolo said. "Not likely, though."

"So, this isn't a demon."

"Most likely not."

He expected Jackson to get frustrated by the revelation, or to argue with him, but the young priest seemed genuinely relieved.

"Thank God," he said.

"Yes," Niccolo said. "Thank God."

"Then, thankfully, it looks like whatever happened here is over," Father Jackson said. "Perhaps Rose had a mental breakdown or a temporary illness like she said. Or maybe something else happened. I feel grateful that she seems to be doing better now."

"So, you believe you got it wrong about the exorcism?"

"It seems I had it entirely wrong," Jackson said. "And, I've never felt so happy to get it wrong. I willingly revoke my request to the Church for an exorcist."

Niccolo hesitated, and then nodded. He felt uncomfortable about the entire situation, but he also knew that, more than likely, Jackson called it true. Something odd *was* happening to this woman and in this city, but jumping from oddities to demons meant a leap he didn't feel remotely willing to make.

"Then, the matter is settled. I can report back that you have dropped the notion and no longer wish to pursue an exorcism for Rose Gallagher."

"That sounds excellent."

"You should also apologize to Bishop Glasser for your rash decisions and for going against his request."

This time, Jackson proved slower in responding. Clearly, he didn't like that course of action.

Finally, though, he nodded. "Yes, of course. I owe him an apology at the very least. Would it be too much trouble to ask that you accompany me when I go visit him? I would appreciate having you there. The man seems quite unnerving."

"Of course. I don't plan to leave for another day or so at the earliest. We can visit and have dinner with him tomorrow night if you like."

Jackson nodded. "Of course."

"I'll call him when we return."

Jackson reached down and tugged at the metal opening at the bottom of the house. It covered about a three-foot-tall entryway, and the grate fit snugly into position. It looked old, with part of the metal broken and bent out of position.

Niccolo knelt and helped, and together, they tugged it loose. The smell here overpowered, wafting out of the hole and causing him to gag. He covered his nose with a handkerchief and squinted.

"That is terrible." Jackson turned away from the crawlspace and covered his mouth.

"Yes, it is."

"The animal must have been in there for a while now. I can't believe her son wouldn't come out to help her get it out."

"Doubtless he is quite busy. Everyone has to fit their priorities into their lives."

"I suppose."

Jackson flipped on the flashlight and aimed it into the hole. The flashlight did little to illuminate the utter blackness within. The floor of the crawlspace looked covered in loose gravel, dirt, and sand.

"Well," Jackson said, "here goes nothing."

He knelt to move into the crawlspace, and right then the screen door to the house opened. Someone spoke, and it sounded like a man's voice. It came from too far off to make anything out, however.

"Father Jackson," Rose called from the front of the house. "I have a guest asking for you. Could you come here for a moment?"

The two men exchanged a glance, and then Jackson sighed. "One moment," he called back, then turned to Father Paladina. "Hang on. I'll come right back. I must find out what she needs. Probably just a concerned neighbor."

"I can go in and retrieve the animal," Niccolo said, holding out his hands for the flashlight and trash bag. "It should only take a few moments."

"Are you sure?"

He shrugged. "I rarely get the chance to help someone out in the real world like this. Helping, though, is something our duty entails, so I would consider it a generosity and privilege for you to allow me to do this."

Jackson hesitated for another second.

"Besides," Niccolo said, and then attempted a joke, "I am quite a bit shorter than you, so I should have an easier time navigating the small space."

Jackson nodded. "You have my thanks."

He handed the items to Father Paladina, turned, and disappeared around the corner toward the front of the house. Niccolo watched him go, and then turned back to the hole leading beneath the house and into the crawlspace.

Claustrophobic, he also had a mild fear of the dark, so he hoped the animal wouldn't lay too deep into the darkness.

He knelt and flashed the light into the crawlspace. It didn't give a powerful glow, and hardly split through the black, but enough that he could see it would make for an uncomfortable fit. Niccolo took a deep breath, rubbed his face, and then moved closer to the hole.

Gently, he lowered himself to the ground and crawled into the hole. It only took moving a few feet across the ground until the darkness consumed him. The only sound came from his breathing as he pulled himself further in.

The smell continued to intensify, making it difficult to breathe. To make matters worse, it only took a few minutes for his muscles to cry out in exhaustion. Though not averse to physical labor, he'd not done something like this in many long years. As such, his muscles proved ill prepared for activities like this. He slid his way forward, keeping the light facing ahead with one hand and dragging the trash bag in the other.

Only a short while later, he crawled into the first cobweb. Though he had expected it, it caught him off-guard nonetheless when his face pushed through it. He tried not to envision the spider that had built the web with its myriad of eyes. And refused to imagine it crawling across his face, on his hands, down his shirt ...

Priest ...

He stopped crawling and blinked, hesitating in the darkness. Had he heard the word, or simply imagined it? The darkness and silence got to him, but he couldn't feel sure if he'd imagined the voice.

It sounded as if it had gotten spoken aloud, but that didn't seem right. No other sounds reached him; nothing but the silence. Moreover, a soft feminine voice had uttered the word, and he didn't remember ever having heard it before.

He waited, tilting his head and straining to hear anything else in the crawlspace, but nothing came. With a frown, he crawled forward again, though more cautiously this time. The smell grew worse, overwhelming his senses. He must have come close to the rotting animal.

You don't belong here. This is our city.

The voice again, soft and delicate, yet he still couldn't tell if the words got spoken aloud or only in his head. His ears told him that they hadn't heard anything, but he didn't believe that he had imagined it, either. He just didn't know.

What he *did* know, however, was that he wanted to get out of this crawlspace. The hairs on the back of his neck stood up.

Part of him just wanted to turn around and leave now. He wanted to get out of this hole, though consciously, he recognized that this most likely came down to his fear and claustrophobia manifesting this situation. The mind had created a scary situation because he felt afraid already.

That didn't make it feel any less real, however.

The moaning sound of a gagged woman somewhere in the darkness in front of him followed the words. He shone the flashlight back and forth ahead of him, but it couldn't penetrate deeply enough to make out anything.

This time, he grew certain that the sound was real and not in his head. It came from a real woman, and she must lay gagged and crying in front of him.

"Hello?" he whispered, his words dampened by the crawlspace. He spoke quietly, but they still sounded like yelling in the small area.

His flashlight flickered.

Priest!

"Who's there? Show yourself."

No response; nothing except the oppressive emptiness and darkness.

The light flickered again, and he smacked it into the palm of his left hand. He dropped the trash bag and waved the light forward. His breathing had sped up, as well as his heart rate, and he became lightheaded.

"What the *hell* is that smell?" he muttered, gasping for air. It seemed worse now, and whatever caused it couldn't lay more than a few feet in front of him. Yet, when he waved the flashlight, he saw nothing. No animal, no person, not a thing. He remained alone in the empty crawlspace, with no one and nothing down here with him.

Cut and run, Priest. Cut ... and ... run ...

He forced his body to relax and closed his eyes. Then he focused on his breathing and fought to regain control over his mind and fear. Not real. None of this had any reality. All in his mind.

All in his mind.

The sobbing sound disappeared all at once, leaving him in complete silence. He felt certain it had never been there in the first place; just something unreal. He had imagined it. A mere product of his fear of the dark and claustrophobia.

Even though the sobbing had disappeared, the anxiety and feeling that he wasn't alone persisted. Even though he *knew* nothing had joined him here under this house, the sudden overwhelming fear that had wracked his body a few moments ago proved hard to deal with. It felt as though he lay trapped and suffocating, and the air in the crawlspace felt way too hot.

Niccolo tugged at his collar, trying to loosen it, and wiped the clammy sweat from his forehead. Then he crawled forward a few feet further. A shape lay on the ground a short ways up ahead.

It looked like an animal, about the size of a large cat, and lay unmoving. Doubtless, it had caused the horrible smell.

"There you are," the priest muttered.

He crawled toward the animal, intending to scoop it up and get out of the crawlspace as fast as possible.

His flashlight flickered once more, and then went out. The area plunged into darkness, a suffocating blackness that surrounded him.

The sobbing sound returned, all around him but just out of reach. He gasped, the fear returning, and pounded the flashlight head against his palm. The crying sounded louder now, everywhere, and then the sobs morphed into laughter. Maniacal and crazed guffaws.

Still gasping and panting, he slammed the flashlight against his palm again and again, willing it back to life.

"Come on," he muttered, tugging at his collar. "Come on, come on, come on."

Run, Priest. Cut and run!

"Come on," he muttered. His hands shook. Terrified, he slid toward losing control.

This is our house. Ours.

Niccolo twisted the cap, tightening it and putting more pressure on the batteries. Another slam on his palm and the flashlight flickered back on, shining a beam in front of him.

He glanced up and saw that no animal occupied the crawlspace, but instead, the body of a woman lay there, rotting and decaying. How had he missed that? A woman. And the woman had lain there the entire time. Oh, God, how had he missed that?

The corpse looked like it had been down here for months, trapped in the crawlspace, and her skin had sloughed off and fallen to the ground in piles.

"Oh, God," he muttered. "Oh, God, oh, God ..."

The woman's eyes flew open, and her body moved, lifting up and reaching for him. She'd died, though. He knew she lay there dead. She had to be dead. The body moved unnaturally fast, seeming to flash forward and glide across the dirt and gravel. Only the top half of her body moved, and her legs looked lifeless.

Numb with terror, he stared into her cold eyes. Lifeless eyes. Not alive, just empty. She reached her hand out, and her hands brushed his cheeks, cold and dead.

"Hail, Priest!" the woman said, the sound coming out with a wet hissing sound. "You should have run."

He flailed back, trying to get away from the corpse, and his head slammed against one of the beams at the top of the crawlspace. He dropped the flashlight, and the light went out as it rolled away.

And then he hit the ground face first, dazed and disoriented. He struggled to crawl away but felt himself sinking into unconsciousness. The corpse crawled closer, rotting skin hanging from her face.

"We're going to have so much fun ..."

His eyes fluttered, and then the world went dark.

Chapter 6

Father Paladina came back to reality slowly. The world flitted back into focus. His head ached and throbbed where he had bashed it against the ceiling of the crawlspace, and when he touched the spot, he felt a welt forming there.

The sun seemed extremely bright, and his eyes tried to adjust. It took him a moment to realize where he lay and what had happened to him. He came to on the grass outside Rose Gallagher's home, a few feet from the external crawlspace entrance.

Details came back to him, flooding his mind and causing him to gasp. He remembered going underneath the house to retrieve a dead animal that had gotten trapped there ... but he hadn't seen an animal.

He had, however, seen a human body.

Except that didn't make any sense. He *had* seen an animal lying there, but then his fear and anxiety had overwhelmed him. The animal had lain on the ground, illuminated by the beam of his light, and yet the other reality also felt real.

Niccolo recalled the body of a young and decaying woman; he also remembered that she had slid across the ground toward him, scraping and scrabbling in the dirt to get to him. Ugh, the way it had touched his skin—

Something touched his shoulder.

"Father Paladina?"

With a yelp, he jerked away from the touch, thrashing his body awkwardly. His head throbbed even more from the sudden motion, and he let out a sharp cry of pain. Dizzy and disoriented, he tried to get away from his attacker.

"Sorry, I didn't mean to startle you," Father Reynolds said, kneeling in the grass beside him with a concerned expression on his face. "Are you all right?"

Niccolo sucked in a steadying breath, shaking his head, and then sat up. *Was* he all right? He didn't know, but he also had no idea how he might express his fear of a situation when he didn't even know if it held any reality.

"I ... I believe so," he said, the fear and confusion trickling away. His fear ebbed, unable to maintain its grip on him under the scrutiny of the sun. His breathing eased, and he regained control. "What ... what happened? How did I get here?"

"I was about to ask you the same thing. We were in the living room, talking, when we heard a loud thud beneath the floor. When he found you, you lay unconscious and looked to have hit your head against one of the beams."

"You dragged me out?"

"Not me. *He* managed to get you out, and he got the cat, too. Looks like the poor thing had been down there for at least a week after it died."

Jackson gestured toward the trash bag that Niccolo had taken with him beneath the house. It looked lumpy now, and someone had pulled closed the drawstrings. It looked about the size of a small dog or large cat.

Even sealed up, though, Niccolo could still smell the rotting stench of decay in the air. It made him queasy.

"What about the girl?"

"The what?"

"The ..." He tried again, "Did you find anything else down there with me?"

Father Reynolds tilted his head to the side in confusion. "Like what?"

Niccolo opened his mouth to explain about the corpse of the woman, and then changed his mind. They couldn't have missed it if they had gone down there to retrieve him; it became obvious to him that nothing else had joined him down there. Only himself and the dead animal. Whatever he had seen or thought he'd seen, it had no reality.

It had felt real, though. He could still remember the way her cold fingers had brushed his cheek, her voice, and the way her words sounded wet and horrible. In his mind's eye, he could see her, dragging her lifeless legs across the dirt and gravel to get to him. Not to mention the way her skin had hung loose from her face. It had seemed so real, and he didn't feel ready to chock all of that up to only his overactive imagination and fear of the dark.

But saying the words out loud wouldn't do any good, either. It would only serve to make him sound crazy or paranoid. Instead, he changed the subject.

"What did you mean, 'not you'?" He turned his body in the other direction. Rose stood there with her walker, looking down at him with a concerned expression on her face. Niccolo doubted she had gone into the hole after him. "You said *he* got me. Who else was with you?"

Niccolo shifted his body to the side again in the opposite direction. A man stood there. This man wore a loose-fitting gray shirt, black pants, and military boots. He had thick brown hair and gray eyes.

The sight of him sparked an immediate feeling of familiarity, but it took Niccolo a moment to register the identity of this other man. However, when he did finally realize that he knew him, Niccolo felt a welling of disbelief and anger in the pit of his stomach.

"You?" he muttered, scrambling on the grass and pushing himself up to his feet. His head throbbed, and he felt dizzy, but now he also felt angry. Furious, in fact, as emotions flooded back to him that he hadn't felt in weeks. "What in God's name are you doing here?"

Father Reynolds looked confused, glancing between the two men. This must have been the house guest, the person who had come to Rose's door before Niccolo went underneath. All thoughts of the corpse and his fear flew from his mind, replaced by his mounting anger.

"You know him?" Jackson asked.

"Of course I know him. This is Arthur Vangeest."

"Hello, Niccolo," Arthur said. He looked none too pleased to see him, either. That didn't surprise Niccolo, however, because he had made his utter disgust for the man clear in their last encounter. "It's been a while."

Jackson turned to face Arthur. "So, you aren't a reporter?"

Arthur shook his head, looking like a guilty dog who had peed on the rug. "I apologize for misleading you."

"You mean lying," Niccolo said. "It's what you do best, right? Why have you come here?"

"We should speak in private."

"*We* have nothing to speak about. You have overstayed your welcome already."

"I'm afraid I must insist," Arthur said. "It is incredibly important, and a matter of some urgency."

"No," Niccolo said, vehemently. "I will not speak with you, nor will I listen to anything you have to say. I also know that you aren't supposed to be out on a job. Any job. Which means you're not sanctioned, are you?"

The look on Arthur's face told him everything he needed to know. "You don't understand—"

"I understand perfectly. If you do not get in your car and leave Everett in the next few seconds, I will notify the Vatican of your presence and report that you have interfered with Church affairs."

"I'll go, but after you hear me out. This is important."

"No."

"It's a matter of life and death."

"All you understand is death, Arthur. I was there. I saw the bodies and what you did."

The words spilled out before Niccolo could restrain himself, and when he turned to look at Jackson, he saw a look of horror on the young priest's face. He took a deep breath to regain control over his emotions and realized he had overstepped. Never should he have had this conversation in front of Jackson or Rose.

Strangely, though, when he glanced over at Rose, it didn't look like the conversation fazed her in the slightest. She wore a small frown and didn't seem to pay them much attention at all.

He turned back to face Arthur. As much as he hated the man, he also knew that ignoring him could become problematic, if not downright dangerous.

In all honesty, pissing him off might prove even worse.

Niccolo turned to Jackson. "Would you please give us a moment?"

"I should explain myself to Father Reynolds as well," Arthur said. "He should hear this."

"No," Niccolo said in a firm voice. He had said too much in the presence of Father Jackson, and whatever Arthur had to say, it lay well beyond the young priest's purview. "You may speak to me, and then you will leave. Understood?"

Arthur hesitated, and then he nodded. Jackson had a look of confusion and concern on his face, but he didn't object. He turned, took Rose by the arm, and then helped guide her back toward the front stoop of the house.

"I will be in right behind you," Niccolo called out as they left. "This will only take a moment."

Father Reynolds didn't respond. His body language made it clear he felt uncomfortable with the entire situation, but he didn't object. Niccolo realized he would have much to explain now after his slip and berated himself for speaking in anger.

He waited until he heard the front door shut before addressing Arthur once more. "Why did you come here?" he asked. "In Everett, of all places. Don't you have more important things to do? More cultists to murder?"

Arthur frowned, almost imperceptibly, but he ignored the remark. "You got it right that I'm not on the books, but I *am* on an investigation. An important one, and it led me here."

"What investigation?"

Arthur hesitated, and then said, "This is something personal."

"If you won't tell me—"

"I'm hunting the people who murdered my family."

Niccolo took a breath, unsure how to respond. He didn't know a lot about Arthur other than that he worked for an organization that did dirty work for the Church. He had gotten called out a few months ago to a rundown manor in the woods of West Virginia.

He worked as one of a group of priests and civilians that the Church sent, though Niccolo hadn't known why at the time. What he did know was that when they got there, they found dozens of dead bodies. Men and women, some riddled with bullet holes and others hacked apart with some sort of bladed implement.

Cultists, he had come to find out, and dangerous ones responsible for multiple kidnaps and murders. The Church had utilized the organization to help eliminate them, and they'd sent Arthur. All of the dead people, he discovered, had gotten murdered in their sleep by one man.

One.

But that didn't make for the worst of it. The worst part came from the fact that Niccolo got tasked with helping to clean it up. His job dictated that he help hide the evidence, destroy the bodies, and pretend like nothing had ever happened. It didn't turn out the first time the Church had done that, either. He found out that they had covered up things like that regularly. Arthur worked as an assassin for the Church, and Niccolo had become a part of his cleanup crew.

It hadn't sat well with Niccolo, and just thinking about it made him sick. He hadn't even had the courage to object. The order came down from way high up in the Church, and Niccolo had just gone along with it.

He held just as much guilt, he knew.

"I'm sorry for your family," he said. "But that doesn't explain why you've come here."

"The person who betrayed me is here."

"In Everett?"

"Yes."

"You expect me to believe that?"

"It's the truth."

"I fought to have you turned over to the authorities, you know," Niccolo said. "After you murdered those people. I became one of the few who thought you the monster. Not the cultists. You."

"They kidnapped and murdered children. They'd gone beyond salvation."

"All of them? Can you stand there and tell me that *none* of them could have been saved?"

"It isn't my job to save people."

"No, I forgot. It's your job to kill them."

Arthur didn't reply, but the look that crossed his face seemed tinged with shame. Niccolo, however, felt no pity for the man. Not after what he'd done.

"I wanted for you to spend the rest of your life in a jail cell. Where you belong."

"I don't blame you for feeling that way," Arthur said.

"You *murdered* those people."

"I did my job."

"You think *that* matters? God will not forgive you for what you did."

"It seems to me like *that* conversation should happen between God and me."

"I won't forgive you, either."

"I'm not asking you to. I just ask for you to hear me out and make up your mind."

"Why should I hear you out? So you can tell me more lies?"

"So, I'm a liar now, too? I thought I was a murderer."

"You can easily be both."

Arthur rubbed his face, silent for a long moment. "This is getting us nowhere. We're just going in circles. You hate me, and I'm a murderer. I get it. But it doesn't change what's happening right now, right here in this city."

"What?"

"Someone betrayed the Church and me."

"Why should I believe you?"

"I think he works with the Ninth Circle. They could have operatives in this area."

"Could have? You mean you don't know?"

"I only just arrived in the city, but the evidence pushes in that direction."

"I thought you took care of the Ninth Circle when you murdered everyone."

"I eliminated one group, but they have a lot more cells in the world. One might be here. And, if not that cult, then something else."

"You just can't help yourself, can you?"

"What?"

"You see cults everywhere. No matter where you look."

"Look, I get that you don't like me, but you need to listen—"

"You are broken, Arthur. Just a broken, sad, little man. You can't even tell right from wrong anymore, can you? You should leave the city and get help. I get it. Your family got murdered, and you wanted revenge, but you crossed *every* line that separates people from monsters. You are a monster."

Arthur stared at him. "Maybe. But I'm also *right*. Something is going on here, and they have a powerful ally."

"Who?"

"Bishop Glasser."

✱✱✱

A moment passed, and then Niccolo let out a disbelieving laugh. He turned and walked toward the front door of Rose's home. Arthur moved to follow, and Niccolo held up his hand to stop him.

"Your two minutes are up. Get help, Arthur. I'm begging you. I won't forgive you for what you did, but I will pray for you. And I don't have time to listen to these ridiculous accusations."

"Leopold Glasser betrayed me and got my family killed," Arthur said. "He sold information to the Ninth Circle and has worked with them for years. I also know that he has allies *here,* and he plans something big."

"You have proof?"

"A confession from the bishop's sister, Emily."

"And how did you obtain that, might I ask? It hardly offers compelling evidence unless I can speak to her directly."

"She isn't here. The Council have detained her and will, no doubt, transfer her to the Vatican in a few days."

Niccolo sighed. "Until—if—that happens, how can I possibly believe anything you say? What other proof do you have?"

"We don't have time for proof. She confessed everything to me. You need to believe me."

"I don't care. This confession you speak of is, doubtless, coerced. I would never believe a single word you say."

"I wouldn't lie about something like this. We have a real threat here in the city and—"

"Have you spoken to the Vatican? You said you turned Emily over to your organization, so, no doubt, they can get you permission to be here, can't they?"

Arthur hesitated before saying, "I don't have *time* to run this through the proper channels."

"Then, make time. How did you know to find me here?"

"I didn't. I had hoped to speak with Father Reynolds and find out if he knew anything about the bishop. *This* is just an unfortunate coincidence."

"For the both of us," Niccolo said. "What did you plan to speak to Jackson about? Did you plan to tell him about what you do or all of the people you have murdered? I can assure you that

that makes a terrible idea."

"I wanted to ask him a few questions and see if he worked with the bishop."

"He doesn't."

"I know. I spoke with him inside. He hates the man and seems oblivious to what's going on."

"Or, maybe, *nothing* is going on. If you feel you have evidence against the bishop, then contact the Vatican. If they have any interest in having you operating in Everett, then I will work with you. Until then, however, I suggest that you get out of the city before I report you myself. Now, if you will excuse me, I must get back to Father Reynolds and Rose Gallagher."

Father Paladina walked toward the front door, leaving Arthur standing alone on the lawn. This time, Arthur didn't follow.

"I'm only trying to help."

Niccolo stopped and turned back, feeling a burst of anger. "Help? The way you helped those innocent people to find God's love when you murdered them in West Virginia?"

"They would have killed me. I had no other option."

"You didn't wait for help. I saw the report when the Church sent me to help cover it up. You were not supposed to go in alone. You lost your family, you were grieving, but that gives you *no right* to kill all of those people."

"What was I supposed to do?"

"Wait for backup. Take the cultists by force so that they could have had a chance to repent. How many have you killed with your shoot-first-ask-for-forgiveness later modus operandi?"

"Not everyone can have redemption."

"Not *anyone*, by your estimation. Twenty-three people, Arthur. That's how many people you murdered that day. That's how many people I helped the Church pretend never existed so that *you* wouldn't get punished."

"Are you mad at me, or at yourself?"

This time, Niccolo didn't respond. A moment passed in silence.

"That's what I thought," Arthur said. "I get it, I do. I regret what I did, and many more things in my life. I've made a lot of mistakes, but the Church sanctioned my actions. I felt ready to accept whatever punishment they sanctioned, but the Council I serve, and myself, received exoneration."

"And what happens when your actions don't get sanctioned? What happens when you cross *that* line? I can assure you, Arthur, that when *that* day comes, there will be no turning back."

Arthur stood, unmoving and unblinking. "It will never come

to that."

"It *always* comes to that. I don't trust you, and I want nothing to do with you."

"You need my help."

"I don't need *anything* from you, least of all your kind of help."

"Then, at least, heed my warning. You are in danger."

"Consider the warning heeded," Niccolo said. "Now, leave."

Arthur nodded and set off again through the grass to the sidewalk. A moment later, he climbed into a car and drove off, heading down the road away from Rose's home.

Niccolo watched him go, frowning, and rubbed the back of his head. The welt there felt tender and painful. It had swelled up and throbbed; he had a headache, but he couldn't tell if it came from the welt or his conversation with Arthur Vangeest.

That made for the last thing he had expected on this trip, and it left him feeling angry and annoyed. Niccolo felt furious with himself more than Arthur, however, because even with how angrily he'd just spoken to Arthur, he hadn't spoken up when it truly mattered.

Arthur seemed like a cancer on the world, a sanctioned murderer working on behalf of powerful men. A weapon that the Church pointed at its enemies, claiming to do God's work.

However, that didn't provide the only reason Niccolo felt so unsettled by the encounter with Arthur. His heart still pumped rapidly when he recalled what he had seen beneath the woman's house, although he felt positive it hadn't been real. His overactive imagination had gotten the better of him and created a terror to match his fear of cramped and dark places.

At least, he told himself that.

Part of him—a small part—remained worried that maybe Arthur had it right. Maybe something *was* going on, and maybe something dangerous. Could the bishop have involvement in something so horrible?

His gut said no. Niccolo didn't like the bishop, but if Arthur had it right, then the man had stepped too far over the line. Leopold Glasser didn't exactly make a good servant of God, but that remained a far walk from betrayal of the Church.

Still, it was possible. And, if that were the case, then having a weapon like Arthur around might not be a bad idea.

That didn't offer a route that Niccolo felt willing to take just yet, though. Arthur remained dangerous, and even though some strange things had happened, he saw no reason to believe it anything supernatural or dangerous. Not yet, at least.

Niccolo shook the concerns away, focusing once again on the task at hand. He hadn't seen any signs to make him think that Rose suffered a possession, and after Father Reynolds had found and dealt with the dead animal, it looked like he might not have anything else here to investigate.

He would report his findings to his superiors back in the Vatican, find out what they wanted him to do next, and go from there. Hopefully, they would want him to return to the Vatican, and right now, that sounded like an excellent course of action. Let someone else deal with all this strangeness. He missed his home and sleeping in his bed and eating good food. All he had to do now was accompany Father Reynolds to meet one last time with Bishop Glasser, and then all of this would lay behind him.

Chapter 7

They didn't stay long after Arthur's departure, having no further reason to continue pestering the old woman. They thanked her for her time and headed out to return Niccolo to his hotel room.

His first course of action would be to call the Vatican and report all of his findings. Whether or not Jackson wanted to call off the investigation didn't matter where the Vatican was concerned, and his first duty was to give an accurate report back to his superiors.

How much or how little he told them, however, he hadn't yet decided. The thing was: something strange was definitely happening, and the entire city made him feel uncomfortable. But none of it offered concrete evidence that he could bring up to them. It all came down to more little things that seemed to happen to him and a feeling he had.

His feelings had no importance, though. The Vatican wanted evidence of omens or possession. Aside from maybe a bit more rain than normal at this time of year, and a few people acting oddly, he'd seen nothing here that made him think demonic possession.

Besides, the odds of an actual possession taking place in this town seemed negligible, especially not on the level that Jackson had presented. That video had chilled, but he had found no evidence at the woman's house to reflect what he had seen—

"Who was he?" Father Reynolds asked Niccolo as they drove away from Rose's home.

Niccolo barely heard him, as he'd gotten so distracted in his thoughts. He blinked back to reality, glanced over at Jackson, and then frowned. Then he realized his mistake in bringing up anything about Arthur—everything about the man remained on a need-to-know basis, and Jackson didn't come under that umbrella.

Niccolo had only ended up in the know because of the circumstances surrounding the assault in West Virginia. Each and every thing about that event had felt wrong to him, and it became clear, even at the time, that the Church scrambled to cover it up. They expected those events to happen, which meant that Arthur proved a liability at best.

At worst ...

"Arthur?"

"Yeah. He told me he was a reporter, but he wasn't, was he?"

"No."

"You said you saw the bodies. You know what he did?"

Niccolo hesitated, and then said, "It's probably best that you don't ask any more questions."

"For you?"

"For both of us. I don't have the authority to talk about this, and just asking puts you in danger. He told you he was a reporter, and for your safety and sanity, you should take him at his word."

"How do you know him?"

"I don't. At least, not personally."

Niccolo had met Arthur a few weeks after the incident. The meeting had awed him. After seeing the devastation wreaked on the cult in the woods, the idea that Arthur would be a normal-looking man had seemed unthinkable. He'd imagined a larger-than-life, terrifying figure; Arthur looked more like a suburban house dad.

He had still sported injuries during that meeting and needed to recover from his wounds. On that day, the Church officials had told him they wouldn't investigate the issue any further and would let Arthur go. Barely a slap on the wrist. Niccolo had felt flabbergasted and objected strongly, but his words fell on deaf ears.

He couldn't tell any of that to Jackson, however. Just knowing that someone like Arthur existed could prove dangerous for the young priest.

"He wouldn't tell me why he came here," Jackson said. It seemed he had decided not to continue pursuing the issue. "He just asked me a bunch of questions and seemed worried when he found out that you'd come here."

"I guess he remembers me, too. What did he ask you about?"

"Mostly Bishop Glasser," Jackson said with a shrug. "He said he was writing a story about the bishop and called him a 'rising star.' He wanted to know how well I knew the man and if I had interacted with him much since taking this post at Saint Joseph's."

"What did you tell him?"

"I told him that I knew Leopold from a few previous encounters but had rarely interacted with him on a personal basis."

"You didn't tell him anything about Rose?"

"Rose? No, why would I?"

"You're sure? Nothing about your concern that she might have become possessed?"

"Definitely not. I make it a habit not to talk to reporters about Church business. Nor did I tell him about my recent disagreements with the bishop. He asked what you were doing here, but I didn't tell him that either. I didn't know who the man was, but he seemed to know quite a bit about me."

"That's good."

Father Paladina felt relieved that Jackson hadn't told Arthur anything that could have come back to haunt them. When he made his report later, he fully intended to alert the Vatican that Arthur had arrived here in Everett, though he doubted it would come to anything. Already, he had seen to what lengths they would go to protect the man, and his word meant nothing where Arthur was concerned.

It remained unthinkable that Arthur had gotten fully exonerated of his actions in West Virginia. The Church had berated him and the Council he served for acting rashly, but it amounted to little more than a slap on the wrist. Arthur had managed to dismantle a dangerous cult responsible for death and mayhem, and for that, they felt willing to forgive almost anything.

But, if Arthur did the same thing, did that make them any better?

They'd made the wrong call in forgiving Arthur as far as Niccolo was concerned. Arthur remained dangerous, and even though he had dealt a sizable blow to an enemy of the Church, he had gone about it in the wrong way entirely.

At the very least, he hoped his threat had worked and that Arthur wouldn't come back to Everett anytime soon. With luck, Arthur would have gone before he even made his call to the Vatican.

As Niccolo sat in Jackson's car, thinking, he had to admit that his annoyance about West Virginia didn't make for the only reason that seeing Arthur had made him feel out of sorts. In truth, having someone like Arthur in Everett terrified him. He'd only met the man a handful of times in his life, but he'd heard stories about him.

Arthur, brutal and ruthless, had the willingness to do anything to accomplish his mission. Also, he had become the best at what he did, which meant whenever he rolled into town, bad things were about to happen. If Arthur had come here, then it indicated that something dangerous had set in motion.

"You used to know him?" Jackson asked after a few minutes of silence, attempting once more to spark Father Paladina into conversation. "He seemed surprised to see you out here. You must have history."

"We do."

"Why did he ask me about the bishop?"

"No clue. All I know is that he's dangerous, and you should avoid him at all costs. If he comes looking for you again, let me know, and don't answer any of his questions."

Jackson seemed uncomfortable by Niccolo's answer, and he wanted more information about Arthur, but Niccolo had gone as far as he felt willing to in the conversation. Finally, Jackson nodded, conceding that the issue had closed, and they drove the rest of the way back into town in silence.

✳✳✳

Jackson dropped off Niccolo at his hotel a short while later, and then he went back to his church. Though still early in the afternoon, it looked like it would turn into a clear night. Jackson wanted to finish some paperwork and prepare for his Sunday sermon, and Niccolo needed to make his call to the Vatican to report his findings. He could have used the phone at Saint Joseph's Cathedral, but just now, he wanted to stay alone for a while.

Niccolo passed through the lobby and upstairs to his hotel room, kicked his shoes off, and then relaxed back onto the bed. He didn't place the call back home just then, though, wanting to spend time sorting through his thoughts and deciding what he would tell them. Perhaps he could turn on the television to distract him and so the room wouldn't seem so quiet? Then he changed his mind.

While sitting there, alone in the quiet hotel room, he couldn't hide his concerns about the day quite as easily as he had done out in the daylight. The town had something unsettling about it, not to mention the events that had taken place, starting with the diner and culminating in the crawlspace beneath Rose's home. He hadn't spent much time in Everett, but it grew clearer that something had gone awry.

Alone, he found his mind wandering continually back to what had happened to him beneath the house. The grotesque visage of the corpse crawling out at him had seemed lifelike and horrific and unlike anything he'd ever seen or experienced. It couldn't have had any reality, or he would have died, and yet, it had *felt* real.

The woman, her eyes, and the way she crawled over the dirt and gravel ... the memory stuck with him, and each time he closed his eyes, she was there. It terrified him, and he wavered back and forth between believing he had imagined it and wondering if, maybe, something else *had* joined him down there in the crawlspace.

Yet, admitting that something might have happened meant allowing him to admit that supernatural creatures existed. He believed in evil, and he believed that people could be evil, but he did not believe that demonic creatures lived out there, trying to ruin humanity. If they did exist, then surely he would have seen them; after all, he was an exorcist.

Nevertheless, he found it difficult to focus on anything else. The longer he sat there in the dark, the more he realized how terrified he felt. This trip hadn't turned out how he had expected, and right now, he had endless questions and few answers.

What was more, as much as he despised Arthur Vangeest, the man wouldn't have come here if he didn't have a good reason. He must think that the town had a problem that needed his sort of expertise.

Finally, Niccolo reached over and placed a phone call. He held the handset to his ear, at the end of the cord, and listened to it ring. After several rings, someone answered.

"Hello?"

"Hello, Bishop Glasser," Niccolo said. "How are you?"

"Quite well. And you?"

"The same."

"To what do I owe the pleasure?"

"I have met with Father Reynolds, and he would like the opportunity to speak to you in person."

"Oh?"

"Yes."

"About what, might I ask?"

"That would be best coming from him. I hoped that we might arrange a meeting."

"Of course. How about tonight?"

"Tonight?"

"Yes. Maybe around seven?"

Niccolo glanced over at the clock—just after two. "Sure. That should work."

"It isn't anything serious, is it?" The bishop's voice sounded playful, and the words in jest, but something about the way he spoke put Niccolo on edge.

"No, no, nothing like that," he said.

"Excellent. Then I shall see you tonight."

They hung up, and Niccolo sat on the edge of his bed, frowning at the phone. Bishop Glasser couldn't *possibly* have involvement in events in the city—no matter what Arthur said— and yet, just speaking to the man had made him uncomfortable.

After speaking to the bishop, Niccolo phoned the Vatican. His superior, Father Desmond Affretti, answered after a few rings, "Hello?"

"Hello. It is Niccolo."

"Ah, Niccolo, I have tried to get hold of you. I called your hotel room for hours."

"I went out with Father Jackson," he said. "My apologies. Why did you want to reach me?"

"We received a report earlier that could affect your mission. I need to know what you have found."

"Father Jackson has decided to drop his request for an exorcist in Everett."

"Good. What else?"

"I feel that something is happening in this town, which deserves the attention of one of our brethren."

Father Affretti remained silent for a long while, to the point that Niccolo grew afraid that the call might have disconnected.

"Are you in immediate danger?"

"What? No," he said. "I don't believe so."

"Why do you feel that way? What omens have you seen?"

"Nothing outright, but a few strange things have made me concerned."

"Strange how?"

Niccolo frowned. The line of questioning seemed considerably more direct than he'd expected or had grown used to from the older priest. It felt more like a test than simply asking questions.

"I don't know how to explain it. First, I spoke with a restaurateur who referenced details about my childhood—which she could not have known—and I also met with Arthur Vangeest. He said he believes the bishop—"

"Stop talking," Father Affretti said in clipped, harsh tones. His voice held an edge of concern, which Niccolo had never heard before from the priest.

"Excuse me?"

"You have concerns and have said enough. Damn it; I had hoped the report would prove wrong. Okay, I have all I need to know."

"Yes, but—"

"You must leave immediately," the older priest said.

"What? So soon?"

Father Affretti ignored his question, "What about Father Jackson? Do your concerns about the city extend to him as well?"

"No," Niccolo said.

"Good. He should come with you. I can schedule your flight in an hour for yourself and Father Jackson."

"We can't leave yet," Niccolo said. "We have plans to meet

with Bishop Glasser."

"When?"

"Tonight."

"He expects you?"

Niccolo hesitated before replying, "Yes. I called him before I called you. I can cancel, though."

Another long pause came from Father Affretti. The conversation worried Niccolo, and he developed a sinking feeling in the pit of his stomach.

"No, that would make it more dangerous. It would look like you were running. You need to keep up appearances until we have assets to keep you safe."

"Safe from what?"

Father Affretti didn't answer that query either, "Have you noticed anyone following you?"

"No."

"Any people acting strangely?"

"A few."

"Did they pay you special attention?"

"Yes."

"This is of vital importance, Niccolo. You *must* continue to act normally. Go to the bishop's house tonight but say *nothing* of your investigation. Act naturally and as if nothing has gone amiss."

"*Is* something amiss?"

"I don't know yet. I have to await more information and don't have any good answers. Tonight, I will call you at ten with the details of your flight. *No one* must know you plan to leave so soon."

"Why? What's going on?"

"Hopefully nothing," Father Affretti said. "But I don't feel willing to take any chances. Be careful, Niccolo. Don't let your guard down."

Then, Father Affretti disconnected.

Niccolo sat on the bed in stunned silence, holding the handset in his hand and listening to the dial tone. He could hardly believe the conversation he had just had, and a sickening feeling lay in the pit of his stomach.

Father Affretti never feared anything. Ever. For him to feel worried about something ...

Maybe Arthur had called it correctly. Maybe something *had* gone wrong in this town. Worse, maybe the bishop did have an involvement. If that proved the case, then he had just set up a dinner arrangement between himself and Jackson in the middle of the hornet's nest.

All of a sudden, the dial tone clicked off, and the line went dead. Niccolo didn't register it until he heard the soft sound of breathing on the other end of the line. In and out, barely audible. Gradually, the sound increased, and slowly mounting laughter replaced the breathing.

Niccolo looked at the phone in horror and slammed it down on the base. *What in God's name is going on?*

He needed to get to Jackson and make sure he remained okay. With grim determination, he gathered up his coat, slipped his shoes back on, and headed out of the hotel room and down toward the lobby. He wanted to tell the priest about the goings on, but a part of him warned him that such disclosure wouldn't turn out a good idea.

Act normally, Father Affretti had said. Niccolo didn't know how to act naturally when he felt so terrified, and the worst possible option would lay in alerting Jackson that he might face danger, too.

Chapter 8

Father Paladina walked through the streets of Everett toward Saint Joseph's Cathedral, hoping to gain a sudden insight into the situation and what he should do next. His conversation with Father Affretti had worried him quite a bit, and now he couldn't help but glance around to see if anyone followed him.

But that was crazy, right? Why would anyone tail him?

Father Affretti seemed concerned at the situation, like the news he had received meant Niccolo had come into danger. He felt at a complete loss; something that didn't happen to him often. Part of Niccolo felt like he had jumped in over his head and had gotten stuck in a situation for which he remained wholly unprepared.

Except, that didn't run quite true. He had received training for something like this. Had prepared for this sort of situation his entire life, and to recognize omens and demonic activity and deal with it on behalf of the Catholic Church.

That would involve risk, they had told him. People would want to harm and stop him, and it could come down to reasons other than anything demonic. What he represented from the Church put him at risk. However, hearing his teachers tell him that and actually experiencing it remained vastly different things.

He had never dreamed that something like this might happen. In every case he had ever worked up to this point in his life, the situation had turned out as something entirely mundane or a hoax. The priest had investigated, found the culprit, and then returned home.

This differed, though. This would make for his sixteenth investigation. Had his luck run out at last?

Could Father Affretti possibly have assumed correctly that his life was in danger?

He didn't know. What he did know was that he felt terrified and at a loss. His mind kicked into overdrive, and he replayed events. People acting strangely or paying him special attention? He had only spent about a day here, but he could think of circumstances that fit that description.

Everett either had to be a strange place, or something had gone badly wrong.

The wind felt chilly, and his nose had grown cold and tender from long exposure when he finally came out of his reverie and realized how much time had passed since he'd set off walking. He had missed the turnoff to get to the church and walked several blocks farther.

Annoyed, he chided himself for getting lost in his thoughts and quickly headed in the opposite direction. His feet and body felt exhausted, and a layer of sweat covered his skin, but he also felt better. Always, he became less prone to anxiety and worry when he grew physically exhausted. It helped him think more clearly.

While he walked, his brain avoided the problems at hand and focused more on the people around him on the street. They looked normal enough. Just ordinary people going about their days. Nothing dangerous about them, right? A fair number of them lingered on the streets, more than he would have expected in this cold, but maybe they had business to attend to? Some carried grocery bags; others, briefcases.

Did it represent an abnormal amount? Or had Niccolo become paranoid in seeing things where nothing existed? All the people looked as if used to the cold weather and constantly blowing wind, bundled up tight with thick scarves pulled up to cover their mouths. The city most likely looked like this regularly at this time of day.

Niccolo had packed several scarves for this trip and regretted that he'd forgotten to grab any of them out of the luggage before heading out. Instead, he rubbed his hands and then pressed them to his cold and numb cheeks and nose.

He retraced his steps through the city, made the correct turn, and stood at Father Reynolds's church a short while later, exhausted and ravenous. And still, he didn't know what he would tell Father Reynolds, if anything, about the goings on.

✻✻✻

Father Jackson Reynolds sat in his office when Niccolo arrived, looking over a stack of papers. He wore a pair of large-rimmed glasses, which he removed promptly when Niccolo entered the room. He stood up from behind his desk and frowned.

"Apologies; I must have lost track of time."

"Don't worry; I wasn't supposed to stop by until later," Niccolo said. "I had planned to call first but then decided just to walk over."

"I could have come and got you."

"I didn't mind the walk," Niccolo said. "I just went out for a bit and thought I might spare you having to make the trip."

"Ah." Jackson rubbed his face. "Did you speak with Bishop Glasser?"

"Yes." Niccolo nodded. "He expects us at his house tonight at seven."

Jackson glanced at his wristwatch. "So, a few hours."

"Is that all right?"

"Of course. It just means I might have time to make part of the game."

"Game?"

***

A youth baseball game hadn't factored as something Niccolo could envision attending with Jackson before their meeting with Bishop Glasser. His first reaction came as disbelief, considering their situation, but the more he thought about it, the more he realized it offered a perfect way to pass the time.

Right now, he didn't want to spend time alone. The more people they surrounded themselves with, the better, and it served as a mild distraction to keep him from worrying about what Father Affretti had said.

The game had importance for Jackson. They ended up at a high-school baseball game, and many of the students and parents were members of his congregation and close personal friends. Evidently, the young priest did this on a regular basis—going out to support his congregation in their life events, and Niccolo could respect that.

It also served as a perfect way to blend in and keep a low profile, given his instructions to act naturally, and having Jackson take him to the game seemed like a perfect cover.

Many of the parents greeted Jackson warmly when the two priests first arrived, and everyone seemed genuinely pleased to see them. It all fell outside of Niccolo's comfort zone—he cared little for sports and had to struggle to keep his fear in check—but he had grown both willing and used to stifling his worries. They could go to the game, and then the dinner with the bishop, and then in the morning, they would leave the city with no one the wiser.

Then it would become someone else's problem to solve.

The most surprising part about the baseball game, though, came in the fact that Niccolo enjoyed himself. He still worried that someone might sit watching him, but after they had sat there for a while, he calmed. It all felt so normal. The mood seemed light and happy, and he even bought a hotdog when he grew too hungry to think straight.

A first for him—the hotdog, while not that good, tasted edible and quite different from what he had expected. His expectation had taken it as akin to sausage, and instead, the hotdog proved unique. He chocked it all up to a pleasant distraction to keep his mind occupied.

The parents grew loud and cheerful as they watched their children play, and even though Niccolo had little idea of what events on the field meant, he found the excitement contagious. Jackson cheered and clapped when certain things happened, and on occasion, stood up or laughed.

"You're a baseball fan?" Niccolo asked during one of the lulls in the game.

"I grew up with it," Jackson said. "Not here, though."

"Oh?"

"I was born in Boston, so I rarely miss a Red Sox game on the television. What about you?"

"Baseball? Never played. I don't even know what's going on."

"I mean sports in general. Are you a fan?"

Niccolo shrugged. "Not really. It never seemed important in my life. I don't mind watching it, but I rarely turn sports on at home."

"You come from Rome?"

"Yes. Born and raised, and I've rarely ventured outside of it. How did you end up here, in Everett?"

"The Church asked me to take this parish shortly after my Seminary education. They didn't give me much of a choice in the matter. It came down to this or nothing. At first, I was ..."

He seemed to realize what he was saying and glanced sideways at Niccolo.

"Furious?" Niccolo said.

Jackson laughed. "Displeased," he said. "This didn't make my first choice of places to go."

"Why not?"

"No professional baseball team in the area, for one thing." Jackson smiled. "Plus, the town has a lot of people who ... let's say, who are different from me."

"You mean white. Is that a problem?"

Jackson shook his head. "It took some getting used to for all of us, but I didn't mean that. I'd imagined that I would work in the communities I'd grown up in and help kids like me. Then, when the Church asked me to come here ... well, I almost thought it belied a race issue."

"Do you regret taking the job?"

Jackson shook his head. "No. As I said, it took some getting used to, but I realized that it brought a blessing and not a curse."

"What do you mean?"

Jackson took a moment to consider his words, sipping his water. "I grew up an angry kid. Didn't have the best upbringing, and I almost fell in with the wrong crowd. I used to look at the world around me and hate everything. All I wanted to do was change it."

"I can sympathize."

"Don't get me wrong, I became an ambitious kid, and I thought myself special. I wanted to go back and fix things, and when they told me I had to come here to take over Saint Joseph's Cathedral instead, I grew furious. I pushed back and demanded to go home. They gave me an ultimatum, and I figured they just wanted to punish me."

"Now, you don't think they did?"

Jackson shook his head again. "Not anymore. When they put me *here*, I had to take over a well-established parish full of good people. I had arrogance, though, and felt ready to do something great. Like I could go out and fix the world, but the thing is, I remained just a confused kid. If they had put me back in Boston when I first left Seminary, I would have fallen back into bad practices and old habits, and I would have stayed just as angry as the day I'd left. I needed ... separation from that."

"So, will you go back?"

Jackson nodded. "Yes. That brings us to the other reason they didn't send me to Boston, which I didn't know at the time. They plan for me to take over the Cathedral of the Holy Cross, close to where I grew up. One of the oldest and most important churches in New England. They've already cleared it and begun setting plans in motion, but it won't happen right away. I haven't told anyone here, yet, but in a few years. Father O'Connell will retire soon, and his church stands only a few blocks from my old house. I think when I finally do go back, I'll have grown ready to make a proper difference."

"I know you will. From all reports, you've done a tremendous job here. Your congregation loves you. I've heard only glowing reports about you in the Vatican."

Jackson waved his hand in the air, brushing away the praise. "You exaggerate, but I appreciate it nonetheless. The people here are great. I feel lucky to get to spend my days with them."

"Nevertheless, many important people see great things in your future."

"You mean, until this," Jackson said with a self-deprecating chuckle. "Until I freaked out and cried 'demon' to the Vatican? I feel fairly certain this will stain my reputation in the future."

"How so?"

"Well, they sent you here to help me see the error of my ways," Jackson said. "I claimed that we needed an exorcist in Everett, and they sent you, and you've found nothing here."

"I ..." Niccolo had been about to say, *I wouldn't be so sure,* and then stopped himself. He still felt unsure how much he should tell Jackson about their circumstances, and now he leaned toward withholding everything until they set off on their way out of the city.

The people here didn't know Niccolo, so if he behaved oddly, they could chock it up to his personality. But, if Jackson realized that they might have come into danger, then he would have a much more difficult time in hiding his true feelings from the people around them.

Better for both of them if Jackson didn't know that they had something to hide. Not yet, at least.

"You did your duty," Niccolo said, instead. "That's all the Vatican can ask of you."

"Who will see it that way? Bishop Glasser will never forgive me for what I did, going behind his back like that, and he's been known to hold a grudge."

That held truth, Niccolo knew. Leopold Glasser had grown famous for nursing grudges for years after an event had occurred. Most likely, Leopold would attempt to ruin Jackson's career.

That, of course, depended upon Arthur getting it wrong, and Leopold not having any involvement in whatever went on in Everett.

Either way, agreeing didn't seem the most prudent thing to do for the young man.

"You acted the way you did because you wanted to help protect a member of your congregation. Even though you might have gotten it wrong, your intentions remain unquestionably good. We can't second-guess the decisions we've made. We can move forward and learn from them."

"I suppose," Jackson said. "Still, I felt so *sure*. I mean it *felt* like a demon, you know?"

Niccolo frowned. "What do you mean?"

Jackson glanced at him, tilting his head to the side, as though he'd only just realized what he'd said, and his eyes widened in concern. "Never mind."

"You mean when you visited with the woman? With Rose Gallagher? What did you mean, it *felt* like a demon?"

Jackson hesitated and fidgeted. "I don't know. Nothing. It isn't a big deal."

"You felt something inside of her? Like another presence?"

Jackson's expression shifted to suspicion, as if Niccolo had tried to back him into a trap. Niccolo pressed at the idea, "What did you mean, you could feel the demon?"

"Not exactly sure. When I sat with Rose, I could sense something ... wrong inside her. It seemed like I could reach out and touch it like something evil lived there."

"And you think it was the demon?"

"I did at first. But not anymore."

"What do you mean?"

"I mean ..." The young priest shook his head and laughed at himself. "You must think me crazy, going on about this. As we said, we have no demon here in Everett, just me overreacting."

They sat in silence for a few moments, watching the game. Niccolo got lost in his thoughts, trying to come to terms with what Jackson had described. The idea that he would feel demons and reach out and touch them.

He'd heard of such abilities before from some of the most famous exorcists throughout history, and the way they talked about what they did in old documents and reports. He hadn't met anyone living who described things that exact way, as reportedly, it made for a rare gift.

Still, what Jackson had described highlighted the idea that something felt wrong about the woman, not that he had sensed an actual demon. And, he didn't seem to think it relevant anymore. Niccolo had jumped to conclusions.

Niccolo hadn't sensed anything strange about the woman, but he also didn't believe the accounts that some people could sense and interact with demons. It seemed too far-fetched, and considering he didn't believe in demons, he refused to accept the prospect of people with special gifts.

Of course, he'd also never imagined ending up in a situation where his life might be in danger, either.

"I'm off to get another hotdog," Jackson said. "Would you like one?"

"What?" Niccolo asked, distracted. Then he caught up, "No, thank you."

"All right, I'll get back in a couple of minutes."

"Wait a second. When we spoke to Rose earlier today," Niccolo said, as Jackson rose from the uncomfortable metal bench. "Did you ... could you still sense the evil presence inside her?"

Jackson frowned at him. "Why do you ask?"

"Humor me. Could you still feel it there, or did things seem different this time?"

The young priest hesitated for a second before nodding. "Yes. When we went into her house, I could still sense it. But it couldn't possibly have meant she's suffered possession, though. I got it wrong."

"Why? What do you mean?"

"Because she's not the only person that seems like that in the city anymore."

Then, Jackson headed down the stairs toward the concession stand, leaving Niccolo sitting alone on the aluminum bench. Uncomfortable from more than just the hard metal. Father Paladina sat there, watching him leave, and couldn't keep his hands from trembling.

✳✳✳

Quite a while passed, and still Jackson hadn't returned from the concession stand. Niccolo sat there alone, trying to act normal and aware that he failed miserably.

Fear for his life brought a double problem, he realized. First, it made it difficult to do anything because his entire body shook like a leaf. That didn't bring the worst part, however, but more the longevity of the situation. To have his senses heightened by fear for such a long time made him exhausted and weak, and he didn't know how to turn it off.

Everything felt like a threat. He didn't know if people watched or plotted against him, and now Jackson had gone missing—even though only for a few minutes. Niccolo could understand why people with deeply ingrained paranoia would have so much trouble functioning in daily life.

Most likely, Jackson remained fine. The line had looked rather long when they'd first gone up, but he should have come back by now, and Father Paladina began to worry. It grew close to the time they would need to leave to go see Bishop Glasser, and he didn't want to arrive late.

Plus, the game wound down and many parents were packed up and made ready to leave. Niccolo couldn't take it any longer. He stood and headed for the concession stand, hoping to find Father Reynolds and make sure he remained all right.

He spotted him as soon as he walked off the metal bleachers and headed toward the concessions. Jackson stood near the fence around the field and spoke with a middle-aged couple. The man looked squat and overweight, wearing a Hawaiian shirt and baggy shorts, and the woman stood a head taller than him and wore long business pants and a precise white blouse. She would have appeared quite attractive except that she seemed to have had too much plastic surgery in the past.

Niccolo assumed them married as he walked up toward the three of them. Jackson had a wadded up napkin in his hand and looked to have finished eating his hotdog at some point during the conversation. When Niccolo drew closer, all three of them turned to face him.

Jackson glanced over. "Ah, Niccolo, allow me to introduce you to the Spencers. Mary and Tim. Mary, Tim, this is Father Niccolo Paladina. He comes from Rome."

Niccolo nodded and shook their offered hands, smiling as pleasantly as he could manage.

"A pleasure," he said, raising a questioning eyebrow toward the young priest.

"They asked me about the sermon this Sunday. Tim acts as one of my Deacons and had planned to help me repair one of the pews."

"Oh?"

Jackson glanced over at Tim. "We hadn't settled on an actual time? Would tomorrow work for you?"

"Yeah, that works well," Tim said. "It's Saturday, so I'll grab Brad, and we'll meet you there first thing in the morning. I just need to remember to bring my tools. Shouldn't take more than an hour to fix the pew up."

"Excellent," Jackson said. "I'll meet you there in the morning."

"We should get going," Niccolo said. "We don't want to end up late for our appointment."

"Of course," Jackson said. "Mary, Tim, I will see you both later. Thanks again!"

Father Reynolds turned away from the couple and headed toward the cars. Niccolo nodded politely at the man and then turned to follow, but he stopped when a look of anger flashed across the woman's face.

Pure rage, and she'd directed her look at Jackson's back as the young priest walked away. Her eyes filled with it, though it only lasted for a second before her expression returned to normal.

She hadn't realized that Niccolo stood watching her, and when she looked back at him, she smiled pleasantly.

"It was nice to meet you, Father."

He cleared his throat. "Likewise."

Her husband turned and walked away toward the fence,

turning his attention back to the game.

Mary watched him go, and then turned and smiled at Father Paladina. "I wish you all of God's love and all the luck in the world."

"Thank you," he said.

She turned and headed toward her husband, then paused and glanced back at Niccolo one last time.

"You're going to need it."

✳✳✳

"What did you mean?" Niccolo asked when they'd climbed into Jackson's car and got on their way to Bishop Glasser's estate. He felt queasy and weak, not sure what to think about everything happening around him. What had Mary meant by saying he would need God's love? What was going on? "When you said Rose wasn't the only one who seemed different, what did you mean?"

Jackson frowned, thinking. "I don't know how to describe it. When I first met with Rose in her home when she started acting weird, she gave me this vibe ... like ..." He shook his head. "I don't know how to describe it. It seemed like I could sense what lived inside her, and it felt *wrong*."

"But not just her?"

He shook his head. "No, not anymore. It has become a general feeling now. Not everywhere, exactly, just in a lot of people; and, I have this sense of foreboding. As far as I can guess, it started when I first went to visit Rose, and then my mind ran away with the idea and set me off in imagining it. I don't know, like maybe I'm searching for the worst in people now, you know?"

Father Paladina nodded. "Did you get that feeling from Mrs. Spencer?"

"Mary?" Jackson asked. He took a long moment before pausing. "Yes. How did you know?"

He spoke reluctantly as if tattling on a friend. Niccolo stayed careful not to let his face give anything away, but it made him feel somewhat sick to his stomach. "But not her husband?"

"No. I mean, I don't know. As I said, it doesn't seem to mean anything. It just comes down to this feeling I get sometimes. But Mary is one of the nicest people I've ever met, so I know it doesn't have anything to do with her."

"Probably not," Niccolo said. "Most probably nothing."

Inside, however, he didn't feel at all certain. Right now, all he wanted was leave Everett behind forever.

One last dinner. He only had to make it through tonight.

Chapter 9

The rain sprinkled lightly when they arrived at the home of Bishop Leopold Glasser a short while later. The gloom and misery outside filled him with dark thoughts and worries. He believed their best option lay in canceling the meeting and going to the Airport, but Father Affretti had warned him most specifically against that. Their best option dictated that they act normal.

The trees flanked their car as they headed up the drive, and Niccolo couldn't help but feel that they'd come alive. He felt like a prisoner heading to his death, no matter how ridiculous a thought. They just had to get through a simple dinner engagement and everything would turn out fine.

"I've only come here a handful of times before," Jackson said, turning the car off after parking in front of the bishop's house. He looked at the estate with an expression of mixed awe and disgust. "Each time I see it, it makes me feel ..."

Father Reynolds, once more, grew aware that he'd nearly voiced out of place. He glanced sideways at Niccolo, a guilty expression on his face.

"Ostentatious?"

"I didn't mean to ... it isn't my place to judge—"

"I agree completely," Niccolo raised a hand. "It is ostentatious and designed to draw attention. Men such as Glasser believe that their relation to God entitles them to luxuries not befitting such a station. He should live in a humble way, and this home is not one of humility."

"We're supposed to live within reasonable means, aren't we? It isn't our place to flaunt our wealth."

"It depends on the outlook you have. Some believe that a show of privilege benefits their congregation by showing them that worship of our Lord has tangible rewards. I, however, don't make one of those people. I believe that faith is its own reward."

"So do I. I would rather the money get put to good use in helping those in need. Our reward isn't to be found in this world."

"Are you ready to go in?" Niccolo asked. "I hope we don't have to stay here for too long."

Jackson seemed surprised by that. "I thought I was the one who didn't like the bishop."

Niccolo didn't respond.

Father Reynolds and Bishop Glasser had a strained relationship. Jackson seemed rather on edge by the situation even without knowing the whole story, and that made Niccolo worry.

Supposed to act normally, it wouldn't prove good if one of them acted off. Niccolo wanted to make sure that Jackson relaxed and remained in control before they entered the estate. He didn't want to push Jackson into a confrontation for which he hadn't prepared.

To be honest, though, he felt unsure whether or not he'd prepared. The last few days in Everett had provided some of the strangest and most worrisome of his life, and he had no idea what he would do in response to everything happening. He had come here with the belief that anything abnormal happening could get explained mundanely, but now he doubted if he could make it out alive.

"We just need to inform him that the investigation got dropped and that everything can go back to normal," Niccolo said, finally.

Jackson smiled, but it looked a strained smile. "Of course. What sort of man would I be if I proved unable to admit when I got it wrong?"

Niccolo nodded and opened the car door, stepping out into the rain. Though not heavy enough to warrant an umbrella, and his coat being waterproof, it still felt uncomfortable when the cold water ran down his hair and beneath his shirt. The rain wouldn't have bothered him at all, in fact, if not for how cold the night had grown. Only a few moments after stepping out of the car, he felt chilled to his bones.

A well-dressed man awaited them at the door, perhaps another butler, and opened it to allow them entrance. It surprised Niccolo to see a different man than he had met last time. Maybe the bishop had multiple people on staff for different nights?

Surely it didn't give a sign of anything amiss?

"Please, come in," the butler said. "Dinner is nearly prepared."

They followed him into the foyer, and then through a set of double doors, and ended up in a large dining hall on the first floor on the opposite side of the building from where he had met Bishop Glasser during his first visit here. That felt like a lifetime ago.

A table ran the length of the room, easily capable of seating thirty guests while having room to spare, but for now, only three place settings lay at the far end of the hall.

Staff had set them near a cozy hearth, and a fire blazed and crackled within. Even from across the room, Niccolo could feel the warmth spilling out, and it felt glorious on his cold skin. The butler took their coats and disappeared, leaving the two priests standing in the entryway of the dining hall.

Bishop Glasser stood next to the hearth, watching the flames. He glanced up at them when they came in and smiled. He wore red formal robes and had a shiny substance in his thinning hair to keep it in place.

"Welcome," he said, striding across the hall to meet them. He shook hands with Father Paladina. "It is good to see you again."

"Likewise."

"It is great to see you as well, Father Reynolds," Leopold said, offering his hand to the young priest. "It has been entirely too long since we've sat down and conversed. It pleases me to no end to see you once more."

Jackson grew visibly uncomfortable but accepted the offered handshake and nodded. He swallowed back his discomfort and put on a calm face.

"I agree, it has been too long since we've talked. I came here to apologize in person for—"

Leopold waved his hand in the air. "Come now. There is absolutely no need for that whatsoever. You need never apologize for actions taken while guarding your flock. Your first duty is to them, not to me."

"I went over your head," Jackson said. "An action unbecoming of someone in my position."

"You did what you felt was necessary, and I will *never* blame you for that. I trust in your judgment, and though I wish you had consulted me further regarding what steps should get taken, I do not blame you for taking the steps you did. Apology is not necessary, nor is forgiveness. Let us simply put it behind us and move on to the next chapter."

Jackson hesitated, and then said, "I thank you for your understanding."

"Of course, my friend. I trust this brings the end of the matter."

"Yes." Jackson took a deep breath before continuing, "I became severely mistaken in my belief about Rose Gallagher's condition. I ... overreacted, and as such, I have changed my mind about seeking an exorcist or help from the Church. I plan to speak with Rose's family and determine if we can find some other way to help her outside of the Church."

Bishop Glasser smiled. "It is of no concern. Please, have a seat and relax. Our food will be brought forth shortly. Do you enjoy lamb?"

He guided them over to the three place settings, and they all took their places. The bishop sat at the head of the table, Niccolo to his right, and Jackson to his left. Niccolo felt grateful to sit so near to the fireplace, as the waves of heat radiating out felt heavenly, though he would have preferred more distance from the bishop himself.

Bishop Glasser lifted a small bell and shook it once, giving off a soft tinkle. A moment later, a side door opened, leading to the kitchen. Servers came into the room, carrying trays, and set them down in front of the three men.

Underneath, the plate held a Caesar salad—and a traditional one at that, replete with anchovies and a light drizzle of sauce. Niccolo's mouth watered. The hotdog at the game seemed weeks ago.

Part of him wondered if he should eat the food at all, but he experienced too much hunger to care. Also, he had to act naturally, and turning down the meal would get taken poorly. So, he would eat it and do his best to seem like nothing had gone amiss.

They barely spoke as they ate, and as they finished up the salad, the servers returned to replace those dishes with a lamb pasta with pesto sauce, which tasted delicious and earthy and authentic. The servers moved silently and with ease, ghosts in the room, continually filling their wine glasses and removing empty plates.

During this course, Bishop Glasser spoke lightly and courteously about nothing of substance. He asked Niccolo about his home in Italy and the food he enjoyed. Niccolo answered as courteously as he could without giving any long responses. Though normally a talkative person at the dinner table, right now, he found it difficult.

The conversation turned to what the weather was like, and if Rome compared to what he saw in Everett, and then there came other pleasantries that kept the conversation and wine flowing.

Niccolo loosened up as the meal continued, letting his guard down and enjoying himself. This acting normal business became easier because everything seemed normal. He had felt terrified coming into this situation but now believed it all unfounded. The bishop remained polite and courteous. No way did Arthur have it right. The bishop couldn't possibly have become involved.

The last several days had proven stressful, and it felt nice not to worry for a time. Jackson felt much the same way. Leopold Glasser had an easy charm about him and behaved in an incredibly courteous manner. Soft spoken, he seemed polite with a sort of old-fashioned affect easy to get along with.

Once they had finished their lamb, the servers returned and replaced that with a dessert course—butter cake with raspberry syrup and mixed berries. Niccolo, though full by the time dessert arrived, still found himself devouring the cake in its entirety.

Certainly, it made for one of the most enjoyable meals he had experienced in a long while. While the servers cleared off the table, he leaned back in his chair and patted his stomach, pleasantly full. Somehow, it felt like everything would turn out all right. Consciously, he recognized the feeling as wrong and realized that every second they stayed in Everett they remained in danger; however, he still half-believed it.

If the bishop had no part in events, he realized, then it became possible that he had also come into harm's way. Maybe he should speak with Father Affretti about getting the bishop a ticket to Rome as well. Just in case.

"Well, gentlemen," Bishop Glasser said. "If you would like, we can retire to my study and have a drink and continue our conversation."

He stood, and the two priests followed him across the hall into another room. Still raining, the wind and water pattered softly against the windows, and Niccolo found himself growing rather sleepy.

From the wine, he assumed. He hadn't drunk anything since first coming to Everett, and only had wine occasionally back home in Rome. A lightweight, his comfort at the entire situation had diminished his judgment.

Bishop Glasser poured out a few glasses of brandy, and they took seats in comfortable, reclining chairs. For a while, they relaxed in silence, sipping their drinks and enjoying the quiet.

"You should come visit us sometime in the spring or summer," Bishop Glasser said to Niccolo. "It looks quite beautiful out here when everything comes out in bloom."

"I would like that," Niccolo said.

He doubted he would ever return to Everett, Washington, but it didn't seem a prudent thing to say.

"When will you return to Rome?"

"Tomorrow," he said, the answer slipping out before he could stop himself.

The bishop frowned. "So soon?"

"Yes. I need to return to report my findings."

Bishop Glasser looked down at the glass in his hand, twirling a finger around the rim. "And what will that report say?"

In Niccolo's mind, warnings flashed. Perhaps his worry came from his run-in with Arthur at Rose's home. However, it seemed prudent to keep his concerns to himself. He felt that the bishop remained on the up-and-up and that everyone had overreacted. Also, he wanted to stay safe and hold certain details back.

At least for now.

"Precisely as Father Reynolds explained," he said, nodding toward the young priest. "I have found nothing abnormal happening in Everett, and thus, my recommendation will lean toward dropping the investigation."

Bishop Glasser nodded and sipped his brandy, but the motion appeared stiff and awkward. Niccolo frowned, realizing that something about his tone or what he had said had given the other man pause.

"Nothing? You didn't find anything to report?"

"No."

"Hmm. I would have thought you might find a few oddities in every city that you should take to your superiors. The idea that you found *nothing* at all seems quite ... peculiar."

Niccolo took a steadying breath. "Nothing of substance, at least."

"Ah. Well, I'm glad to hear it," the bishop said, finally, "though I will be sorry to see you go."

"I've enjoyed my time here quite a bit," Niccolo said. "Perhaps I will take you up on that offer and come to visit in the future."

"I would like that, as I'm sure would Father Reynolds."

The conversation turned to idle things. Jackson seemed relaxed while they spoke, though Niccolo fell silent and brooded. Something about the meeting felt off to him, as if more went on than he had anticipated.

The bishop didn't say or do anything that caused him to second guess the man's intentions, but he couldn't shake the feeling that the man withheld something. It came not from what he said but the way in which he spoke.

Maybe he didn't like the bishop's personality and demeanor and had let it rub him the wrong way, but part of him knew that wasn't it. No, it came down to something else.

By the time they had finished conversing, it had grown late. It had stopped raining completely, and all three men felt exhausted. The bishop walked them to the front door—the house had emptied of staff now, and Niccolo assumed the butler and serving staff had gone home—and bid them farewell. He wore a small smile that didn't quite reach his eyes as he shook Niccolo's hands, and then they stood out in the cold.

The gravel crunched underfoot while they walked back to Jackson's car.

"That went well," the young priest said, a note of surprise in his voice. "A lot better than I expected."

Niccolo didn't respond for a few seconds. "I'm glad," he offered, finally.

"I had expected a chastisement, or maybe a punishment, but he seemed reasonable about the whole thing."

"Yes," Niccolo said.

Too reasonable, in his estimation. What Jackson had done had made an affront to the bishop. Moreover, Leopold did not seem like the kind of man to forgive so easily.

So, why did he let Jackson off the hook so quickly?

They climbed into the car and drove away from the manor. With a growing sense of foreboding and worry, Niccolo watched the estate disappear behind them in the side mirror. Had he said too much and been too open with the bishop? He shouldn't have said anything about his travel plans. Had he just added to their risk?

"Are you leaving tomorrow for real?" Jackson asked while they traveled.

"Yes," he said.

"A shame. I've enjoyed having you around. Someone else I can talk to that understands what our lives are like."

Niccolo didn't reply. A part of him—a large part—wanted to open up to Jackson about his fears and concerns and tell the young priest that he had to travel with him. He wanted to explain the odd things that had occurred, the bad omens, and admit that he believed something crazy was going on.

But he didn't. Not yet. They wouldn't leave tonight, and he would tell Jackson first thing the following morning. He would get one more night of peace before his world crumbled around him. They would need to have the conversation eventually, but he wanted to postpone it until he got outside Everett and had Jackson safely away from the city.

Father Reynolds dropped him off at his hotel and then headed home. Niccolo tried to relax on his bed and get some sleep, but after a short while, he found himself pacing back and forth across the room. The last few days played over and over in his mind, along with Arthur's warning.

They had reached the homestretch, though, and soon they would get safely on their way to Rome.

Chapter 10

The next morning, Father Paladina felt quite a bit more on edge about what he was about to do. It made him quite relieved to have a plan of action to get out of the city, even though it still seemed as if he held onto a small thread and the entire situation had begun to unravel.

He needed to speak with Jackson and explain what would happen next. He had spoken with Father Affretti the previous evening, and he had scheduled their flight to leave at noon. Tickets would wait for them at the counter, so they only had to make it to the airport, board their flight, and they would be home free.

The decision to bring Jackson along but leave the bishop behind didn't make for an easy one when he got down to it. They didn't want to leave Jackson alone in the city, and he felt confident that the young priest had not become involved in anything that had gone on. A team of specialists would assemble to come to the city and investigate.

The things Jackson had told him the previous night at the baseball game had unsettled him more than he wanted to admit. And, thus, he feared he would drown he was so worried, because he didn't know if a possibility even existed that Jackson might have it right. Had Rose gotten compromised? Could more people in the city have become compromised than just Rose? How deep did all of this go?

More than that, however, he thought it important that the Church speak directly with Jackson for the purposes of what he had told him. If it were the case that Jackson had managed to sense something in these people ... then, well, that became something entirely above his status within the Church to handle. It would make Jackson quite valuable, so getting him out of the city went beyond just keeping him safe.

Niccolo finished packing up his things but left them in the room. He would need to walk to the church and didn't want anyone to see him with his belongings. They could pick them up on their way to the airport.

Or not. To be honest, if they didn't get the opportunity and simply left the luggage behind, he would consider it a minor loss.

He found Jackson in the main area of the church, moving pews around to create space around one in particular. Jackson greeted Niccolo when he came into the interior.

"Father Paladina, I hadn't expected you so early. Is there anything you need?"

"We need to talk," Niccolo said.

"Oh, about what?"

Niccolo started to explain that they had to leave the city in a few hours, but then didn't get the chance. Just then, the front door opened, and Tim Spencer and his son, Brad, arrived. Tim wore another ridiculous shirt, but Brad had dressed in much more comfortable clothing. He didn't look particularly happy to have to spend the morning like this.

Brad carried a toolbox that looked quite a bit too heavy for him, and he set it awkwardly on the floor not too far inside the room.

"Which one am I looking at?" Tim asked.

Jackson pointed toward the pew that he had pulled out of the way. "That one. The leg has come loose. I cleared as much space as I could manage so that you have room to work."

Tim went over and tested it, lifting the wooden bench off the ground with ease. He tested the leg, and it tilted sideways with a little bit of pressure.

"One of the screws broke at the head, and the wood has started to rot. I'll have to remove it, drill some new holes, and set a couple to anchor the leg.

"I could just throw it away."

"Then they wouldn't be even. We'd have an odd number of pews."

"This isn't too much trouble, is it?"

"Not at all. Not as bad as I thought. Doesn't change the fact that these are way old. I told you, just let Brad and myself build you some new ones."

"I can't afford it right now."

Tim grunted. "I told you that I'll buy the materials."

Jackson shook his head. "These ones work fine for now, and when I *can* afford to replace them, I will buy the materials, and you can help put them together. Maybe sometime in the future, but, until then, these will serve us just fine."

Tim grumbled some more, but he didn't object. He dug around in his toolkit and pulled out a drill and fit in a long bit. He directed Brad to work on getting the broken screw out and separating the pieces, and reluctantly, the kid set to work with the wood to pry it out.

Niccolo watched, feeling much like a fifth wheel in the situation. Tim barked orders at his son, and they worked with a practiced efficiency that struck him as impressive.

After a while, Niccolo turned to Jackson. "We need to talk."

"Okay."

"In private."

Jackson frowned, but he did move away from Tim and his son. Niccolo followed, speaking quietly.

"I spoke with my superior last night. Father Affretti."

"Oh? What did he say?"

Niccolo lied, "He said they agree with us that nothing is going on. They also mentioned that they would like to meet with you in person for a full debriefing. They already sent a ticket, and you're to leave with me this afternoon."

Jackson's face fell. "About what I did? They want to chastise me, don't they?"

Niccolo almost disagreed but changed his mind. It provided the easiest lie to get Jackson moving, and once they had left Everett behind, he could explain the rest of the situation to him. Tim and Brad had put a snag in his plan, and he didn't want to risk anything while they were here.

"I doubt you will receive any serious punishment, but you can expect a stern conversation."

Jackson frowned and nodded. "I shouldn't leave my parish, though. Tomorrow is Sunday."

"It will only take a few days. You'll come back in a few days."

"What about my congregation?"

"Perhaps you could ask Tim to handle the sermon for you. It would give good experience for him as well, I imagine. Keep in mind, however, where this request comes from. It isn't one you should refuse lightly."

Jackson thought about it for a moment, and then nodded. "I understand. I can speak with Tim and get him up to speed. It will be the first time he's stepped in for me, so it could prove good practice for him. When do we leave?"

"At noon."

"So soon?"

"They didn't want to take up much of your time and were quite insistent about the timing."

Jackson sighed and nodded. "All right. I can speak with Tim and give him my notes, and then I should call Bishop Glasser and let him know—"

"I think we will have to skip that, for now."

"I would much prefer to speak with him about it sooner rather than later, if possible. After everything I did, I don't want to get back on his bad side."

Niccolo frowned and sighed. "All right. We can call him from the airport and let him know, but for now, let's just get everything situated so that we don't end up late. How long do you think it will take you to pack a bag?"

"Not long."

"Go and do that now."

"What about Tim and his son?"

"I'll stay here with them until you come back. Hurry, though. We need to get moving. You can tell him that he's to give the sermon when you've packed."

"Okay. See you in a minute."

Jackson stood and headed for the exit. He disappeared out of the church, and Niccolo watched Tim and his son work. Tim's wife, Mary, might have become involved in whatever was happening, but did that mean Tim had? Jackson hadn't given him a clear answer about that. He thought not. Tim seemed quite normal.

Not that it mattered. Who could he trust?

Could he trust anyone?

Suddenly, the power in the church went out. The main room fell into darkness. When the central fans turned off, it also fell into silence.

A loud thud sounded when something got knocked to the floor.

"Damn it," Tim said in the blackness in front of him.

"Are you all right?" Niccolo asked.

"Yeah," Tim said. "Just stubbed my toe."

"What happened?"

"Breaker flipped. I think we drew too much power with all of the tools. Not the first time."

Niccolo frowned. "That has happened before?"

"Happens all the time," Tim said. "Whoever wired this place had no idea what they were doing and screwed up a lot of the connections. Father Reynolds won't let me gut the place and redo the wires."

"So, we have to flip the circuit back on?"

"Yep. It's in the basement. I'll go—"

Tim cut himself off with a curse, and then came a scratching sound as one of the pews slid roughly across the wooden floor.

"Are you all right?"

"Yeah," Tim said. "Fine. I just tripped again. Damn toe is killing me."

"You said I'd find the breaker in the basement?" Niccolo rose from his seat. His eyes adjusted to the darkness, and a little light came in from the stained glass windows. The day had started out gloomy, though, and so not a lot of sunlight reached them anyway. "In the back?"

"Through the father's office and down the stairs," Tim said.

"Just behind you."

Niccolo stuck out his arms to feel in front of him and headed for Father Reynolds's office. After a few steps, he felt the door, and then reached for the handle. He pulled the door open and stepped inside.

It seemed even darker inside the office, having only a small window high up on the wall. Niccolo steadied himself, took a deep breath, and then moved across the room, treading carefully until he came to the door leading to the basement.

"Where will I find the box?"

"Bottom of the stairs and a couple of steps to your right. Open the box, flip the breaker that blew, and it'll all come right back on."

"Hang on," Brad called from the room. Niccolo heard some pews slide across the floor, and then footsteps came in his direction. "I'll get it. I know where the box is."

The young man came through Jackson's office toward him, and then, suddenly, Brad stood there beside him. He opened the door to the basement. Inside lay pure blackness. Niccolo couldn't even see the first step leading down.

"You sure?" he asked.

"Yeah. There's a handrail," Brad said. "It'll only take me a minute."

"Be careful down there," Tim called from back in the central area.

"I will, Dad," Brad called back. Then, quieter, so only Niccolo could hear, he added, "He worries too much. Jesus."

"Want me to go with you?"

"Nah, the staircase is narrow. It'll be easier on my own."

"You sure?"

"Yep."

Niccolo had to admit that he felt incredibly relieved. He would never make the kid go into the basement, but since he had offered, Niccolo allowed himself to admit how scared the prospect of going down there alone made him.

Brad's clomping steps resounded as the kid descended the staircase. It sounded like he trod on old wooden steps that seemed to go on a long way down before reaching the floor.

Niccolo moved away from the basement entrance, waiting for the lights to come back on. A minute passed, and then another, and then he realized that the basement had fallen too quiet. He couldn't hear Brad at all anymore, and it had taken a lot longer than it should have to get the lights on.

He moved forward a short ways, putting his hands on the wall to steady himself, and tilted his head to the side. He strained to hear, listening for any sound of movement in the basement below.

He heard nothing. It seemed utterly still.

"Brad?" he called down the stairs. His voice echoed back up to him, louder than it should have.

No response. Then it hit him that the air coming from the basement felt too cold. It seemed a lot colder than it had a moment ago, and it caused him to break out in shivers.

"Brad, are you okay?"

Still nothing. No response or sound at all. He waited a second, teeth chattering, and then turned back toward the main area of the church where Tim waited.

"Tim, I can't hear anything from Brad. Does the basement have another exit?"

Huh. No response from Tim either. Niccolo squinted, and it appeared as though the lobby stood empty. He couldn't see any shapes that might have defined Tim or his son out there, and neither could he hear anything.

"Tim?"

He took a step away from the basement entrance. The air had grown even colder now, yet beads of sweat formed on his skin. His collar felt too tight around his neck, and he tugged at it, trying to loosen it.

It wouldn't budge. The cloth pinched now, and Niccolo struggled to breathe. He let out a gasping sound and staggered away from the basement doorway, stumbling across the floor of Father Reynolds's office. He tripped on something and fell to the ground, and when he looked back, he saw a body lying there.

Brad's body.

Niccolo's eyes had mostly adjusted to the darkness now, and he could make out the kid's expression. His eyes stared glossy and empty, and his mouth hung open. He looked dead.

Niccolo kept tugging at the collar, trying to loosen it, and let out a shuddering gasp of terror. It felt the same as it had in the crawlspace under Rose's home, but so much worse. It seemed as if he had something inside his head, rooting around and mucking with his thoughts and fears.

It isn't real, he told himself, dragging himself away from the body. He became short of breath and weak from the lack of oxygen, and it felt pretty damn real, but he fought back against the terror. *This isn't real. None of this is happening. You are imagining it.*

The air grew frosty, cold enough that his entire body shivered. He kept gasping and tugging at his neck for short breaths of air as he crawled away from the body. It looked like the kid had been dead for hours, though Niccolo couldn't even imagine how he had gotten back up here.

What the hell was happening?

It isn't real. That isn't Brad. I'm imagining this and just need to regain control.

For a few seconds, he forced the fear away and felt better. The collar loosened, and he managed to suck in a ragged breath of air. In his mind, he begged God to give him the strength to resist. He prayed for the willpower to push back against the weakness and regain control over his mind and body.

It isn't real, and if I just disbelieve, I can push it all away. None of this is happening.

It worked. The air didn't feel as cold in the room, and he could breathe once more. He closed his eyes, praying and thanking God for the strength to overcome. With breaths through his nose, he cleared his mind and focused on the situation. The body on the floor wasn't real, and when he opened his eyes, it would be gone.

There is no body. None of this is real. Brad is in the basement and is fine.

He opened his eyes.

Brad's body remained there with his glassy eyes and open mouth. Niccolo gasped again. His belief about the events unfolding and perception of what had happened clashed violently in his mind. He couldn't reconcile the two, and it made him feel dizzy.

Then something moved inside the kid's mouth. It sat deep in the back of his throat. At first, Niccolo thought it was Brad's throat or tongue, but then he realized that something else lay back there. Though he could barely see its shape in the darkness, he knew instinctively what made the shadow.

A giant bug. A locust. It crawled out of Brad's mouth, flapped its wings a few times, and then took off into the air. It came straight for Niccolo, and he swatted at it, trying to keep it away from him. It flew away, and he felt a moment of relief, but when he glanced back at Brad's body, his heart fell into his stomach.

The kid's throat expanded, and now more locusts fluttered in the back of his throat, crawling and fighting their way to the surface and spreading their wings.

Niccolo let out a gasping whimper, crawling away from the body.

It isn't real! This isn't real!

Then, the swarm of locusts came flying out of Brad's dead mouth.

✳✳✳

Hundreds of them, maybe thousands, came straight out of his mouth and at Niccolo. He could hear the flapping of their wings, the buzzing roar in his ears, as they surrounded him and landed on his skin.

Then, they burrowed.

The pain proved immediate and intense when they dug into his tender flesh, a white-hot fire covered his entire body and made him gasp and cry out in agony. He swatted at them, brushed them off his skin, but more came every second. For every one he knocked away, two more took its place.

They consumed him and ate him alive while he thrashed on the floor. The sheer terror and helplessness of the situation washed over him, filling him with a dread he had never experienced in his entire life. Here came the moment of his death. This meant the end of everything.

It isn't real!

This time, though, no strength of conviction reached the thoughts. Logically, he knew that it all remained in his imagination, but right now, logic played no part in what he experienced.

"This, Priest, is just a taste of what awaits you."

The pain lessened for a moment, giving him back some of his faculties. The voice came from nearby, but Father Paladina couldn't see anyone else in the room. The voice sounded familiar, but for the life of him, he couldn't place who it belonged to. He kept thrashing and crying, closing his eyes and trying to crawl away from the locusts.

"You've been very naughty, Father."

The voice again, and this time it sounded closer. Tim Spencer, he realized. The voice of the man helping to fix Father Reynolds's pew. The Deacon of Jackson's church.

Only, *this* wasn't Tim. It couldn't possibly be Tim.

Could it?

The locusts disappeared all of a sudden. It took Father Paladina a second to realize that they had gone, had never existed, and he kept swatting at his limbs to get them off and gasping in terror. No cuts or scrapes marred his body; no wounds of any sort.

Even Brad's body had gone, leaving the room empty.

They had never been there, he realized. It all happened in his head, but, it had felt *so* real. He had felt the locusts burrowing into his skin, and the memory of that came strong and powerful. He lay there on the carpet, shaking and trying to regain some semblance of control over his emotions.

Not everything had happened in his head, he saw, a few moments later. Someone else occupied the room with him. Tim stood in the doorway of Father Reynolds's private office, watching him. He had a blank look on his face and a hammer in his hand as he stared lifelessly at the priest. Though still dim, more light came in through the window now as the clouds parted.

"Tim?" Niccolo asked breathlessly, grabbing onto the corner of Father Reynolds's desk to pull himself to his feet. "What ... what's wrong?"

Tim didn't reply, except to raise the hammer into a threatening position and take a step toward Niccolo.

"Stay back!" Father Paladina shouted, moving away from the man and circling the room, which had only two exits. The basement and the main entrance.

Tim blocked the main entrance back into the church proper. Which left the basement—somewhere Niccolo didn't want to go.

He didn't see any other options, however. Tim kept walking toward him, moving slowly but with a clear purpose, and he backed Niccolo toward the stairwell leading down into the darkness.

Niccolo raised his hands in the air, waving them as though trying to calm a wild animal. The problem was, Tim looked perfectly calm right now and barely seemed to notice the gesture. There seemed something vacant about the way he moved, like he didn't fire on all cylinders.

"Tim, listen to me. You don't want to do this."

"Oh, yes. Yes, I do," Tim said, and again Niccolo got struck by how *wrong* the man's voice sounded. It used Tim's vocal chords, but the sound came out wrong. The inflection, the tone, everything about it seemed off. "I really, really do."

"We can talk about this."

Tim raised his hammer and grinned. "I have a better idea."

Niccolo turned to the staircase and sprinted to it. He grabbed the door handle and stumbled onto the basement staircase. When he looked back, Tim hadn't set off in pursuit. Tim just stood there, grinning and watching.

"What do you think will happen? Where will you run?"

Niccolo didn't answer. He slammed the door shut. As soon as the door had closed, the entire world went dark. No windows or lights to let in the light down here. Niccolo couldn't see more than a few inches in front of his face. He felt around, praying for a lock to seal the door. Unfortunately, he couldn't find one, at least not on this side. Then he turned and rushed down the stairs as fast as possible.

"Come on, Priest. Is this necessary? You *know* what is about to happen."

Niccolo used the handrail to guide himself down, which proved lucky because, about halfway, he missed a step and stumbled forward. He hit his shin hard against one of the stairs but caught himself after only a small fall. The shin ached and throbbed, but he didn't stop. He rushed to the bottom until he felt cement underfoot instead of wood.

Should he go to the right or left into the basement? Which direction offered the most safety? Might other things in the darkness trip or harm him? The idea of running off into the basement without knowing what might lie in wait terrified him.

What had happened to Brad? Was he okay? Did he form a part of what was going on, or had he become a victim like Niccolo?

He turned back toward the staircase and felt around. A storage space nestled next to the stairs and extended underneath. Better than nothing. He worked his way into the space, maneuvering around boxes and loose decorations. The stairs were wooden and hollow, and he hoped he would find a decent spot underneath where he could hide.

Luck stayed with him, and he managed to use his hands to guide him toward the wall beneath the staircase. There, he came across more boxes and other things stuffed there, but enough room remained for him to bend down and duck out of sight. Then he crouched into position in front of some boxes. Next, he stopped moving, going completely silent.

Not a moment too soon, either. There came a thudding sound against the door of the office above, followed by raucous laughter, and then it swung open. A sliver of light flitted down the staircase in front of Niccolo, and he watched through an opening between two of the stairs when it lit up the church basement.

"Come out, come out, wherever you are!"

Father Paladina knelt in his uncomfortable position beneath the staircase, eyes closed and struggling to control his breathing. Each gasp sounded like the cracking of a tree branch, and he couldn't fight down an occasional sob of terror. His heart beat in his ears, and his veins seemed about to burst open.

"I can smell you, Priest. I know you didn't run far. Where are you?"

The voice came from upstairs in the local priest's office. Niccolo couldn't remember a time in his life when he had been so on edge and afraid. It felt like a sickness in his stomach, as all of his muscles tensed simultaneously. It made his body shake, and he worried that he might throw up at any moment.

"We both know how this will end. If you come out now, I'll do it quick. If you make me come and find you, though ..."

Niccolo struggled to control his breathing as hot tears ran down his cheeks. He reached into his front-right pocket for the single item he kept there. His rosary, which he held between his fingers and pressed against his lips, praying as hard as he could for the strength to deal with whatever was happening to him.

Not to overcome it, though. Part of him—if he were honest, a *large* part—knew he was about to die alone in this church, and the only thing he prayed for was the strength to die well.

After all, right now, not only his life hung in the balance: so did his everlasting soul.

"This basement has no exits. I know this church. This is *my* church. Not yours," the man—if still a man—said from just upstairs. "I never thought I would actually get to kill a priest here. This is delightful!"

What is he waiting for? Niccolo wondered, in fear. Tim Spencer—or whatever controlled him—seemed to enjoy taking his time. Every muscle in Niccolo's body ached, and he had to fight to keep from sobbing. *Why is he doing this? Why is he waiting up there?*

It felt like he'd been hiding under the stairs forever, but it had probably lasted for less than a minute.

"We're having fun, aren't we, Priest?" Tim asked.

Niccolo couldn't contain a shudder, and the movement caused his shoulder to bump against one of the boxes behind him. The noise it made wasn't that loud, but to Niccolo, it rumbled like an explosion in the stillness of the basement.

If his pursuer heard, though, he didn't let on. Tim hummed to himself as he took his first step down the staircase. It creaked heavily underfoot, and Father Paladina winced when dust fell on his head.

Another step; the sound of the boot on the stairs sounded like a nail in the priest's coffin. Tim kept on coming, humming a tuneless tone, until the father could see muddy boots in front of his face.

"Priest? You know I'll find you. You can't hide from me."

Niccolo's whole body trembled, and the man had called it true. His hiding place seemed weak and pathetic now. As soon as Tim reached the bottom of the staircase, he would spy Niccolo. The priest had backed himself into a corner and had nowhere to go.

He shouldn't have stayed here at Saint Joseph's Cathedral alone. Should have gone with Father Reynolds to his home; splitting up had turned into a terrible idea, one that might well cost him his life.

Father Reynolds's life, too, Niccolo realized. Jackson had gone home, but no doubt, whoever had sent this creature after Niccolo had gone after him as well. Father Paladina hadn't warned his friend of the danger. He regretted that, now. Jackson had no way of defending himself and knew nothing of the danger. Niccolo had led him like a lamb to the slaughter.

Tim Spencer reached the bottom step, and Niccolo could see his back through the gap in the risers. He had nowhere to run and no possible way to get out of this. It was over. He was about to die.

He should at least face his death head on.

As a servant of God.

Easier said than done, however. His body struggled against him. The priest forced his wobbly legs to move and rose from his crouched position, stepping out from beneath the stairs to confront his pursuer. Tim heard him and turned.

"Well, then. There you are." The man grinned and bared his teeth. He looked more feral than anything. "Well done, Priest. Found a little courage after all. Are you ready to meet your maker?"

Father Paladina opened his mouth to speak, to pray, but no sounds would come. His voice had abandoned him, and the words he'd studied and practiced for years caught in his throat.

"What? Cat got your tongue?" The man stepped closer to him and continued to grin that insane grin. "Let me get you started: Our Father, who art in heaven ..."

"Vile abomination, you don't belong here," Niccolo muttered. "By the power of Christ, I compel you." He held up his rosary, hand still shaking. "In the name of the Father, the Son, and the Holy Spirit, I order you to leave this place."

The man stopped moving forward, his grin fading. "You think that will work? You, of all people, think that a prayer could compel *me* to just drop everything and leave?"

Father Paladina grew emboldened, feeling momentary strength while the words poured out of him. The demon was lying, and the words did have some impact. They gave Niccolo courage and knowledge that, despite everything, he did not stand alone. It had an effect, the power, the prayers, and his faith. They held the man at bay.

Maybe he *could* get out of his alive. If his faith held up.

"You do not belong here, creature. Return from whence you

came. Through the power of Christ, I demand that you leave this holy place."

A long moment passed, the only sound Niccolo and the man's breathing. The priest held his rosary forth, hand unwavering and back tall. They stared at each other, locked in place, as the seconds ticked by.

"Silly priest," the man said, finally, his grin returning. "Don't you know you have no power here?"

The man reached up and grabbed the rosary in Father Paladina's hand. A sizzling sound filled the basement, as though flesh burned, and the priest could feel the metal heating in his hand.

Niccolo watched in horror when Tim stepped closer to him, pressing the cross against his forehead. The metal burned Tim's skin where it touched, and he burst into a wild and maniacal laugh.

Father Paladina released his grip on the rosary and jerked back in disgust. The man let it fall to the floor, a sizzling chunk of metal, and there it lay.

"How does it feel?" The man took another step closer to Father Paladina. Still grinning that sick and toothy grin. "How does it feel to know you are truly alone?"

He reached forward, grabbing the priest around the throat and squeezing. His grip felt like iron, crushing down on Niccolo's windpipe.

"How does it feel to know that God has abandoned you?"

***

Niccolo's imminent death loomed large. The end had come. The world closed in around him, and the lack of oxygen made it impossible to think straight. He closed his eyes, praying softly to himself and trying to mumble out the words.

Tim just kept laughing and squeezing with inhuman strength. Niccolo could feel his windpipe collapsing and knew it was almost all over. He swatted at the arm, trying to break the man's grip, but he might as well have swatted at a brick wall.

Suddenly, the hand had gone. A sound of something heavy thudded against the ground, followed by a grunt, and then nothing. A moment passed while he regained his breath, and then, oh so slowly, Niccolo opened his eyes.

Arthur stood there, staring at him with a slight smirk on his face.

"Aren't you glad to see me?"

✳✳✳

"What happened?" Niccolo asked. "What's going on?"

"I don't know," Arthur said, looking tense.

"Is Jackson okay? Please, don't tell me I got him killed."

"He's fine. I left him sitting safe in my car with no clue."

"He tried to kill me," Niccolo said, clutching at his throat. It made him wince in pain, and the skin felt tender.

"I'm aware," Arthur said. "I'm also on something of a clock, so we need to get moving."

"What?"

Arthur didn't respond. Instead, he walked over to the breaker box, flipped open the lid, and threw the blown fuses back into the correct position. The lights flickered to life with a humming sound, and Niccolo blinked from the brightness.

When his eyes adjusted, he saw Brad lying on the ground in the corner of the room. Arthur walked over and touched his fingers against his neck, feeling for a pulse.

"Is he …?"

"He's alive," Arthur said. "The other guy, too. I just knocked him out."

"This is insane. He tried to kill me."

"We've established that."

"Why? Why would he kill *me*?"

Once more, Arthur didn't respond. He stepped over Tim's body and headed up the staircase and out of the church.

"Wait. How are you here?" Gingerly, Niccolo stepped over Tim's unconscious form and followed Arthur. "Why did you even come here? How did you get involved in all this?"

Arthur hesitated and glanced back. "That's a long story."

Chapter 11

A few days earlier

Arthur stood on the lonely sidewalk a block away from the residence of Jun Lee, an enormous apartment complex in the center of Yokohama, Japan. Jun had become one of the longest-standing members of the Council of Chaldea.

Arthur served that Council as one of their Hunters, protecting the world against supernatural threats. His duty was to follow, unquestioningly, any order given to him by the Council. Anything less, they would consider as treason against the Council, which could be punishable by death.

Stood outside Jun's house, Arthur balanced on the edge of a knife. If he went inside the apartment without the consent of the Council, he would cross a line, and he didn't know if he would have any way of coming back.

But he couldn't leave. Not yet. Not without the answers he needed. Already, he had disobeyed Frieda by leaving Germany, and he needed to see this through, no matter the outcome. Arthur needed to do this for his family, if not for himself.

At just after ten o'clock in the evening, he still had jetlag from his recent flight into the country. He had only traveled to Japan once before, a few months ago, and it also became an occasion to visit Jun Lee; though, that time, on drastically different terms. Back then, his family was alive, he hadn't been labeled a butcherer, and Jun had been one of his most trusted allies.

Jun Lee would have multiple bodyguards inside and outside the complex to keep himself safe. Some of them Hunters like Arthur, and others mercenaries from private firms hired to protect the Council's most valuable assets. Arthur took no issue with any of them and wouldn't hurt any if he didn't have to.

He hated coming out here like this, because when everything got said and done, he considered Jun one of the few respectable Council members. He doubted Jun had anything to do with the deaths of his wife and daughter, and if he could find any other way to get the information he needed, he would have done that instead. Jun had always behaved in a friendly way with Arthur, and he'd even sided with him when it came to the vote about whether or not to have Abigail, the young girl Arthur had rescued from the cult, executed.

However, Arthur didn't have any other way of getting the

information he needed. As for why it needed to happen in person, this wasn't a conversation he could have had with Jun over the phone. He wouldn't dare announce his intentions ahead of time. The Council would never approve of his actions, and if they knew what he had planned after this visit to Jun, they would actively work to stop him.

He couldn't have that. Not until he had his answers. Not until he had killed the person responsible for the murder of his family.

✳✳✳

Nine months had passed since he had raided the decrepit manor in the woods and killed all the cultists. A principle cell of the Ninth Circle had used the place as a hideout for running multiple illicit operations, including kidnapping and murder. Some of their most important leaders had hidden out there, and Arthur had killed more than two dozen people.

He hadn't expected—or intended—to survive the raid. It had happened from a rash decision in response to his family getting murdered by the cult, and his only hope had lain in taking as many of them with him as he could when he went out.

It hadn't gone that way, however. He had rescued Abigail Dressler, a little girl that the cult had tortured and abused for months, if not years, and it had opened his eyes to just how insane his suicidal plan had been. After what she had gone through, how could he possibly just give up the way he had?

Then, as time went by, he realized he had another reason to go on. Vengeance. Yes, the cult had killed his family, but from where did they learn about his loved ones? Only a handful of people inside the Council of Chaldea had known about his family—where they lived and who they were. Those few people had the task of keeping the families of Hunters and members of the Council safe and away from their enemies, which meant they must have betrayed him.

Jun Lee knew the names of those Council members tasked with protecting their families, which meant he could give Arthur a list of who might have sentenced his wife and daughter to death. Arthur had never dreamed he might manage to track down the name of his betrayer, much less dole out punishment for her or his actions.

But here he stood, close to the answers and desperate for revenge.

They didn't send him out on assignments anymore, and

hadn't tasked him with anything since his raid on the cult. The council had shelved him while they tried to decide what to do with him. Forced into early retirement, so to speak. They felt furious that he'd disobeyed their direct orders and gone off after the cult on his own.

But they had also grown shocked and amazed at what he'd accomplished. Arthur had struck a tremendous blow to one of the most dangerous cults, and his street reputation had gone through the roof. He became something of a living legend—something which made him feel awkward—and probably the only reason they had kept him alive and exonerated him of his disobedience. They couldn't afford to distance themselves from him after he'd sent their enemies running in fear, but they also didn't want to deal with him.

That seemed okay, though, as he was done with the Council, too. He had given his life to their cause, and they had given him nothing but heartache and despair in return. His plan gave him a way to get vengeance for his family, and then live a normal life.

✳✳✳

Arthur had left Abigail in Germany with Frieda when he took this trip. Up until now, he'd felt unwilling to leave her side because the threat of execution by the Council still hovered over her head. He had made it clear that no matter how the Council voted on the matter, they would have to go through him if they intended to put the young girl to her death.

The Council had, finally, voted to give Abigail a stay of execution, pending further investigation into the issue and consultation with the Catholic Church. He didn't trust them—it had come down to seven voting to spare her the death sentence, and six wanting to kill her immediately—but he, at least, knew he had some time to spare before the issue came up again.

What made this situation worse, though, was that Jun had made the deciding vote in sparing Abigail's life, and this made the trip so much more difficult. He didn't want to harm Jun, but he would if it became necessary. He would get the answers he needed and give his family the justice they deserved.

✳✳✳

Arthur circled to the side of the apartment complex, searching for a back entrance he could use to slip in unnoticed. He didn't intend to siege the place or pick a fight if not necessary. This late at night, not many people populated the sidewalks, or vehicles the streets. The entire block appeared quiet and serene.

He had a revolver tucked into his waistband. And though difficult to smuggle such items into the country, it didn't prove impossible when using the international credentials that the Council supplied for him. For all intents and purposes, he traveled as an Air Marshal or a UN operative whenever he needed to.

He also had a few hidden blades on his person. One in his boot, another at his hip, and a backup strapped to his chest. Hopefully, he wouldn't end up needing any of them.

Jun, as one of the longest active members of the Council, had great value, which meant he would have at least four guards on hand at any given moment, and doubtless, one of them would be a fellow Hunter.

Arthur didn't know their identities—Frieda Gotlieb had charge of such assignments, and she remained incredibly tight-lipped about such information—but, doubtless, he would find someone he'd worked with or trained in the past.

He rounded the back of the apartment complex. A large group of residents milled around a patio just outside the rear entrance. At first, he felt annoyed, but then he realized it would work in his favor. Some of them sat on benches or huddled around talking.

It looked like a party or cookout of some sort, and string lights dangled from the trees around the area, casting the entire place in a colorful glow. A table held various potluck dishes, but most of them had gone already. The event seemed to be winding down as they all turned in for the night.

Arthur could use the distraction to his advantage. He stuck out in the crowd, but didn't appear the only obviously foreign person at the party. The distraction would help him slip into the building unnoticed and without a confrontation.

Most likely, though, at least one of the guards would have watch on this entrance to stop this sort of ingress, and if any good, they would blend in with the party-goers. He just needed to figure out who they were.

On this breezy night, most of the residents had bundled up in jackets or leaned away from the wind. With such a party, he had hoped a guest might have propped the door open for restroom usage, but no such luck. It stood closed up tight and would be locked at this time of day. He would need a resident's key to get inside, or to slip in with a group of them.

However, to Arthur's surprise, he also didn't spot any guards hiding out near the door or amongst the partiers. Maybe he'd come to the wrong place, and maybe Jun had moved in recent weeks. Not likely, though. Jun had lived in this same apartment complex for at least the last ten years, and Arthur had come here not too long ago.

If Jun had moved, it meant that they had relocated him for some security reason. That would, most likely, mean because of Arthur and what he might do, which meant they knew his intentions. If that proved the case, then this was, no doubt, a trap.

Not an encouraging thought.

It seemed much more likely that Jun hadn't moved at all, but that his security hadn't gotten on top of their duties. Had they just dropped the ball and assumed their charge safe since it had grown so late in the evening? If he hadn't come here outside his normal duties, he would have chastised them for their mistakes.

Arthur took a little extra time studying the crowd, hoping that maybe he had it wrong and one of the residents was a guard in disguise and just doing an excellent job of blending in. If Arthur had charge of Jun's security, he would have handled the situation in that way.

After a few moments, he felt satisfied that they all lived here as normal residents and partiers enjoying an evening get together. None of them seemed to pay much attention to other guests, and neither did they watch the surrounding area.

So, he came back to square one—either the security was lax, Jun had moved, or they had set a trap. He considered abandoning his plan entirely and leaving the situation alone. It could turn out that he risked his life without even the possibility of finding out who'd murdered his family.

On the other hand, if he left now, then he might miss the perfect opportunity to get the answers he needed.

After a short internal debate, Arthur decided to go forward with his plan. Already here, it made sense to go through with his first plan and find out what had happened. If they had set a trap, he could deal with that when the time came, but for now, he couldn't turn around and leave empty handed.

Arthur slipped through the group of milling residents, timing his entrance as one of the small groups of the complex headed inside, and he caught the door just before it closed. He took one last glance outside to make sure no one watched him.

No one did.

A chill of concern gripped him, and without a doubt,

something wasn't right about the situation.

Cautious, he headed into the apartment complex and made his way down the empty hallway. The lights seemed bright even at this time of day, giving it an eerily quiet feel.

Jun lived on the third floor. Arthur made his way past closed doorways, careful to stay as quiet as possible so that he didn't wake any sleeping residents.

The quietness made him uncomfortable. It felt more and more like a trap. He crept to the stairwell, hand resting on the revolver strapped to his side, and made his way up.

The walls of the apartment complex, painted brown, stood around old hardwood flooring that creaked with each step he took. The hallway, uncomfortably narrow, made the entire place seem like a claustrophobic nightmare. That didn't bother him normally, but right now, he felt on edge. The hot building made the air seem even more stifling.

He moved slowly, listening for any out of place sound. The old building, like many such structures, had a unique plethora of strange sounds and smells, but nothing stuck out as misplaced. He didn't see any guards posted in the stairwell, which made him worry even more.

Jun must have moved, he decided but didn't quite believe. He liked to think that if something so major had happened, Frieda would have told him. Even if he made the reason for Jun's move, at the very least, she would tell him to warn him off such an action.

It also didn't feel right because it didn't mesh with Jun's personality. Even if they wanted to move the old man for fear of Arthur coming to his home uninvited, he would have refused.

Which meant that he'd walked into a trap.

So, why had they let him get so close before springing it?

The hairs stood up on the back of Arthur's neck when he reached the third-floor landing. He moved down the hall, drawing his weapon and holding it ready, as he came to Jun Lee's apartment. Still no guards, or any other sign that something had happened.

The door stood closed but unlocked. With a frown, Arthur eased it open and crept inside.

Jun had a small apartment with sparse furnishings. A pair of padded rocking chairs rested in the living room, but no television. The Councilor hated it, considering shows and movies a complete waste of time.

Off to the right stood a kitchen that looked tidy and neat with stained marble counters, considerably more expensive than what had come originally with the space, and a hallway led off to the left further into the apartment. Memory informed him that only a single bedroom and bath lay down there.

Nothing had changed since the last time he had come here. An old fan circled lazily overhead, pushing warm air and dust around the room.

In one of the rocking chairs in the living room, he saw the top of Jun Lee's head, facing away from him and toward the window. The chair rocked gently, but Jun didn't move.

Arthur edged deeper into the apartment, trying to determine if this were, indeed, a trap. No guards, the lights turned off, and everything entirely too still for his liking. He held his gun ready and circled the chair to see if Jun remained alive.

Jun frowned up at him, definitely alive and seeming more annoyed than worried to see Arthur standing there. A brown blanket wrapped the old man, who looked exhausted. A long and gnarled wooden cane leaned against the chair next to him.

"Did you have to get here so late in the day? This is *well* past my bedtime."

"What?" Arthur asked, surprised.

"I'd begun to fear I'd gotten it wrong and that you hadn't planned to come here when you left Germany. Glad to see that I hadn't misjudged."

"Where are your guards?"

Jun waved his hand in the air with a shrug. "Somewhere. I don't feel too sure, in fact. I sent them to a nearby establishment to purchase some refreshments, so no doubt, they're drunk at this moment."

"You sent them away?"

"I had confidence you wouldn't have done irrevocable damage to any of them if I had kept them here, but I felt a confrontation both unnecessary and wasteful."

"You knew I would come?"

Jun nodded. "Of course. Frieda called me."

"I didn't tell her where I planned to head."

"Nor did she know. She grew worried and called all the Council members because she didn't know where you might go or what you had planned, but I surmised the rest."

"How did you know?"

"I've waited for this encounter since the day your family died. When you left Germany yesterday, I knew the time had arrived. Though, I do wish you had come earlier. This chair feels uncomfortable, and my old bones can't handle these late nights too well."

Arthur shook his head in confusion. "I don't get it. Why

dismiss your guards? If you *knew* I would come here, why not hire more security instead of less? You could have had thirty men waiting for me."

"Because, no matter what, you would have come, and I have confidence you would have found me. I figured the best chance of this meeting ending amicably was to make myself easy to find."

"If you hold any guilt in betraying my family, then you have severely misjudged why I came."

A moment passed in silence. "If you thought me guilty of such a crime," Jun said with a slight waver in his voice, "then, I would be dead already."

Arthur stood in silence for a long moment, and then he blew out a breath of air. He had known Jun Lee for a long time, ever since he began training to become a Hunter. The man had no capability of such a crime. Not against anyone, and definitely not against him.

He'd felt terrified that maybe Jun had some hand in what had happened, but now he grew confident that it wasn't the case. The palpable relief seemed like a weight had lifted from his chest.

However, Jun gave his only chance of finding out the identity of the real betrayer.

"Please." Jun Lee gestured toward the empty rocking chair. "Have a seat."

Arthur hesitated, and then walked over to the chair. He slipped his revolver away and sat down, facing toward the old man.

"You know why I came."

"And you know I'm forbidden from giving you what you desire."

"Someone betrayed my family, and now my wife and daughter are dead."

"A terrible tragedy. I feel beyond sorry for your loss, but they entrusted me with this knowledge because of my unwillingness to divulge it. I cannot help you, Arthur. I cannot give you any privileged information without risking the lives and families of others."

"Clearly, someone else didn't share your scruples, Jun. Now, my family is dead. All I want to know is who else knew?"

"Telling you would betray the Council."

"Not telling me would betray me," Arthur said. "And you know I stand on the right side here. We're friends, Jun. We've known each other since I was a child. If you won't help me, then ask yourself, honestly, which would prove worse right now—betraying me or the Council."

Jun sat in silence for a moment, slowly shaking his head. "Look how far we've fallen."

"What? What do you mean?"

Jun didn't seem to have spoken to Arthur. He looked out of the window. "Is this what we've come to? One of the most loyal men I've ever met stooping to threats because of the situation he's gotten pushed into? Has the corruption of our Order run so deep?"

"I have no desire to threaten you," Arthur said. "If I knew any other way to get the information you have ..."

"No, but you do feel desperate. And, yet, here I sit defending the people who murdered your family because archaic rules dictate that I must act in such a manner. A sorry lot I've drawn in life that I get tasked with defending murderers and betrayers at the cost of doing the right thing."

"Then, tell me what I want to know."

"So you can kill them back? How do we break the cycle when all we seek is vengeance? Where is the justice?"

"I came to you in the dead of night and completely off the record," Arthur said. "What part of that made you think I wanted justice?"

Jun hesitated, and then shrugged. "Fair enough."

"And you let me into your room without any conflict or objection. I have a feeling you don't want justice in this matter, either."

A heavy silence hung in the air. Arthur studied Jun, praying that he would give him the answers he needed. He'd come too close to turn back now, and if Jun refused him ...

"I don't know what I want anymore," Jun said, finally. "What I do know, Arthur, is that I have no intention to make you my enemy. Nor do I wish to betray my duty to the Council."

"Three people knew the names of my wife and daughter. You, Frieda, and one other person. I know you and Frieda would never betray me, so who is the last person on my list? I need a name."

"Frieda also knows the answer you seek. Why not ask her?"

"She would never break her oath to the Council. She would rather die."

"And you think me any different? She withheld the information from you, but you think I will tell you?"

"I know you, Jun. I know it sickens you to become party to any of this. Your silence on the matter amounts to the same as guilt. You are a good man, and you believe in virtue. The guilt of what happened to my family weighs heavy on your soul, and you know the traitor in our midst. Whose family will die next?"

"This is not your matter to attend to. We are looking into the possibility that this didn't make for a singular event, and you have my word that whoever did this will get dealt with accordingly."

"*You* know who it is. Tell me and let me help you do your duty."

"My hands are tied."

"Mine aren't."

"Arthur ... please, trust that I *will* handle this," Jun said.

Arthur recognized this as the real reason that Jun had let him in. The man had hoped to talk Arthur out of doing anything crazy.

Most likely, Frieda lay behind it. Jun had said that Frieda didn't know where Arthur planned to go, but he didn't believe that for a second. Frieda, brilliant and cunning, no doubt all of this—from sending away the guards to what Jun told him—she had orchestrated.

"That's not good enough," Arthur said. "My family got *murdered*. I found their bodies in my home. I will not leave here without the name."

Jun stared at Arthur, frowning and thoughtful.

"If something happened to this other person, they would know I divulged the information that pointed you in that direction."

"Tell them I tortured it out of you."

Jun shook his head. "Such wouldn't prove sufficient."

"What do you propose?"

"For this crime, the person in question cannot get accused without irrefutable proof or a confession."

"This person betrayed the Council. You know so."

"We have no proof, only speculation and correlation."

"That's good enough for me."

"But not for the Council. If I give you this name, I need full assurance that you will bring this person before the Council for justice and not murder him or her in the streets. If this person turns up dead, then I won't have the ability to get the answers I need. You turn in this person with evidence. On this, I will not negotiate, Arthur. I need your word."

"What good would a trial do?"

"It would hold meaning beyond us finding a body in a river, and it will help me find out how our security got breached and what we can do to fix it in the future. If I name this person, then you will collect evidence to bring to me, and together, we will bring down this person."

"Who is it?"

"Your word, Arthur. I won't say anything without it."

Arthur considered. Jun wouldn't tell him otherwise, but he

hated the idea. Still, it seemed the best offer he would get.

"You have it. I will bring the evidence to you to deal with. I swear it on my life."

"Swear it on Abigail's life."

"I don't want to bring her into this. She doesn't deserve it."

"Which is why I know you will keep your word. Swear."

"Fine. I swear that I will not kill this person, if you swear you will do everything in your power to have them pay for this crime with their life."

Jun nodded. "That promise I can make easily. I have confidence you will have little issue finding evidence that proves this person's guilt. But, as soon as you go after her, you will have kicked a hornet's nest. When that happens, a firestorm will come down on your head; but, if you get me sufficient evidence, then I should manage to protect you from the worst of it."

"You need to guarantee me justice," Arthur said.

"I can and will," Jun said. "If you can prove her guilt, then her punishment will be execution. You will get the justice you want."

"Very well," Arthur said. "Who is it?"

Jun nodded. "Emily Glasser."

Arthur felt as if he'd received a punch in the stomach. He coughed in disbelief. "What?"

"She made for the third member of the Council tasked with protecting our familial assets."

"You're kidding."

"I wish I were."

Arthur composed himself, feeling a seething anger growing in his chest. The news had come completely unexpected, but it also made perfect sense. It infuriated him beyond anything he had ever imagined.

"Very well."

"Know that I don't give you this information lightly, Arthur. Both of us want to see her punished for these crimes."

"I understand," Arthur said. "I will deal with things accordingly."

"I have great respect for you and consider what happened to your family a terrible travesty. But you coming into my home uninvited makes for a one-time situation. Should you ever try to come to my abode like this in the future, your visit will prove considerably less welcome."

Arthur stood. "I don't think that will become necessary."

"I should hope not."

Arthur bowed his head toward Jun and headed outside. Emotions raged inside him, including a feeling of helpless betrayal.

In the hallway outside Jun's apartment, five armed men in casual clothing leaned against the wall and watched him. Jun's crew, and not drunk. They looked ready for a fight while they surveyed him. He recognized some of them, but many more he'd never met.

Despite everything Jun had said, he had felt much better prepared for that conversation than he'd let on.

✳✳✳

Council member Emily Glasser had a dubious past. She made for the sort of person he'd known better than to trust since first meeting her many years earlier. Self-centered and cruel, she always looked for what she could get for herself out of every situation.

She also had as a brother Leopold Glasser, a wealthy Catholic Bishop who lived in Washington State to the North. Leopold had responsibility for keeping the Council's coffers full and had become one of their largest proponents in recent years. Every year, he donated a fortune to the Council on behalf of the Church, and they considered him a prized friend. That made things so difficult on Frieda and Jun Lee in bringing a trial against Emily.

Emily had joined the Council on Leopold's special request, which meant she could get away with a lot because of her familial ties. Drastically unqualified, she did not take her position seriously. She always seemed to avoid punishment because her brother felt she could do no wrong and made his donations contingent upon her position.

The Council felt terrified of angering Leopold because he had provided almost three-quarters of their annual operating budget. Such disgusting and blatant nepotism, and it infuriated Arthur to no end.

He'd hated Emily from the day they'd brought her into the Council, but he'd always justified it by believing Emily only held a token position. Never had he dreamed that they would give her any sort of true responsibility.

Arthur had never even considered her as a suspect in the betrayal of his family. He'd had a few names in mind when he went to confront Jun, but she hadn't factored on his list. Emily should never have known his family existed, much less become privy to their location or tasked with protecting them. If he had felt certain of anyone who could never get raised to such status on the Council, it would have been Emily Glasser.

Yet, he didn't feel half as furious at her as he did at Frieda for keeping him out of the loop. Frieda had known about Emily's position. She should have warned him about Emily gaining access to familial information the moment the Council voted on it. Then he could have done something about it. He would have had the ability to protect his family. Perhaps he could have moved them, or made his home more secure, or done *something* to keep them safe.

Instead, she had kept him in the dark while his family got slaughtered, and even now, Frieda had attempted to keep from him the information he so desperately needed.

Could he ever forgive her?

In any case, he had a clear agenda now.

Find Emily Glasser.

As soon as Arthur got back on the street and away from the apartment, he called Frieda. She answered on the second ring.

"Hello?"

"You knew," he said, shaking his head. "Frieda, how could you not tell me?"

The line fell silent for a full minute. "Arthur, let's talk about this."

"Why the hell would I talk to you now? You knew about Emily, and you didn't tell me."

"I told you I would take care of—"

"All those times you told me you were looking into the issue of my family's death, you lied, didn't you? You knew the culprit as Emily the entire time and that you would never get to touch her."

Frieda hesitated, and then said, "I *have* collected evidence against her, with Jun's help, but she covered her tracks so well. She seems genuinely surprised by what happened and doesn't act like a guilty person. We have no evidence linking the murder at your home to Emily or any of her acquaintances."

"Why didn't you tell me?"

"In your fury, you would have done something rash."

"You're damn right. I knew the Council as incompetent, but this takes it to new depths entirely. She killed my family, Frieda."

"We don't have enough evidence. She has the support of the Catholic Church, Arthur, and they've forbidden us from investigating her. Who do you think the Church will believe if we hold a trial?"

"We *know* she's dirty. Remember what happened in Atlanta?"

"Nothing ever got proved."

"It shouldn't have to have. If you had any doubts at all of her trustworthiness, why would you entrust her with the fate of our families?"

"Three members of the Council get entrusted with the list of names of the Hunters and their families. Her name got suggested a few years ago, and she got voted in despite mine and Jun's opposition. We fought to keep her out, Arthur, and we lost."

"If you knew, why didn't you warn me all those years ago? Why didn't you tell me so that I could better protect my family?"

Frieda didn't reply for a while. "I'm sorry," she said, finally, and devastation laced her voice. "If I had imagined it would come to this ..."

Arthur took a steadying breath. He felt unsure if he would ever forgive Frieda. In his heart, he understood that she had nothing to do with what had happened to his family and that no way could she have known, but at that moment, he felt as furious and heartbroken as ever before.

"I need to go."

"Arthur, please, let me deal with this. I beg you to let this go. I swear to you that I *will* take care of this. Don't do anything stupid."

"You had your chance. Now, it's my turn."

"Emily has powerful friends. A poor excuse, I know, but there it is. The Council has had three meetings dealing exclusively with your family's murder, and each time her name gets brought up as a suspect, they dismiss it immediately because of her brother. The sister of a bishop couldn't possibly be guilty. The feeling is that the betrayer must have come from outside the Council."

"Outside the Council?"

"Your brother."

"Mitchell? Are you kidding me? He would never betray me like this."

"I know. But, so far, I haven't managed to find any evidence against Emily that will convince the Council or the Church to take a closer look. It's risky for me to even search."

"For you, but not for me."

"If you do this, I will not have the ability to protect you. Please, Arthur, think about what you're about to do."

"Goodbye, Frieda."

"Wait, hang on—"

He hung up before Frieda could finish, breathing quickly through his nose and trying to regain control over his frantically beating heart. He had to hurry now because Frieda would try to stop what he planned to do.

Chapter 12

As soon as his plane touched down in Sacramento, California, it hit Arthur that he now operated without a lifeline. It seemed a crazy realization for him, as he had grown used to being able to contact any number of assets all around the world at a moment's notice.

Worse, Frieda would actively try and stop him from confronting Emily. She would think that she did it for his own good, but it would make his job considerably more difficult. Did the Church have any Hunters in the area that she might send after him? Even if not, it wouldn't take long before she flew some in.

The sunny and warm day didn't feel too cold even though winter loomed large. Not a single cloud dotted the sky. Raised in the Midwest, he'd spent quite a bit of time out there with his family, and it would be cold and windy this time of the year.

He left the airport late in the afternoon, and the sun had begun to set, but he didn't expect it to get a lot colder in the hours of darkness. This close to Los Angeles, the weather made California so desirable. Though he loved coming to the sunshine state and enjoyed the pleasant climate, he would hate living here. His personality contained something dark that craved more dangerous weather. His favorite activity involved him sitting in his home and listening to a thunderstorm, cradling his daughter in his arms while she slept.

The daughter he had lost.

Frieda had tried to get hold of him several times since he'd left Japan, but he hadn't answered any of her calls to his satellite or cellular phones. He didn't want to hear what she had to say, and she would just try to talk him out of what he had to do.

Part of him regretted making his deal with Jun Lee to spare Emily. The flight out here had given him time to think, and the more time he spent mulling over what Emily had done, the more furious he became about the entire situation. If he had known Emily Glasser as the person who had betrayed him, he would never have agreed to hand her over to the Council alive. No way could Jun or Frieda give her the sort of justice she so richly deserved.

But Arthur was a man of his word. He would do as Jun had asked and bring Emily in. The only thing it changed was that he needed irrefutable proof of Emily's betrayal so that they had no choice but to put her to death. And acquiring that information brought something that Arthur looked forward to.

He had to bring her in alive. Not unharmed.

Without the Council or other assets to help him, though, he would have to remain cautious about his next move. He did this completely on his own and out on a limb. The fact that he had cash on hand meant he could avoid using any of the traceable cards the Council supplied him with. Also, he had multiple identities and aliases that he could call upon to stay undercover for a while, some of which the Council knew nothing about. Still, it gave him much less than he had gotten used to working with.

His biggest worry, however, came from whether or not Frieda would give the Hunters searching for him orders to bring him back alive, or to kill him.

He hoped for the former but suspected the latter.

If lucky, he would never have to find out. He had a head start on her and knew where he would find Emily Glasser. She frequented a huge and obnoxious nightclub known as Afterlife.

***

Emily Glasser often hung out in the nightclub Afterlife, located in downtown Sacramento. The seedy and unsettling place, dark and vibrant, provided a venue where a lot of illicit dealings took place. It offered a haven for unsavory types, including fixers and dealers who worked in the underworld.

A respectable member of the Council wouldn't get caught dead in such an establishment, but Emily Glasser proved anything but respectable. This would be the place to find her, or at the least, the club's owner would know where he should search next.

A man named Elgin Fortman owned Afterlife, a smuggler and trafficker in all sorts of drugs and paranormal paraphernalia, he had built the club a dozen years ago. The small man had a big ego and thinning brown hair and still spoke with a Brooklyn accent despite living in California for more than half of his life. Arthur couldn't remember a time that sweat didn't cover the man, even in the air-conditioned environment of his club.

Arthur found himself there at just after ten o'clock that same evening after a fairly long drive. He felt exhausted after spending so much time on international flights and in transit, but at the same time, had become used to operating in sub-optimal conditions. Without any thought, he could handle his discomfort.

By the time he got there, it had grown dark and muggy. Sacramento looked a beautiful city, but it had a few districts less than hospitable.

A line hadn't formed outside the club yet, but he saw bouncers posted, and the doors stood open. It wouldn't get going until around midnight and would stay crowded until at least seven in the morning. Arthur had visited Afterlife quite a few times on behalf of the Hunters, and Elgin had become a font of resources and information for the Council, but this time, things would turn out differently. Elgin would never harm a member of the Council, but if he knew Arthur had come here on his own ...

Elgin hated him.

Two bouncers waited at the door, and he recognized both of them. They had a strong loyalty to Elgin, which was fine, but they'd also worked here the last time Arthur had stopped by, which seemed less fine. Heavy and muted bass tones spilled out through the door behind the pair.

"Hey, guys," Arthur said as he walked up to the door. "I need to get inside and talk to your boss."

Tony, a burly Italian man, wore an expensive jacket a few sizes too small. It looked like he had ignored the dry-clean-only tag. He had also donned sunglasses and looked like he'd walked out of a nineties "B" movie. He acted mean, but Tony had shown himself one of the laziest and least intuitive people that Arthur had ever met. He could tell right away that Tony didn't recognize him.

Carmen made for the dangerous one. A petite woman, she had brown hair and mousy features. She looked pretty, wearing a white sweater.

For sure, she looked more like a soccer mom on her way to pick up her kids than a club bouncer for a place like Afterlife, but she'd spent several years with the Sacramento police before getting discharged for extreme use of deadly force. She had a powerful temper and knew how to handle herself in a fight, and Arthur knew better than to piss her off.

Also, she had a long memory.

"I didn't expect you to show your face around here again," she said when Arthur walked up. The words came out smooth, but her eyes belied her worry at seeing him.

Tony cast Carmen a sidelong glance, unsure of to what she referred. Arthur felt unsurprised that the big guy didn't recognize him.

The last time he'd seen Arthur he had gotten knocked unconscious after only a few seconds. Arthur's last job had brought him here to question Elgin about some of his shadier clients, and it hadn't turned into a social call.

"I'd hoped I wouldn't need to."

"They let you off your leash?"

Tony still looked confused as he watched the pair talk, and then, suddenly, his eyes widened with recognition.

"No way. You are *that* Arthur?"

"What Arthur?"

"The one who killed all those people."

Tony's statement caught Arthur a little by surprise, but the more he thought about it, the more sense it made. This den catered to the underworld, and they traded in illicit information, which meant that they would know about what he'd done to the cult in the woods of West Virginia.

It also explained why Carmen looked so afraid of him, though he only understood her fear in a clinical way. What he'd done to the Ninth Circle that day almost nine months ago had become legendary in some circles, and a lot of inaccurate rumors had spread. Each time he heard the story, another dozen people had gotten added to the body count.

These days, people almost always seemed deferential or scared around him, even his fellow Hunters, who he had known for dozens of years. A bond used to exist among them all, but now, they treated Arthur as an outsider. He had become infamous. Not a good feeling, but it beat the heck out of being dead. A little unsettling, the negative fame made him look forward to the day when people finally dropped the issue and forgot about it.

To make matters worse, it gave a constant reminder of what he'd done. Each time someone brought it up, it made him feel ashamed. When he went on that raid, he had been in a bad headspace and had killed a lot of people who probably didn't deserve it. If he could take it back, he would.

When he weighed his reputation against *that* reality, then the street cred it garnered him proved not worth the price.

"No other options," Arthur said. "I need some information, and Elgin is my only resource to get it."

"You think he wants to talk to you after the shit you pulled the *last* time you came here?"

"I had a job. Elgin harbored a fugitive we thought was a demon, and he told me I couldn't come in."

"The guy *wasn't* a demon."

"I didn't know that, and I sure as hell couldn't take Elgin's word for it. He only had to let me in for a couple of minutes, let me splash some salt and holy water, and I would have gone on my way. He's lucky it didn't get worse."

"You shot Elgin in the shoulder."

Arthur shrugged. "He's still alive, isn't he?"

She narrowed her eyes. "You shot me, too, if you don't

remember."

"I said sorry. When will you let that go?"

"What do you need? Maybe I can help you, because I sure as hell won't let you inside."

"I need to get in there, Carmen. I can't take 'no' for an answer."

'That won't happen."

"Maybe not easily," he said. "But it *will* happen. How's your other leg doing?"

Tony grew visibly unsettled at the way the conversation went. He didn't like conflict and shifted half-a-step back from Arthur and glanced at Carmen, unsure what to do next.

"Maybe we should just let him—"

Carmen held up her hand, cutting the big man off, and kept her eyes focused on Arthur. "You think you can just come here anytime you want and waltz inside?"

"I'm not asking. I'd love to stay here and bicker with you, but—"

"Frieda called," Carmen said. "We know this visit is off the books. We made our deal with the Council, not with you, and we don't have to let you in."

He took a breath. Though he had expected that, it still hurt to hear. "Look, let me explain—"

"Nah, I don't think I will. You should just scurry on back to your mommy's dress and beg her forgiveness. You aren't getting inside, and if you try anything stupid, I'll shoot you."

She shifted her coat to the side, letting him see the grip of the gun she wore tucked into her pants. Arthur struggled to keep his face calm, but he had become annoyed and frustrated.

"If Frieda called, then you also know why I've come here and who I want. I need to talk to Emily. Do you know where I can find her?"

"No."

"Does your boss?"

"No."

She didn't even try to pretend like she hadn't just lied, but Arthur didn't expect anything less. She still wore a slight look of fear on her face, but the normal cockiness that he'd come to expect out of Carmen replaced it gradually. The woman had built Arthur up in her mind after the news of the raid, but now she saw him as just a man once more, and the edge slipped away.

"All right, Carmen, I'm just being honest here. I will walk through that door, head up the stairs, and speak with Elgin about Emily Glasser," Arthur said, speaking slowly and clearly. "If Elgin helps me, I'll go on my way. If he doesn't, then I'll shoot him again, and this time it won't hit his shoulder. The question comes down to whether you will let me in peacefully, or if this needs to get messy first."

The words gave her pause, and she mulled them over.

"I'll have to go and check with him first," she said, finally. "Elgin has a meeting with some clients tonight and won't have an opening, but I reckon he'll see you tomorrow night if you come back."

Arthur frowned. "Emily is up there with Elgin right now, isn't she?"

Carmen winced.

"I only want to talk," Arthur said, trying one last time to get in civilly.

"You said that the last time you came here, too, and I still got shot."

"This time, I mean it."

Carmen frowned. "You said *that*, too."

"Look. I don't have any issues with either of you, and you remember what happened here. Back then, I was a man with a family just doing my job. I had something to lose, and I still didn't feel afraid to throw down. This time around, I consider myself significantly less encumbered. You told it right; I didn't come here on behalf of the Council. I came here on behalf of my family. My *murdered* family. What do you think will happen if you don't let me in?"

Carmen hesitated, and Tony looked downright scared. Finally, she rubbed her temple. "Damn it, Arthur."

"If Emily comes with me quietly, then I'll get out of your hair in a couple of minutes. If not ..."

Carmen stood there for a long while, thinking.

"I think we should let him in," Tony said.

Carmen flashed him a look that silenced him, and he gulped.

"We don't have any beef with you, Arthur," she said. "But it looks like you've got some beef with Emily, and she's a friend. You *know* we can't let you in if you plan to hurt her."

"I know," he said. "These don't make for normal circumstances, though. If it helps, I give you my word that I won't kill her. One time offer. So, how do you want to play things from here?"

Carmen stepped aside. "Don't make me regret this."

She waved her hand, shooing Tony out of the way so that Arthur could pass. Tony pulled the door open, and the music tripled in intensity and volume.

"You won't."

"You'll find them in the VIP," Carmen said.

"Thanks." Arthur nodded.

"Two of your own are up there as well. Hunters. They came in a couple of hours ago, but Emily wouldn't tell us why. We figured to protect her against you."

She sized Arthur up for a second. "I figure we don't have to guess anymore."

"I guess not."

He made to walk through the open doorway, but Carmen grabbed his arm as he went, stopping him.

"So help me, Arthur, if I find so much as a scratch on Elgin, I'll pay you back for it in full."

"I have no issue with Elgin," Arthur said. "If he leaves me be, I won't touch him. You have my word."

She nodded, released his arm, and then beckoned for him to go inside. Arthur slipped past the two bouncers and headed into the nightclub.

✳✳✳

Inside the nightclub, it looked smoky and dim. The ground floor of the establishment, comprised of a large dance hall with a raised DJ station along the right-hand side, had a bar on the left. No one tended the bar right now, and the dance floor stood empty, but in a few hours, the whole place would fill with scantily-clad bodies grinding against one another.

A balcony hung above, looking down over the dancers with a solid metal railing for people who liked to watch. Tables lined it. The VIP section sat on that level, enclosed with windows looking outward. It had the best view of the entire place.

Arthur had been up there before, and the last time, after shooting Elgin and Carmen in the VIP room, he'd barely made it out with his life.

Hopefully, this time would go a little smoother.

Strobe lights ran across the ceiling, casting the entire place in a spasmodic glow and giving it the constant sensation of movement. It disoriented Arthur, and he couldn't understand why people would come to a place like this for entertainment. Too much happened all at once for him to enjoy himself, keeping him constantly on edge.

Arthur headed to the stairs that led to the balcony, climbing quickly and going for the VIP section. By now, Carmen would have warned her boss, which meant he couldn't dilly dally. He considered drawing his gun just in case but then changed his mind. It wouldn't do to come across as threatening, and he still hoped they could end this conversation amicably.

He weaved around the empty second-floor tables before finally reaching the entrance to the private rooms. Another bouncer stood guarding the VIP, but this one, Arthur didn't recognize. Short and stocky, he wore a suit that looked made for a much taller man. He had drenched himself in enough cologne to make Arthur gag.

"Who're you?"

Arthur ignored the guy and kept walking, heading for the open doorway next to him that led into the VIP rooms. This time, he wouldn't try and talk his way through. He didn't have the minutes to spare.

The bouncer moved to block the doorway, holding up his hand to Arthur's chest. Arthur caught the man's hand, bent the wrist back at a painful angle, and then twisted the man around to face the opposite direction. The guy let out a cry of pain, staggering forward, and Arthur shoved him through the open door into the VIP section. Arthur followed him inside, tapping his leg where his gun rested for courage.

Four people sat in the room, including Emily, Elgin, and two Hunters that Arthur recognized: Jim Fronson and Michael Epplinger. Two of his least favorite allies, and it came as something of a relief to come across them and not one of his close friends. The fact that he didn't like either of them would make things a lot easier if it came to a confrontation.

Of course, they didn't like him either, so the odds of a confrontation just went up.

Jim, a short guy, had rough features and ruddy cheeks. Mike stood tall and ugly.

Emily leaned back in her blue padded chair, sipping on a cocktail and smiling smugly at Arthur. She seemed under the impression that the two bodyguards Frieda had sent to keep her safe would make for more than enough to keep Arthur at bay.

He couldn't wait to prove her wrong.

Emily looked pretty with almond-colored eyes and black hair, though a little overweight. In her mid-forties, she had the dignified air of someone born into wealth. If he looked at her hands, he wouldn't find the signs of even a single day's labor.

Elgin sat in one of the plush chairs opposite Emily. He looked particularly greasy and unkempt tonight, steepling his hands in front of his face and frowning. The man appeared considerably less assured about the situation than Emily, which probably came from both past experience and Arthur's reputation. He leaned forward when Arthur entered.

"What's the meaning of this? You think you can just barge in whenever you want?"

"Hello, Elgin."

"Why have you come here?"

"I didn't come here for you," Arthur said. "I came for Emily."

"I am his guest," Emily said, smiling pleasantly at Arthur. "And a well-paying one at that. I am here with my friends and don't appreciate this intrusion, especially by one of our own."

Arthur glanced over and saw that Jim and Michael had both stood. Jim had dialed into his phone and held a whispered conversation with someone on the other end. Michael had a hand rested on his hip, no doubt inches from his concealed weapon.

"I just need to talk with her," Arthur said, looking directly at Elgin and ignoring Emily. "Let us walk out of here, and this doesn't have to get messy."

"About what?" Elgin asked, rubbing his chin.

Emily shot him a look. "About *nothing,*" she said. "I'll not go anywhere with you, Arthur."

"I don't expect you to refuse, Elgin. This doesn't concern you. Think it through. You do remember what happened before, don't you?"

"Last time you stormed in here with your goons and used your position with the Council to browbeat me. This time, you've come all alone and outnumbered, and the Council doesn't have your back. *You* should think it through."

"I won't leave here without Emily."

"And you won't leave here with her. You can ask a couple of questions, but she's staying right here."

Emily scowled. "That wasn't the deal—"

Elgin held a hand in front of her face. To Arthur, he said, "Ask away."

"The kinds of questions I need to ask ... trust me; you'll prefer I don't do it here."

"Those are my terms."

"That won't work for me."

"Tough shit."

Arthur took a step further into the room, releasing his grip on the bouncer and pushing him toward Elgin.

"I promised Carmen I wouldn't provoke a conflict, but if you start something, that lets me off the hook. Are you sure this is how you want things to go?"

Elgin turned to face Emily. "Do you want to go with him?"

"No," she said, sipping her drink. "I'd rather stab my eyes out with a hot poker than go anywhere with Arthur Vangeest."

Elgin turned back to Arthur. "There you have it. She doesn't plan to go with you, and I have no intention of letting you take her anywhere outside this club."

Jim stopped his whispered conversation and held the phone toward Arthur.

"Here. Frieda wants to speak with you."

"See?" Elgin said, all smug and leaning back in his chair in relief. "We all know you didn't come here on behalf of the Council, who are *my* allies, and when these two showed up earlier, it became clear you would stop by at some point. Now, talk to Frieda, take your punishment, and get the hell out of my club."

Arthur hesitated, trying to decide how best to proceed. He had hoped to get to Afterlife before any other Hunters arrived, but these two must have been in the area. The worst possible situation for getting out of here cleanly.

He couldn't afford just to let this go. If he abandoned this now, then Emily would get away, and he wouldn't get the answers he needed, and the next time he did anything, she would have much better protection.

"I'll even forget this little transgression ever happened," Elgin said. "After I get a little something from Frieda for my troubles."

Arthur stared at Elgin, furious. Though confident he could handle the bouncer, and maybe one of the two Hunters if it came to blows, having all three of them would make things considerably riskier. Both of the well-trained Hunters knew better than to underestimate Arthur. He would have few advantages.

If they had gotten sent here on behalf of the Council, then probably, they also had orders to use deadly force if necessary to keep Emily safe. It would become their first recourse rather than a last resort.

He'd wanted to get Emily out of here without a conflict, but it didn't look like that factored in his options. Now, Frieda wanted to talk to him, too, and no doubt, she wanted to talk him out of doing anything stupid.

Too little, too late.

With an internal sigh, he walked over and accepted the phone from Jim. Everyone else in the room stared at him, smug expressions on their faces.

"Yeah?"

"Arthur, you *really* should start taking my calls."

"I've been busy."

"I know. So have I."

"You sent Jim and Mike here to stop me? I thought we were friends?"

"I had no choice. You've put me in an impossible situation."

"At least now I know where you stand."

"You don't know anything. Next time, answer your damn phone."

"Why? So you can talk me out of doing this?"

"No," she said. "I *had* to send Jim and Michael so that Emily wouldn't just disappear. The reason I tried to call you ... I needed to tell you that Jim has a bum right knee from a recent surgery, and Michael has seen a doctor twice in the last month about lost vision in his left eye. He's practically blind right now."

Arthur hesitated. "Oh."

"Next time I call, answer your damn phone."

Then Frieda hung up. Arthur held the phone to his ear for a few seconds. Finally, he offered the phone to Jim.

"She said she wants to talk to you."

Jim reached for the phone, still smiling, but didn't quite reach it before Arthur let go. It fell.

Jim acted on impulse, diving forward to catch it before it smashed against the ground. He never even got close.

Arthur stepped toward Jim, caught his wrist as he leaned in, and yanked him off-balance. Jim fell sideways, stumbling and exposing his bad knee.

Jim tried to react and jerk back, but Arthur moved faster. With his steel-toed boots, he kicked Jim in the side of his bad knee. Even if the joint had been perfect, the placement and power behind Arthur's attack would have done serious damage. Against Jim's bad knee, it proved devastating.

The short man staggered, letting out a half-scream-half-groan and falling into the side of the couch beside him. He tried to catch himself and stop his fall, but with the pain, he couldn't and fell to the ground and clutched his knee.

Arthur didn't hesitate but rushed at Michael, shifting sideways into the man's blind spot. The Hunter tried to adjust to follow him, but Arthur could tell that Frieda had given him a true assessment. Michael had only limited vision out of his left eye, and almost no depth perception.

Arthur waded in and punched the lanky man with a series of rapid hits on his ribcage. Michael could barely defend himself while he tried to turn to face him. Arthur followed the flurry by a sucker punch to his jaw.

With the advantage of knowing Michael and Jim's

weaknesses, it turned out all too easy. To his credit, Michael kept his feet and tried to fight back, but Arthur didn't give him a chance to regain his ground. He kicked Michael in the stomach, grabbed his arm, and threw him face-first into the wall. He hit hard, and then slid to the door, dazed.

Arthur turned and drew his gun just as the bouncer freed his nine-millimeter pistol from his shoulder holster. They aimed at each other. Arthur's hand stayed steady while the bouncer's gun shook up and down in his fear.

"Wait, wait!" Elgin shouted, climbing awkwardly from his plush seat. "No shooting!"

"I'd prefer not to," Arthur said. "Have your man lower his weapon, and we can still end this amicably."

"Guns down," Elgin said, grabbing the bouncer's arm and pulling it toward the ground. "Fine, Arthur, I get it. I get it. Just lower your gun, please."

Arthur did, but he held it ready at his side.

Jim groaned from nearby on the floor, clutching his wounded knee. He emitted a string of curses, aimed at Arthur as he tried to pull himself up using the couch arm.

"Cheap shot, going for my knee like that."

"You should spend more time on those rehab exercises they gave you."

"How'd you know?" Jim asked, dragging himself up onto the couch. His face grew pale from the pain.

"Lucky guess."

Jim winced, touching where Arthur had hit him. "Frieda told you, didn't she?" Then he cursed at her. "That bitch. When the Council hears about this ..."

"The Council won't hear about it," Arthur said calmly, walking over to where Jim lay. "As far as they're concerned, Emily had gone when you got here. Unfortunately, you could do nothing about it. Understood?"

"Like hell I'll let you walk out of here—"

"It's either that," Arthur said. "Or the Council will find a lot of bodies and Emily gone."

Jim fell silent for a minute, refusing to look at Arthur. Finally, he nodded.

"Fine. We got here too late."

"What?" Emily rose from the sofa. Her smug expression evaporated.

Jim ignored her. "You can take her. We won't try to stop you or come looking for you. Just get the hell out of here."

"You can't do that," Emily yelled with wide eyes. "You're

sworn to protect me. Shoot him. I demand that you shoot him."

Jim grabbed her and shoved her toward Arthur. She tripped and stumbled, but Arthur caught her before she fell to the ground. Her body trembled, but he had no pity for her. When she looked up at him, a terrified expression settled on her face.

"What happens to me now?"

Arthur looked her square in the eyes. "Depends on how quickly you tell me the truth."

"About what?"

"About why you had my family murdered."

✳✳✳

Once he had Emily safely under control, Arthur got out of Afterlife as fast as he could. Carmen gave him a look of mild annoyance and disbelief as he left, but after a quick call up to the VIP room to make sure Elgin had sanctioned his actions, she let him go. He didn't breathe easy again until he got Emily into the backseat of his car.

Emily begged with him to let her go, but once she realized that her pleas had no effect, she resorted to screaming. Arthur used duct tape to bind her wrists and cover her mouth. He didn't want to hear her speak, and the more she begged and pleaded, the angrier he became.

Had his wife and daughter begged like this before they got murdered? In his control, he had the woman who had gotten them killed ... how could he possibly let her go? Though he had promised Jun he wouldn't kill Emily, he didn't know what would happen if he had to listen to her pleading and sniveling for too long.

He could barely believe that he had her—the person who had betrayed his family; the reason his wife and daughter had died. She sat in the back seat of his car, completely at his mercy. That, honestly, gave him enough to kill her, but he needed evidence first. He needed answers.

His first and ultimate question, though, was *why*? Why had she sold him out? What price had she set, and to whom had she sold him? Arthur had made a lot of enemies in his time serving the Council, and he needed to know which one of them had gotten to Emily.

He drove them outside of Sacramento to an area where the city currently underwent a lot of construction. They had started a lot of projects, as the fiscal year closed, to guarantee funding, but now they sat on the money since they had more projects than contractors. It made these buildings the perfect place to operate away from prying eyes.

He took her to the skeletons of a dozen buildings that stood unoccupied. No doubt the crews wouldn't come back for months, which meant they would remain alone and undisturbed. Emily would quickly realize that screaming would do her no good.

He found an unoccupied building, broke open the door, and dragged Emily inside.

She didn't struggle anymore, but her face had grown ashen when Arthur brought her into the dim interior of what would, eventually, become an office building. He found a five-gallon bucket and sat her on it, and then grabbed one for himself to sit across from her on the empty ground floor of the building.

Then he just waited, sitting silently in the darkness. He stared at her, letting the circumstances of her situation set in. Terrified, Emily's eyes darted around the room, looking for any way out of the situation.

Finally, after about ten minutes, he reached up and rudely ripped the tape from her mouth. She let out a gasp of pain followed by a whimper.

"Arthur, I don't know what you think I did—"

He held up his hand. "We need to talk."

"You can't do this," she whispered, a hint of whininess in her voice. She sounded like a teenager pleading with her parents. Except for the staring at the floor and making gasping and sobbing noises. "You *need* to let me go."

"Not a chance."

"When my brother hears of this …"

Her brother made for a powerful figure, and having him involved in the situation did worry Arthur quite a bit. He had become the reason that Emily would prove so difficult to prosecute if the Council accused her of betrayal. And stepping on the toes of Bishop Leopold Glasser could have sizable consequences.

Which meant Arthur now tread on dangerous territory and couldn't do anything serious to harm Emily … at least, not without good reason. He intended to honor his promise to Jun Lee and had no intention of killing her.

Although, she didn't need to know that.

"If you don't tell me what I want to know right now, then your brother will *never* find your body."

Emily sputtered. "I swear, I had nothing to do with your family's death."

"You mean their *murder*." Arthur leaned forward. "They got

murdered, Emily, after *you* told the Ninth Circle where to find them."

"I didn't. Someone else must have."

"No one else could have."

"It wasn't me!"

"Don't bother trying to deny it," Arthur said. "We've gone past that point. You're one of three people who knew where I lived, and the other two didn't do it. You had the information, and now I need to discover the motive."

"Maybe they trailed *you* back home," she said. "How do you know *you* didn't give your family away?"

"This will go a lot easier if you let me ask the questions," Arthur said. "I told you; we've gone past the point of arguing or pleading, and you won't convince me of your innocence. You'll only piss me off."

"I *didn't* do it! I swear."

"Did you do it for the money?"

"I didn't do it."

He ignored her. "Your options are to tell me what I want to know, or I'll torture the information out of you."

"You know that doesn't work. You won't get the truth through torture."

"No," he said. "But I'll have a lot of fun trying."

Emily's body shook, and Arthur had to admit a moment of petty satisfaction. She had called it correctly, and torturing her would prove ineffective. He would get her to swear she was the Pope if he went down that road.

Fear, on the other hand, could make a powerful motivator on its own.

Part of him hated doing this at all. It seemed shady and beneath him, and it wasn't who he was. Or, at least, not who he used to be before his family got killed. Back then, he had considered himself an honorable man, willing to do the right thing even when not easy.

Now, he just wondered if his daughter had cried like that before they cut her throat.

"I'm a member of the Council. You can't do this. You are a *Hunter.* You serve *me.*"

"You can argue the semantics and rules of the situation all you want. It doesn't change what will happen. I won't enjoy torturing you, Emily, but make no mistake, I *will* do it. Who was your contact in the Ninth Circle? To whom did you sell the information?"

"Arthur, I *don't* even know what you're talking about. I don't know anyone from the Ninth Circle. I serve the Council faithfully and would never betray you. Do you think I could live with myself if I had a part of what happened to your family?"

"I guess we shall find out the answer to that at the end of our conversation."

He stood and walked over to a table littered with construction tools. There, he picked up a screwdriver, eyed it for a second, and then set it back down.

"I just want to know who you told," he said. "It's a simple piece of information and can save us both a lot of time and energy."

"I didn't tell anyone. I wouldn't."

"If you cooperate, I'll turn you over to the Council and let them deal with you. No doubt they will offer you a painless execution. That's a way better offer than you'll get from me."

"I don't have a contact. I don't know anyone in the Ninth Circle. I don't know *anyone*, period. I swear, I would never deal with that cult or any cult. I would never betray the Council. Arthur, please, you have to believe me. I might not be a perfect person, but I'm not a killer. You *know* that."

Arthur hesitated. She stuck to her story a lot more firmly than he had expected. Emily made a good liar, but under the circumstances, he doubted she could pull off something this convincing without at least a small slip-up.

She had it right, too. He didn't like her. She would screw over a lot of people to get her way, but he also knew she wasn't cold blooded. The woman had never struck him as a killer, and he *knew* killers.

It added doubt to Arthur's mind. The conversation hadn't progressed how he'd expected. With her self-serving attitude, by now he had expected her to give up her information in exchange for something else. She would have, at least, offered a deal.

Maybe, he admitted, she told the truth.

But, if not Emily, then who?

"You had to tell someone," he said, finally. "Maybe not someone in the cult, but someone you weren't supposed to. You were the only one who knew about my family, so you must have slipped up."

"I tell you, I *didn't*. I got sworn to secrecy and would never tell anyone outside the Council. Hell, I don't even know many people outside the Council who would even believe me if I told them what we do."

"Think, Emily. The Ninth Circle didn't find out by accident. Who did you talk to?"

"No one, Arthur. The only person I ever talk to about Council business outside of the Council is ..."

She looked up from the ground and at Arthur. Realization spread across her face.

Horror settled there, too.

"What is it? Who did you tell?" he asked.

Slowly, she shook her head.

"No, he wouldn't."

"Who did you tell?" Arthur took a threatening step toward her. "Who betrayed my family?"

She became a completely different woman now. In only seconds, she had gone from argumentative and scared to broken. Clearly, she didn't want to believe that this person might be capable of something so horrible, but she believed it just the same.

"My brother."

✳✳✳

Arthur felt sick to his stomach.

"Your brother? The bishop?"

"He's the only person I talk to, and I tell him *everything*."

"But why would he ...?"

Arthur failed abysmally in discerning how to continue because it felt so hard to believe. He wouldn't have, in fact, if not for the look of utter betrayal on Emily's face.

Leopold Glasser had incredible power, and people trusted him both inside and outside of the Council. Though arrogant like his sister, he had incredible loyalty to the Church and Council, unlike her. He made for one of their staunchest supporters and greatest beneficiary. The idea that he would betray them seemed inconceivable.

Except ...

The fact that he had so much trust and lived beyond reproach put him in the perfect position to do exactly what he'd done. He had lied, cheated, and manipulated to find out about Arthur's family and use that information against him.

Though hard to believe, in his heart, Arthur saw the truth of it.

✳✳✳

At any given time, the Council of Chaldea had thirteen active Council members. They served the Catholic Church as a secret organization that the Church could call upon to handle sensitive supernatural problems when they didn't want to get their hands dirty.

But they didn't form actual members of the Church. Instead, they made for allies. The Church had played a critical part in forming the Council many centuries ago, but over the years, the Council had expanded to deal with all manner of supernatural threats and worked outside the Church's command. They didn't serve any religion in particular, and nor would they refuse to help anyone based on religious or political principles.

Yet, despite that, the Catholic Church had always been the primary monetary force behind the Council's operations, giving them funding and political clout well beyond their meager means. Most of the Catholic clergy knew little or nothing about their Order, but some of the bishops did. Bishop Leopold Glasser was one such bishop, and he donated significant funds toward keeping the Council in operation.

The idea that he would lay behind this ...

That represented something else entirely.

"Your *brother*? You think Leopold did this?"

She hesitated and shook her head. "No, it couldn't be him. I've gotten it wrong. I must be wrong."

"Did you tell him about my family?"

"Yes. But as an off-handed thing. Something mentioned in passing. We sat talking about the Hunters, and he didn't know if you served as priests and weren't allowed to have families. He assumed familial ties could become a liability, but I told him that you *were* allowed to marry, and your families had protection."

"And then you told him about *my* family," Arthur said.

Emily nodded. "I used you as an example. I didn't think."

"You never told anyone else?"

"No. But my brother would *never* do something like this. No way. Not unless he felt he had no other choice."

"Don't try and justify."

"I'm only saying—"

He raised a hand to stop her words. "What else did you tell him? Did you tell him about any other families you got tasked to protect?"

"Just that. Except ..."

"Except?"

"Leopold asked me a few days ago about a couple of members of the Council. I didn't think anything of it, but he seemed more specific than usual when we talk."

"Did you tell him anything?"

She winced. "I did. I thought he just had an interest in knowing more about the Order since he donates so much money to us. One of the people he asked about was Frieda, but I don't know much about her. She's private and doesn't have any living family members that I know of. But the other ..."

"Who?"

"Aram Arison. He has two young children."

"You told him where he lives?"

She nodded. "Not his family, specifically, just the city where they reside. But I said he was the leader of a congregation and which one. You don't think they could use that information to find Aram's family, do you?"

Arthur didn't answer. He walked away from Emily and pulled out his phone. He called Frieda.

She answered right away. "What is it, Arthur? You have Emily?"

"Yes. Where is Aram?"

"What?"

"Aram Arison. Where is he? Where is his family?"

"He's in India dealing with Council business."

"What about his family? Are they home?"

"Arthur, you *know* I can't tell you—"

"They aren't safe, Frieda. Where are they?"

She hesitated. "Washington State on vacation. They just got there. Aram is supposed to meet them tomorrow."

"You sent him?"

"Yes. So that he can take care of some Council business in the area."

"He's meeting with Bishop Glasser, isn't he?"

"Yes. How did you know?"

"It's a trap. His family isn't safe."

"What do you mean? We have two Hunters keeping an eye on them, and we've had no reports of anything out of the ordinary."

"Leopold," Arthur said. "He betrayed us. He got my family murdered."

Frieda fell speechless on the other end of the line.

"Frieda?"

"That can't be right."

"He's the only person Emily told, and he asked specifically about Aram. He's the only other person who knew about my family, and now he knows about Aram's, too. You need to get me to Washington and send me Aram's family's location."

"Jesus, Arthur. This is …"

"Way bigger than we thought," Arthur said, rubbing his face. "And way worse. We don't have a lot of time. Whatever might happen, it will unfold before Aram gets there."

"You need to stop this, Arthur."

"I thought I was out of commission?"

"Not anymore. Head to the airport. I'll have a ticket waiting for you on the next flight out."

Arthur hung up and slid the phone back in his pocket. He looked at Emily. She sagged on the bucket with a look of utter despair on her face.

"You think it was him, don't you?" he asked. "You think Leopold did it."

She looked up at him. Finally, she nodded. "That's terrible, because he's my brother, but it's true. He's always had a dark streak to him, and these last few years he … changed. We talk less and less, and he always seems to have an agenda."

Arthur didn't know how to respond. "For what it's worth," he said. "I'm sorry."

She gave a sardonic chuckle. "What do you plan to do with me, now? Kill me?"

"No." Arthur picked up a box cutter from the table, walked over, and cut the tape binding Emily's wrists. She rubbed them to help with circulation and pulled the excess tape loose, surprised that he had cut her free.

"What, then?"

"I'll let you go," Arthur said. "And you will call Frieda and turn yourself in. You will tell them everything you told me and throw yourself on their mercy. With luck, they will let you live."

"You know they won't."

He sighed, standing. "I don't care. Either way, my family remains dead, and you're still partly to blame. If you don't turn yourself in, I'll tell them everything, and then I will, personally, hunt you down. Do you want to spend the rest of your life looking over your shoulder? Do you really intend to spend every day listening for my footsteps?"

"What about my brother? What will happen to him?"

Arthur stared at her for a long moment. His hands shook.

"What do you think will happen to him?"

Arthur turned and headed for the exit, leaving her alone in the empty building.

Chapter 13

Arthur found himself back on a plane only a few short hours later. It felt like déjà vu as he'd spent so much time in the air. This time, he flew to Everett, Washington. Frieda had come through with the ticket, and everything ran smoothly.

He had gotten little time to sleep over the last few days and would try and get some shut-eye during the flight. He popped a couple of Dramamine with an inflight drink and soon passed out.

He had no doubt that repercussions to all of this would come back to him, and that Frieda remained far from forgiving him. He had gone behind her back and left her in Germany, holding the bag, so to speak.

He had also abandoned Abigail, which proved even harder for him to stomach. Since he'd rescued her in West Virginia, he hadn't left her side in these last nine months. Though safe now, that didn't change the feeling of guilt he felt at abandoning her.

This paled in comparison, though, to his guilt for what had happened to his family. He hadn't managed to protect them. They'd died because of him and the decisions he'd made.

Part of him wished he *had* killed Emily back in Sacramento; he still felt a seething anger in the pit of his stomach. She hadn't betrayed him intentionally, and didn't seem quite the despicable and hateful person he'd expected, but she remained partly responsible for what had happened to his family.

Even if it not intentional, and even if her brother had manipulated and betrayed her, she still shared the guilt.

She still deserved to die.

However, she hadn't sold him out. Someone else held far more responsibility and deserved the full weight of his ire. Leopold Glasser stood outside Arthur's jurisdiction, and going after him without the Church's permission—even if he could prove that the bishop had betrayed the Council and had the responsibility for what happened to his family—would infuriate the Church and make him an enemy.

On top of that, the man remained dangerous. Leopold had a reputation for being thoughtful and calculating. No doubt he had manipulated things in such a way that it would prove nearly impossible to pin him down for any of his crimes.

Yet, Arthur couldn't just stand by and allow the Council or the Catholic Church to sweep this under the rug, especially if the only punishment Leopold received came down to a slap on the wrist. If it came to that, Arthur didn't know what he would do.

He'd made no similar promise to Jun Lee to spare Leopold's life, and he would be damned if the bishop could walk out of this situation without any punishment.

✳✳✳

First things first, though; he had a duty to the Council to protect Aram Arison's family. Aram was a stuck-up asshole, but Arthur would be damned before he would let what happened to his family happen to anyone else. He seemed to recall that Aram had two children—a little boy and girl. Young. Both under ten. They had raised them as normal with no knowledge of the Council or what their father did.

Arthur had raised his daughter that way too, so he could respect Aram's decision. Arthur's wife had known what he did, but he had hoped to keep this life away from his daughter.

He didn't feel ashamed of what he did—in fact, he loved it—but he wanted her to have a different life. A happier and less dangerous experience. He could understand Aram wanting the same thing for his children.

It wouldn't work, of course. The life followed you, and no way could he protect them from the evil things out there in the night.

Arthur had learned that the hard way.

He didn't like Aram particularly. The man had become one of his primary opponents in keeping Abigail safe. After he'd rescued her from the cult, a long and drawn out battle had unfolded within the Council about what to do with her. Arthur wanted to adopt her and keep her safe, but many members felt that the risk of keeping her alive would prove too great.

Aram stood in the camp of Councilors that felt they should execute Abigail. To Arthur, that seemed unthinkable. Only a child, nothing that had happened to her was her fault. Aram didn't see her as a little girl, though, but rather as a time bomb. And keeping her alive put them all at risk, and it didn't make a risk he felt willing to take.

Aram didn't stand alone in that opinion, either. Several other members of the Council felt the same. Hell, even Frieda would have gone that direction (most probably) if not for Arthur pleading with her. Sure, he understood the risk; that cult had done something to her in West Virginia, and he had no idea what. But that gave no justification to kill her.

***

The plane touched down early the next morning just as the sun rose. He'd managed to get a couple of hours' sleep during the flight, but he still felt exhausted and ran on empty. It had proven a rough couple of days, and he didn't expect it to get any easier until he had dealt with Bishop Glasser.

Arthur picked up a coffee on his way out of the airport and downed it in a few swigs. He hated the bitter taste but needed the caffeine to keep him moving. Frieda had given him the address of a hotel where Aram's family stayed, but no one expected them back until later tonight. Supposedly, they had gone out exploring the city.

He had barely made it into the city when Frieda called him.

"Hello?"

"Did you make it safely to Everett?"

"I'm here," he said. "Have you gotten hold of the family?"

"Not yet. Aram's wife left her cell phone in their hotel room, and it just keeps ringing."

"Why doesn't she have her phone?"

"Aram said she doesn't like it. He insisted she have one, but she often forgets to take it with her."

"What about the Hunters you sent to keep an eye on her? They should answer theirs, right?"

"No answer from either of them. The clerk doesn't remember seeing them since yesterday. He asked if I wanted him to check on them, and I said to hold off."

"I'm on my way to check on them, now."

"I need you to do me a favor, first."

"What?"

"Check on the local priest. A man named Jackson Reynolds. I called the Vatican to tell them everything we know, and they asked me to make sure their priest is okay. Saint Joseph's Cathedral sits in the center of town, and it should only take you a couple of minutes."

"It's a complete waste of time," Arthur said. "Which is in short supply."

"I know, Arthur. But I'm not in a position to say 'no' to the Church right now. Not until we know how the chips fall."

"So, this is a favor for the Church?"

"More or less. I also feel concerned to see what he knows about the bishop. He might be in on it, too, and he could help you come at the bishop sideways if so. We need information, and I hate being this blind about something so important."

"Can't you send someone else to check on him?"

"I have no one else in the area. In case you forgot, you injured the only two people I had on the West Coast yesterday. Both Mike and Jim are in the hospital. You make for my only asset out there right now."

"Fine. I'll stop in on him but only for a couple of minutes. I need to track down Aram's family before it's too late."

"Thanks, Arthur. I'm firefighting right now with the Council, the Church, and everyone else. Emily called and said she wants to turn herself in and confess everything, and I don't even have time to savor that. You kicked a hornet's nest, and everything is falling apart around me."

"If you're looking for an apology ..."

"I'm not," she said, sighing. "You can be a real asshole sometimes, but if you manage to save Aram's family, I'll forgive it all."

Arthur hesitated for a long moment before speaking again, "How is Abigail?"

"Safe," Frieda said. "Worried. She's felt anxious since you left without saying anything."

"I hated doing that," Arthur said. "But I knew you would drill her for information, so I couldn't tell her where I planned to go."

"I did," Frieda said. "I had no clue what you might do or if you were even all right. You scared the hell out of both of us, Arthur."

"Sorry."

"I'm sure she thinks I'm a witch, now. I haven't, exactly, been the best guardian."

"She'll forgive you. She's a good kid."

"I know."

"Keep me informed of anything you find out from the Church."

"Whenever they call me back, you'll be the first to know. Stay safe."

"You too."

He hung up, parking his rental car by the curb in front of Saint Joseph's Cathedral. It seemed a fairly large church, tall and built in a gothic style. Another car had parked out front, a little blue Toyota.

Arthur went up to the huge wooden doors and knocked. After a few moments, it opened, and a smiling young woman stood in the doorway. She had a puzzled look on her face when she saw him.

"You don't have to knock. The doors are almost always unlocked."

"Habit," he said. "I've come looking for Father Reynolds. I had hoped to speak with him."

"He isn't in right now," the woman said. "But he should get back soon."

"It's rather urgent, and I don't have time to wait. He expects me. Do you know where I might find him?"

She frowned. "More Church business? Are you with that priest who came to visit from the Vatican? I don't remember his name. Peregrin?"

Arthur kept his face calm, deciding to roll with the lie. "Yes. I came with Father Peregrin. I had some business to attend to this morning, and they asked me to catch up, though I've quite forgotten where they went."

"Of course," she said. "They went to Rose Gallagher's home. She lives on Richmond Street. Do you need the address?"

"Yes, please."

She gave it to him. He thanked her and then headed back to his car. He checked his map and saw that Rose lived in a housing development just outside town. It didn't lay too far from the hotel where Aram's family stayed.

She had mentioned another priest from the Vatican, though, which set Arthur on edge. He had never heard of a Father Peregrin before. Who, exactly, did she mean?

✳✳✳

A few minutes later, Arthur reached the house that the woman in the church had sent him to. The front door stood open. It had a screen door still in place, but the house inside looked dim and empty. Another car sat in the parking lot as well, and he assumed it belonged to the local priest.

He pulled his little rental car into the driveway, parked, and then walked up onto the porch of the house. He raised his hand to knock on the screen door, but then stopped when a kindly-looking old woman appeared behind it. She stepped out of the shadows like a phantom, blocking his way, leaning on a walker. The old woman smiled at him.

"Hello."

"Hello," he said. "I came looking for Father Jackson Reynolds. One of the congregation told me that I might find him here."

"Yes, he's here." She leaned forward, and then called out into the yard past Arthur, "Father Jackson! I have a guest asking for you. Could you come here for a moment?"

A few seconds passed, and then a handsome-looking black man walked around the corner of the house. He hesitated when he saw Arthur standing there, and then he came forward and offered his hand.

"Hi," Arthur said. "I'm Arthur Vangeest."

They shook hands. "Father Jackson Reynolds. It's a pleasure to meet you."

"Likewise. A friendly young woman at your church said I might find you out here."

"Ah," he replied, relaxing. "That would be Amanda. She helps me take care of the church when I go out and about. Can I help you with something?"

Arthur hesitated. Frieda had asked him to make sure the priest remained alive and safe, but also to find out if he knew anything about Bishop Glasser's recent activities.

What he didn't know, however, was if the priest was in on any of it. He didn't know the best approach to suss out that information.

"I hate to just barge in like this, but I wondered if I could ask you a couple of questions about Bishop Leopold Glasser."

Jackson tilted his head to the side. "Oh?"

"Yeah, I'm doing a piece on him for a local newspaper and wanted to get your take on the man. Do you mind if I come in for a minute?"

Jackson looked to Rose, and she nodded. "Of course, of course. Please, come in."

Arthur followed them into the building and over to a couple of uncomfortable-looking chairs in the living room. Immediately, a smell assaulted him with which he felt quite familiar. The house contained something dead and rotting.

He thought to call attention to it, and then changed his mind. He wanted to get to know the priest a little bit more before raising any provocative questions. Instead, he took one of the proferred seats and turned toward the priest.

"Just some simple questions, really. Let's start with something basic. What is your opinion of the bishop? Do you have a close familiarity with him?"

Jackson thought about it for a second, and then shook his head. "Not really. We live in the same city, but I rarely meet with him."

"When did you last speak with him?"

Jackson hesitated, and then said, "I'm sorry, but I don't think I can give you a lot of information about him on a personal level. As I said, we don't speak that often."

"Just tell me what you think of him. You'll find yourself surprised at the details you might pick up even from a casual acquaintance."

Jackson thought about it for a second. "He is a very ... *distinctive* man." He had the air of someone who had processed one thought and said another, and Arthur could tell that he didn't much care for the bishop.

That gave a good sign. At least it made it less likely that they worked together.

"Distinctive. Do you mean like his personality is distinctive, or—"

A sudden loud thump came from the floor beneath them. Arthur jumped to his feet, hand sliding down to where he had his gun holstered. Or, would have had; luckily, he had left his revolver in the rental outside. He brushed his hand on his legs, disguising the motion.

"What was that?"

Jackson looked quite concerned, standing and heading for the front door. Arthur followed the priest outside and around the house. They walked around the corner to the side from where the priest had first come. A large metal grate lay on the grass next to a hole leading underneath the house and into what looked like a crawlspace.

"Father Paladina," Jackson leaned down to the hole and called into it. "Are you all right?"

At the mention of the name, Arthur's stomach sank. Not Peregrin, Paladina. Father Niccolo Paladina he had met a few times in his life on behalf of the Council of Chaldea. He came across as a hard-liner priest, incredibly opinionated.

He had also become one of the priests tasked with cleaning up Arthur's meltdown in West Virginia when he had killed the cultists. He had met Niccolo under less than ideal circumstances, and he doubted the man would have forgotten or forgiven any of it.

No response came from the crawlspace, and Jackson flashed him a worried look. Arthur cocked an eyebrow but didn't say anything. Might this make an ideal time to make his exit? No ... it might draw more attention to him if he did that.

"Father Paladina?" Jackson called.

"Hang on," Arthur said, kneeling and peering into the hole. A dim yellow light glowed maybe fifteen feet underneath the house.

He couldn't see any movement, though. "I'll come right back."

He crawled into the hole and slid easily over the gravel and dirt floor. Though a tight space, he had grown used to ending up in uncomfortable environments and had little trouble navigating it.

It didn't take him long to find the priest. Niccolo lay unconscious on the ground next to what looked like a dead cat. His flashlight lay next to him, and Arthur picked it up and used it to scan the area.

It seemed quiet and empty. No sign of struggle or anything else that might have been down here with him. Niccolo must not have realized how low the ceiling was and bumped his head accidentally. He checked the priest but didn't see any blood in his hair.

A garbage bag lay underneath him. Arthur extricated it, and then pushed the dead cat inside before tying it closed. This must have caused the horrible smell inside the house, and it looked to have been here for several days, possibly weeks.

Arthur had to drag Niccolo as much as carry him because of the cramped space as he made his slow way back outside the crawlspace. He laid Niccolo on the grass and set the bag down next to him.

"Is he all right?" Father Reynolds asked.

Arthur stood and saw that Rose had come out of the house as well. She and the young priest stood there watching him.

"Yes," he said. "He's fine. Just bumped his head."

Jackson knelt next to Father Paladina, checking his head for any wounds. "He's got a nice bruise, but he looks okay."

"I really should get going—"

"No, wait a few minutes. I'm sorry for this, but I would feel happy to answer any of your questions after I get my friend into the house."

Just then, Niccolo started to wake. Arthur stepped back with a sigh, standing next to Rose. Niccolo blinked his eyes open, squinting them against the light.

"Father Paladina?" Jackson asked.

Niccolo jerked, sitting up quickly and gasping.

"Sorry, I didn't mean to startle you," Father Reynolds said. "Are you all right?"

"I believe so. What ... what happened? How did I get here?"

"I was about to ask you the same thing. We'd gone to sit in the living room to talk when we heard a loud thud beneath the floor. When he found you, you'd fallen unconscious and looked to have hit your head against one of the beams."

"You dragged me out?"

"Not me. *He* managed to get you out," Jackson gestured toward Arthur. "And he got the cat, too. Looks like the poor thing had been down there for at least a week after it died."

"What about the girl?"

"The what?"

"The ..." Niccolo stopped himself. "Did you find anything else down there with me?"

Jackson looked confused. "Like what?"

Niccolo seemed as if about to elaborate, and then he changed his mind and shook his head.

"What did you mean, 'not you'?" Niccolo asked instead, looking around. "You said *he* got me. Who else was with you?"

Then, he spotted Arthur.

"You?" Niccolo sputtered, climbing awkwardly to his feet. "What in God's name are *you* doing here?"

Jackson looked at him in shock, and Arthur could see that his lie just went out the window. So much for his story about Bishop Glasser. "You know him?"

"Of course I know him. This is Arthur Vangeest."

"Hello, Niccolo," Arthur said. "It's been a while."

Jackson turned to him. "So, you aren't a reporter?"

He shook his head. "I apologize for misleading you."

"You mean lying," Niccolo said. "It's what you do best. Why have you come here?"

Arthur took a deep breath. This could work out for the best. Since Niccolo knew about the Order, he could skip the disbelief that normally accompanied situations like this and jump right to the danger. "We should speak in private."

"We have nothing to speak about. You have overstayed your welcome already."

"I'm afraid I must insist," Arthur said. "It is incredibly important, and a matter of some urgency."

"No," Niccolo said, angry. "I will *not* speak with you, nor will I listen to anything you have to say. I also know that you aren't supposed to be out on a job. Any job. Which means you're not sanctioned, are you?"

"You don't understand—"

"I understand perfectly. If you do not get in your car and leave Everett in the next few seconds, I will notify the Vatican of your presence and report that you are interfering with Church affairs."

"I'll go, but after you hear me out. This is important."

"No."

"It's a matter of life and death."

"All you understand is death, Arthur. I was there. I saw the bodies and what you did."

Arthur stifled a sigh and turned to walk to his car. The conversation had gone about as well as he'd expected, and Niccolo hated his guts. He couldn't even blame him, as he would have hated him if the only version he knew was the one from West Virginia. That day, he had functioned at his worst.

Just about to leave, he stopped when Niccolo turned to Jackson and Rose. "Would you give us a moment?"

Arthur couldn't hide a look of surprise. "I should explain myself to Father Reynolds as well," Arthur said. "He should hear this."

"No," Niccolo said. "You may speak to me, and then you will leave. Understood?"

Arthur thought about it for a second and then nodded. Niccolo had it right. If Jackson had no involvement, then it became best he get left out of Council business.

Niccolo turned to face Jackson, "I will come in right behind you. This will only take a moment."

The two disappeared. Arthur cursed his bad luck that he hadn't known Paladina would be here. He didn't know how much or how little to say to convince him that things had grown dangerous.

Why had Paladina come out here at all? He rarely left the Vatican, and only then on some sort of investigation on behalf of the exorcists. Did that make for the reason he had turned up here? Did the Church worry that something might be going on?

Maybe they knew more than Arthur thought.

"Why have you come here?" Niccolo asked. "In Everett, of all places. Don't you have more important things to do? More cultists to murder?"

The words stung. Father Paladina hated him and felt him dangerous and violent. He disliked having his entire life boiled down to one decision he'd made.

"You had it right that I'm not on the books, but I *have* come on an investigation. An important one, and it led me here."

"What investigation?"

"This is something personal."

"If you won't tell me—"

Arthur had only one chance to get through to Father Paladina, and it would take total honesty.

"I've come hunting the people who murdered my family."

His words had the impact he had hoped for. Niccolo appeared completely caught off-guard. He fumbled for a few seconds, looking for something to say, before finally speaking, "I'm sorry for your family," he said. "But that doesn't explain why you've come here."

"The person who betrayed me is here."

"In Everett?"

"Yes."

"You expect me to believe that?"

"It's the truth."

"I fought to have you turned over to the authorities, you know," Niccolo said. "After you murdered those people. I remained one of the few who thought you the monster. Not the cultists. You."

Arthur took a steadying breath. "They had kidnapped and murdered children. They'd gone beyond salvation."

"All of them? Can you stand there and tell me that none of them could have gotten saved?"

"It isn't my job to save people."

"No, I forgot. It's your job to *kill* them. I wanted for you to spend the rest of your life in a jail cell. Where you belong."

"I know. I don't blame you."

"You murdered those people, Arthur."

"I did my job."

"You think *that* matters? God will not forgive you for what you did."

Arthur wondered if Niccolo called it true. He had wondered that a lot since that fateful day.

"It seems to me that that conversation should stay between God and me."

"I won't forgive you, either."

"I'm not asking you to. I just ask for you to hear me out and make up your mind."

"Why should I hear you out? So you can tell me more lies?"

"So, I'm a liar now, too? I thought I was a murderer?"

"You can easily be both."

Arthur rubbed his face. If Niccolo had come here because of a possible exorcism, then maybe things had gone further than he'd anticipated. He needed to try a different tack to get through to him, "This is getting us nowhere. We just keep going in circles. You hate me, and I'm a murderer. I get it. But it doesn't change what's happening right now, right here in this city."

"What?"

"Someone betrayed the Church and me."

"Why should I believe you?"

"I think he works with the Ninth Circle. They could have

operatives in this area."

"Could have? You mean you don't know?"

"I only just arrived in the city, but the evidence pushes in that direction."

"I thought you took care of the Ninth Circle when you murdered everyone."

"I eliminated one group, but a lot more cells exist in the world. I think one might be here. And, if not that cult, then something else."

"You just can't help yourself, can you?"

"What?"

"You see cults everywhere. No matter where you search."

"Look, I get that you don't like me, but you need to listen—"

"You're broken, Arthur. Just a broken, sad, little man. You can't even tell right from wrong anymore, can you? You should leave the city and get help. I get it. Your family got murdered, and you wanted revenge, but you crossed *every* line that separates people from monsters. You are a monster."

Arthur didn't know what to say. Part of him knew that Niccolo had called it correctly. "Maybe. But I'm also *right*. Something is going on here, and they have a powerful ally."

"Who?"

"Bishop Glasser."

Arthur might as well have just punched Niccolo in the face, as the priest looked so surprised. He opened his mouth several times to respond, but no words came out.

Finally, he said, "Your two minutes are up. Get help, Arthur. I beg you. I won't forgive you for what you did, but I will pray for you. I don't have time to listen to these ridiculous accusations."

"Leopold betrayed me and got my family killed," Arthur said. "He sold information to the Ninth Circle and has worked with them for years. I also know that he has allies *here* and plans something big."

"You have proof?"

"A confession from the bishop's sister, Emily."

"And how did you obtain that, might I ask? It hardly gives compelling evidence unless I can speak to her directly."

"She didn't come here. The Council have detained her and will, no doubt, transfer her to the Vatican in a few days."

Niccolo sighed. "Until—if—that happens, how can I possibly believe anything you say? What other proof do you have?"

"I have no time for proof. She confessed everything to me. You need to believe me."

"I don't care. This confession you speak of, doubtless, got

coerced. I would never believe a single word you said."

"I wouldn't lie about something like this. There is a real threat here in the city and—"

"Have you spoken to the Vatican? You said you turned Emily over to your organization, so, no doubt, they can get you permission to be here, can't they?"

Frieda had, but again Niccolo would take semantic-based lies personally. "I don't have time to run this through the proper channels."

"Then, make time. How did you know you would find me here?"

"I didn't. I had hoped to speak with Father Reynolds. This just comes down to an unfortunate coincidence."

"For the both of us," Niccolo said. "What did you plan to speak to Jackson about? Did you intend to tell him about the Council and the Hunters? I can assure you that that makes for a terrible idea."

"I'd hoped to ask him a few questions and see if he worked with the bishop."

"He doesn't."

"I know. I spoke with him inside. He dislikes the man and seems completely oblivious to events."

"Or, maybe, *nothing* is going on. If you feel you have evidence against the bishop, then contact the Vatican. If they have an interest in you operating in Everett, then I will work with you. Until then, however, I suggest you get out of the city before I report you myself. Now, if you will excuse me, I must get back to Father Reynolds and Rose Gallagher."

Father Paladina didn't give Arthur a chance to respond. Instead, he walked toward the front door, leaving Arthur standing alone on the woman's lawn.

"I'm only trying to help," Arthur said, trying one last time to get through to the priest.

Niccolo stopped and turned back to look at Arthur. From the expression on his face, Arthur could see that the conversation had finished. Niccolo had no intention of listening to anything he had to say.

"Help? The way you helped those innocent people to find God's love when you murdered them in West Virginia?"

"They would have killed me. I had no other option."

"You didn't wait for help. I saw the report when the Church sent me to help cover it up. You shouldn't have gone in alone. You lost your family, you were grieving, but that gives you *no right* to kill all of those people."

"What should I have done?"

"Wait for backup. Take the cultists by force so that they could have a chance to repent. How many have you killed with your shoot-first-ask-for-forgiveness-later modus operandi?"

"Not everyone can receive redemption."

"Not anyone, by your estimation. Twenty-three people, Arthur. That's how many you murdered that day. That's how many people I helped the Church pretend never existed so that *you* wouldn't get punished."

"Do you feel mad at me, or at yourself?"

Niccolo stopped talking, and a look of shame crossed his face.

Arthur let out a sigh. "That's what I thought," Arthur said. "I get it, I do. I regret what I did, and many more things in my life. I've made a lot of mistakes, but the Church sanctioned my actions. I felt ready to accept whatever punishment, but I and the Council I serve got exonerated."

"And what happens when your actions don't get sanctioned? What happens when you cross *that* line? I can assure you, Arthur, that when *that* day comes, you'll have no turning back."

Arthur stood, unmoving and unblinking. More afraid of that day than he had the willingness to admit. If he looked back, he would never have imagined himself capable of killing anyone, let alone so many people. The worst part was that it barely even bothered him anymore.

"It will never come to that," he said, though the words didn't sound convincing even to him.

"It always comes to that. I don't trust you, Arthur, and I want nothing to do with you."

"You need my help."

"I don't need anything from you, least of all *your* kind of help."

"Then, at least, heed my warning. You've come into danger."

"Consider it heeded," Niccolo said. "Now, leave."

Arthur couldn't think of anything he might say to get through to the priest. Niccolo had judged him and found him wanting, and no way would he ever understand the pain that Arthur had gone through. The rage that had led him to the manor and his need for vengeance.

He wasn't that man. There was more to him than just a killer, but Niccolo Paladina would never see it that way.

Instead, he turned and walked back to his car. The conversation left thoughts and worries he had long thought buried swirling in his mind. He fought to suppress them because he had more important things to do.

Like check to see if his friends remained alive.

Chapter 14

Arthur drove down the road away from Rose's home on Richmond Street, heading toward the hotel to check on the Hunters that Frida had posted there to keep an eye on Aram's family.

His conversation with Niccolo hadn't surprised him, but the man's words hurt more than he wanted to admit. It had taken Arthur a long time to face up to what he had done in West Virginia, and it had become something of a distant memory for him.

Niccolo had brought it all back into sharp focus, however. Before the raid, he had never done anything that seemed 'wrong' or believed that he had taken anything too far. But part of him—a large part—agreed with Niccolo's assessment of the situation— that he had overstepped.

That didn't change the facts on the ground, though. Bishop Glasser was guilty, and nothing Arthur had done or would do would change that. Niccolo refused even to hear him out or take the situation seriously, which put him and everyone around him at risk.

Not Arthur's problem, however. He had a job to do and felt afraid that he might have arrived too late.

It took another ten minutes of driving to get to Aram's family's hotel. It looked like a quaint little four-story hotel just outside of Everett and near what looked like a state forest. Proudly, they broadcast their access to cable channels and an indoor pool.

He called Frieda again. She had agreed to call him if anything had changed, but he wanted to know if she'd found out anything else. Arthur hated walking into a situation blind.

When she picked up, a hint of worry laced her voice.

"I think you're right, Arthur."

"What do you mean?"

"We've lost contact with the Hunters tasked with guarding Aram's family. I've tried to get hold of them with no answer, and about ten minutes ago, they missed a scheduled check-in and triggered internal contingencies."

"Contingencies?"

"We've called a Council meeting, and everyone now knows that something has gone wrong. Aram feels frantic and won't calm down and is demanding I call in every asset to keep his family safe. Officially, it has moved from worrisome to a crisis."

"Which Hunters did you have out here?"

"Martin Rodriguez and Carl Eztel. I just talked to Martin

yesterday, and he reported that everything remained fine. God, he even thanked me for putting him on such an easy assignment."

"Where did Aram's family go today?"

"From Martin's last report, they planned to go to the movies later today, but that just gives a best guess. Not sure where or when, and he couldn't ask ... not without upsetting the wife. Carl should have tailed them today while Martin rested in their hotel room."

"Which room?"

"Three-four-seven."

"All right."

"I can send some backup to deal with this," she said. "I don't know how long it will take for them to get there, but we're talking fifteen hours minimum. I don't have anyone not currently on a mission, but I can figure out something."

"Don't bother," Arthur said. "By the time they got here, it would be too late. Besides, we don't even know what's going on yet. I'll check things out and let you know what I find."

"Be careful."

"I will."

He hung up just as he pulled his rental car to a stop in the almost empty parking lot and turned it off. Instead of getting out straight away, he weighed his options and tried to decide his next move. He could try to track the family down and talk to them directly, but his job didn't only dictate that he keep them safe, he should also keep the existence of the Council out of their minds.

On the other hand, he could track down the missing Hunters, but that carried risk as well. What if they had died already, and he wasted valuable time trying to find them? What if, while he dallied to find the Hunters, someone murdered the family?

Neither of them offered great options, and it became even more difficult to make a decision with the deep-seated worries swirling around in his head from his conversation with Niccolo. Damn that stupid encounter. Arthur needed to focus on the situation at hand, and the petty distractions did him no good.

The Hunters first, he decided. He had arrived here already and might as well get a sense of how bad things were. The rain pattered gently against his clothes when he stepped out of the car, not heavy enough to warrant an umbrella but enough to cause annoyance.

Arthur headed into the hotel lobby. It appeared a fairly unassuming place, dark and mostly empty. A woman stood behind the counter, reading a magazine. When Arthur came in, she glanced up but dismissed him just as quickly. She didn't even bother asking him if he needed a room, just went back to her magazine.

He would have asked for a key, but he didn't need it. He had a lock-picking kit, and if he did find a dead body up in the room, then the fewer people who he interacted with on his way up, the better. The last thing he wanted was for the girl at the desk to remember him asking strange questions about the room.

He walked to the elevator and pressed the button for the third floor, wondering what he would find when he made it up there. Martin had become a friend, and they'd known one another for a long time, but he had gotten on in years and hadn't worked on a violent assignment in ages. Carl, he didn't know quite so well, but he seemed a good person if a less than effective Hunter.

Martin loved to drink, and when not working, he usually crawled through local pubs. Arthur had spent many long nights out with him followed by painful mornings with few memories. He felt almost certain of what he would find in the room, and it wouldn't bring anything good. He prepped himself for the pain and loss of what he might find if either of the Hunters had died.

Arthur found the room that Frieda had mentioned. It remained locked up and quiet, and nothing looked out of the ordinary. That meant little, though, because all of Arthur's nerves thrummed on edge. The hairs on the back of his neck rose, and something felt not quite right.

He slipped the toolkit out of his pocket and spent a few moments picking the lock. It made for a skill he had picked up early in his career and something he practiced regularly. It took him only a few tries before it popped open.

He opened the door gently, putting his tools away and drawing his gun. Inside, darkness greeted him with the lights out and curtains drawn. The television in the hotel room played but with the sound muted. It showed a stage with dancing people and cast everything in a bright and discordant glow as it flashed across myriad brightness and colors.

At first glance, the room seemed empty. An old and oft-used brown suitcase sat on the floor, still closed, and a few miscellaneous pocket items decorated the countertops where Martin or Carl had tossed them.

Arthur moved over to the door near the restroom, straining to hear anything. It stood closed, but not locked. He opened it up and peered inside.

Martin lay in the bathtub, and it took only a cursory glance to determine that no life remained. Someone had cut open his stomach, and a horrified expression had frozen on his face. From the look of it, he'd lain dead for a few hours, maybe less.

Arthur let out of a sigh, lowering his gun. He hadn't expected anything else, considering they hadn't answered their phones, but it felt painful nonetheless. Martin didn't deserve to die, and certainly not like this.

"Sorry, Marty."

Then, out of nowhere, movement came from the other side of the room. The scuffing of a shoe. Arthur stepped quickly out of the restroom and raised his gun just as a guy took off for the door, trying to push past him.

The guy had hidden huddled behind the bed and used Arthur's distraction to try and sneak out. Unluckily for him, he had clipped his shoe on the divan base.

He looked in his mid-twenties with blonde hair and chubby cheeks. Arthur sprang forward, ducking low to get the guy by the legs. He lifted him up into the air and slammed him on the floor, hard, and then pressed the barrel of his gun against the kid's neck.

"Please, please, please ..." the kid murmured, closing his eyes and making whining noises. "Please don't kill me."

"Who the hell are you?"

"Nobody. I'm nobody."

"Why are you in my friend's room?"

The guy's eyes went wide with fear. "I didn't kill him. I swear."

"Then why are you here?"

"They sent me here to clean up the body. Please, I didn't do anything. I just got here a few minutes before you. Hadn't even had time to start."

"Who killed Martin?"

"I don't know," the kid said.

Arthur pushed the gun harder into the kid's neck.

"I won't ask again," he said. "Better start talking."

"I swear; I don't know. If I knew, I would tell you, but I never got a name. I do know that the guy who hired me drove a blue convertible, and I have his phone number. I can give them to you."

Arthur relaxed the gun against the kid's neck and leaned back. "Body disposal?"

"I work for the local PD, but they don't pay much, so I do some moonlighting on the side. I swear, when I got here and saw the body, I almost left. That ... that wasn't a good way to die."

"You said he drove a blue convertible?"

"Yeah. He was still here when I arrived, but I only talked to his goons. He had a driver, too."

"What did he look like?"

"Balding. Old. I didn't get a good look. Two guys stood with him, and I talked to them. They paid me to dispose of the body. I tried to say 'no, thanks' but they didn't want to discuss it, you know?"

"That guy in the tub is a friend."

"I'm sorry. Look, I don't like this any more than you. I'm sorry your friend died, but I sure as hell didn't kill him. You want the number?"

"Yeah," Arthur said. The guy pulled out his cell phone, scrolled through it, and then handed it to Arthur, who took the gun from his neck for a moment to look at it. He took down the number, and then handed back the phone.

"Can I go?" the guy asked.

"Not just yet. You a local?"

The guy nodded. "Born and raised."

"Where's the closest movie theater?"

"What?"

"Movie theater," Arthur said. "Where is the closest one?"

"Back in Everett. Why?"

"And if someone wanted to see a movie and they stayed *here*, they'd go to Everett?"

"Yeah, definitely. Why?"

"Where is it?"

"Maybe twenty minutes south, center of town."

"All right," Arthur said, dragging the guy off the ground and pointing him toward the door leading out of the hotel room. He gave him a shove, pressing his gun into the small of his back. "Show me."

✳✳✳

Arthur had the cleaner drive his rental car and sat in the backseat, keeping his gun on his lap in case the guy tried to do anything stupid. With any luck, it wouldn't take too long to find the family and make sure of their safety.

Ideally, he would find Carl alive and well, but he didn't hold out hope for that. Someone had come after the Hunters, which meant they had gone after the family, and he felt sure he knew who.

Along the way, he called Frieda to let her know of Martin's death and that he had gone on his way to the theater. He could tell that the news hurt Frieda, though she would never admit it. It lay in her tone.

Mid-call, he hesitated, looking out of the window to his right. "Hang on," Arthur said. "Let me call you back."

He hung up and leaned forward over the seat. "Just up ahead. Turn onto that maintenance road and park out of sight."

"What? Why?"

"Just do it."

They hadn't quite reached the city limits of Everett, but Arthur had noticed a large side road leading into the forest. A rusted old convertible had parked about fifty feet off the main road, and it put him on edge. Though not sure, it looked like someone sat waiting in that car.

He did know, though, that they sat in the middle of nowhere on a not often used road that connected the city to the hotel where Aram's family had stayed. There seemed a good chance that whenever Aram's family finished their movie, they would use this road to get back, which made it a perfect ambush spot.

He would have done it there.

The guy did as told and drove off the road and onto a maintenance path. They didn't go far before a large gate blocked the way, but that didn't matter. Arthur put his hand forward between the seats. "Keys."

"What?"

"Give me the keys and stay here."

The guy let out a sigh, and then handed the keys to Arthur. "It's not like I would have gone anywhere."

Arthur ignored him and climbed out of the car, peering through the trees to see if he could spot the convertible behind them. They had gone about a quarter of a mile, he estimated. The trees grew too thick to see anything.

He circled to the trunk and popped it open. His travel bag held extra bullets, and he poured some out and dumped them into his pocket. He had two quick loaders, about fifteen extra shells, and then a full chamber. Hopefully, he wouldn't need any of them, but better safe than sorry.

"What will you do?" the guy asked.

"Mind your own business," Arthur said.

"You aren't planning to ...?" His eyes widened when Arthur slammed the trunk closed and held up his pistol. "I'm telling you, those guys were armed and looked ready for a fight."

"So am I."

"There are two of them and only one of you."

"They don't know I'm coming. That's more than advantage enough."

"I get it that the guy was your friend, but I don't think you to want to mess with these guys. They're serious and won't think twice about shooting you."

Arthur ignored the kid and opened the door. "Just stay here and keep your mouth shut."

Before the guy could respond, he headed off into the trees, moving through the underbrush toward the access road where he'd seen the convertible. Still gloomy and gray, the rain came down a little heavier now. That made for a good thing, as it would help mask his movement through the area.

The sky grew darker even though only the middle of the afternoon, which meant a storm on the way, most likely. With luck, it would hit later rather than sooner. Arthur didn't want to get caught in it and end up soaked and chilled.

He came up to the edge of the clearing and saw that his instinct had guided him well. The rusted-out blue convertible sat parked off to the side of the access road, hidden away from the main road and barely in sight.

A man occupied the driver's seat, leaning back and waiting. He wore a pair of ugly yellow sunglasses. Thin tufts of black hair highlighted a balding scalp, and the rain had matted it against his forehead.

He had no idea that Arthur stood there behind his car—he focused completely on the road in front of him. Arthur glanced around, looking for the other guy the cleaner had spotted earlier at the hotel, but there seemed no one else around.

An ambush. Had to be. This guy had parked here to wait for something, and Arthur would bet good money that he sat waiting for Aram's family. Probably planning to take them hostage, or maybe just gun them down in the street with his partner.

Neither of those situations would happen, though. Not with Arthur around.

He stepped out onto the dirt access road, walking toward the back of the blue convertible. The rain noise masked his movements, and the guy didn't as much as flinch while Arthur approached. He had made it all the way to the driver's door before they guy even saw him coming.

The man looked a lot uglier up close. He let out a huff and groaned when he saw Arthur, trying to grab a gun tucked between the seats, but he stopped when Arthur leveled the revolver at his face.

"Shout, and I pull the trigger."

"You've got a lot of nerve—"

"Hand me the gun. Slowly. Grip first."

The guy hesitated, but when Arthur moved his gun a few

inches closer, he complied. He handed Arthur the nine-millimeter pistol, and Arthur tucked it into his waistband. A walkie-talkie lay on the seat next to him; probably how he communicated with his partner.

"That too."

The guy handed him the walkie-talkie, and Arthur put it in his pocket.

"Where's your friend?"

"What are you talking about?"

"The other guy you came out here with," Arthur said. "Where is he?"

"I don't know who you mean."

"Yeah, you do. You came out here to kill some people, didn't you? A woman and her two kids."

The guy narrowed his eyes and reached toward the glove compartment where, no doubt, he kept a backup weapon.

Arthur didn't shoot him, not wanting to create more noise than necessary. Instead, he flicked his wrist forward, the one not holding a gun. It held a small and balanced throwing knife, and he embedded it into the guy's shoulder. It sunk deep and would feel incredibly painful.

The guy cried out and collapsed back onto his seat, clutching his shoulder. Arthur stepped closer to the door, keeping the gun ready.

"Think that was bad? The next one will feel a lot worse."

"Screw off."

"Where is your partner?"

The guy cursed at him.

"What about Leopold Glasser? The bishop. Did he hire you?"

The cleaner's description of the main person he'd seen reminded Arthur a bit of the bishop, though not enough for him to feel sure. A look of surprise flashed across the man's face, however, and confirmed what Arthur had guessed. The look only flashed there for a second before he composed himself.

"Who?"

Arthur smiled. "Yeah, I thought so. Where is he? Nearby? Did he stick around, or did he leave you behind to handle the wet work?"

The man didn't reply, but the look on his face said everything. The bishop wouldn't dirty his hands with something like this, which meant that only one other guy remained out here with him to deal with Aram's family.

"Your partner probably went up the road to let you know when he saw them coming. Let me guess, you block off the road with your car, and he hits them from behind? Stay here. I'll come back to talk to you in a couple of minutes, but first, I need to talk to your friend."

"You're crazy if you think I'll just—"

In one swift motion, he bashed the guy on the side of the head with the grip of his revolver. He made sure to hit him extra hard so that he stayed unconscious.

The guy's head lolled uncomfortably to the side, and he fell over sideways onto the passenger seat, making an odd noise. Arthur hit him again, just to make sure, and then turned back to the main road.

It proved impossible to tell where the other guy would stand in wait. Arthur stepped away from the car and scanned the area again. He didn't see any movement, and the existence of the radio made him think the other guy might have gone a decent ways up the road.

He would have taken himself closer to Everett and the movie theater, which gave him a decent place to start looking. The problem was, if Arthur got moving and the other guy didn't, then Arthur wouldn't have the advantage. It made for a cat-and-mouse game that he didn't want to play.

He needed a distraction; something to draw the other guy out of hiding.

Mmm, something like a car rolling into the road.

Arthur reached over and flipped the key to put the convertible into neutral. Then he moved behind to the back and pushed the vehicle toward the street. It proved a heavy old thing, and the rust made it more difficult to get started, but with a little effort, he got the wheels spinning.

Luckily, he stood on the upward side of an incline. Once he got it moving, he just let it go on its way toward the street, and it kept going on its own, gradually picking up speed. Hopefully, it wouldn't meet any oncoming traffic, and there seemed few vehicles on this particular road.

Arthur ducked to the side, moving into the trees and searching for a good vantage point. He turned down the walkie-talkie volume, picked a decent position, and watched.

The car rolled slowly into the street, and then kept going. It passed right through it and went engine first into a ditch on the opposite side. Arthur couldn't suppress the tiniest of chuckles when the guy's head flew forward into the steering wheel. The horn blared, and kept on blaring, when his head came to rest on the button.

A second later, the radio sputtered to life.

"What the hell, man? She ain't here yet!"

Arthur set the radio down and waited, revolver at the ready.

"Ken? What's up with you? Why'd you move the car? Stop with the damn horn."

A rustling came from the foliage on the other side of the road, and Arthur watched a guy step out of hiding. He stood tall and thin, holding a radio up to his mouth. His hiding spot lay about sixty feet from the errant car, but only about twenty meters away from Arthur.

"What the hell are you doing?"

He took a few more steps out into the roadway, moving toward the convertible in the ditch, and looked nervous.

Arthur drew a bead on him. The guy tensed all of a sudden, spinning and drawing his gun. He must have heard some movement from Arthur that gave away his position.

But he moved too slowly. Arthur didn't hesitate, acting purely on instinct. He fired off a single shot. It hit the man directly in the stomach, and he dropped his gun to the roadway, staggering sideways with a shocked look on his face.

If Arthur had to guess, then this guy was maybe around forty years old. He had scruffy facial hair and a big nose. The kind of guy Arthur had dealt with a thousand times before in his line of work. Just a normal guy that got himself in way over his head with the wrong crowd. He made a living by doing dangerous things.

Stuff where he might end up dead.

Arthur moved toward the man, who crawled on his side toward where his gun had fallen, moving away from Arthur and gasping for air. The rain pattered against his face and forced him to squint his eyes.

Arthur walked up slowly, kicking the gun out of reach, and then leveled his revolver at the man. "Did Bishop Glasser hire you?"

The guy rolled sideways, looking up at him in the rain. It came down with fury now and ran through his hair and into his coat. The guy had taken a gut shot, and blood poured out of the bullet hole. Just as quickly as it poured, the rain washed it away.

"You shot me," the guy said. "You killed me."

"Not yet," Arthur said. "Still time to get you to a hospital."

The guy leaned sideways with a grunt and spat at Arthur. It landed on his shoes, and the rain washed it away promptly. "Get it over with."

"Did Bishop Glasser hire you to kill Aram's family? Is that why you came out here?"

The guy didn't respond, except to close his eyes and roll onto his back, holding one hand on the hole in his stomach. He laid back in the street, taking shallow breaths.

Arthur stood there in the rain, watching the man die alone and cold. He could still get him to the hospital, but that didn't fall under his primary mission, and so the Council wouldn't approve of the wasted time. If he followed protocol, he should leave him here and let him die.

Niccolo had nailed it.

He *was* a monster.

✳✳✳

Before now, Arthur had never questioned his duty.

He was born into this life, so-to-speak. It made for something his father did, and his grandfather before him. From the time he could walk, he had gotten prepped for the life of a Hunter and soldier. Not a soldier in the military, though, but rather in the supernatural.

What he did always made sense, and he had never second-guessed any of it. His father had worked as a demon hunter, and so Arthur had become a demon hunter. Home schooled and trained how to survive.

And, he got good at it. It came naturally to him, and he liked doing it. He couldn't imagine doing anything else. At sixteen, he had killed a man for the first time, and it had felt difficult.

The second time, though, hadn't seemed nearly as hard.

Now, however, a new idea entered his mind and seemed set to make his brain its home. The idea murmured that he just provided a tool for the Council. That he had become a monster who liked to kill people. It struck a chord in him and made him wonder about why he did what he did.

Did he want this?

The answer proved easy: no. He wanted for his family to still be alive.

A noise behind him indicated movement, and he spun, raising his revolver. The cleaner stood there in the rain. He stumbled backward in the roadway, throwing his hands in the air.

"Woah!" he said. "Woah, don't shoot. It's me."

Slowly, Arthur lowered his gun.

"Dude, you killed him?"

"He isn't dead. Not yet. Help me move him."

"Where?"

"Off the road. We need to bring the car over and get him to a hospital."

He slid his gun away and hurried over to the dying man. Reluctantly, the cleaner came over and helped him drag the guy out of the road. Damn the Council; he wouldn't let this guy die. He refused to live as just a tool and murderer.

"Car coming," the cleaner said, glancing down the road. Arthur looked up. The vehicle headed toward them from Everett but remained a decent ways away.

Arthur grabbed his keys out of his pocket and tossed them to the cleaner. "Bring over the car."

The guy caught them deftly and took off at a run back toward Arthur's rental. Arthur slid his coat off and put it over the dying man's midsection like a blanket, covering the bullet wound.

The car slowed when it drew close, and the driver's window rolled down. An Indian woman looked out at him with a concerned expression on her face. In the passenger seat sat a young girl, maybe eight years old, and in the back, sat a young boy about a year older than his sister.

Aram's family, he realized. He had seen photos of them but never met them. If they had driven by here twenty minutes earlier, they would have died.

Thank God for small favors.

"Do you need any help?" the woman called through the rain.

"No, thank you," he called back. "Just a little accident."

"Are you sure?"

"Yeah. My nephew just got here, and we've notified the police."

"Is your friend okay?" She looked at the guy on the ground and wore a concerned expression.

"Yeah. He got bumped around bad in the accident, but I'm going to get him checked out at the hospital as soon as my nephew brings the car around. Crazy day, huh? Guess I drove a little too fast for the rain."

She seemed as if she didn't quite believe him, but just then, the cleaner pulled up in Arthur's rental car. He came to a stop just behind her.

"There's my nephew now," he said. "Thank you so much for stopping, but we are perfectly all right."

She shrugged and then nodded. "All right, then. Good luck with your friend."

"Thank you," he said. "And thanks for checking up on us."

She nodded, rolled her window back up, and then pulled off down the road. Arthur watched her go, and then let out a sigh. They would stay safe now. He had done his duty. Of course, he had one more thing to accomplish—get this guy to a hospital.

Together, they loaded the unconscious man into the backseat of the rental. Arthur grabbed the other guy, too, just in case. He bandaged up the gunshot wound as well as he could, but still, a lot of blood spilled over the backseat of the car.

Arthur felt fairly certain that his rental insurance wouldn't cover this but didn't care. He'd had considerably worse in his cars before.

They drove to a nearby hospital, and Arthur left both of the men at the emergency room entrance. He put the gunshot victim in a wheelchair, confident that someone would find him, and laid the other one out on the street.

Then they got out of there before anyone could ask any questions. They traveled in silence for about ten minutes, just listening to the rain, before the cleaner spoke up. He asked Arthur where to head next, and Arthur directed him once more to the movie theater.

They soon ended up back in Everett, heading toward the theater. On his command, the guy drove slowly around the parking lot, and Arthur got a look into all the cars. This late at night, most of the movies had ended for the day, so most of the foot traffic had gone.

It didn't take him long to find Carl.

At first, it looked like Carl slept in the driver's seat of a little red Chevrolet parked near the back of the lot. No other vehicles remained parked nearby, and it looked as if Carl had chosen this spot to stake out the place.

On closer inspection, he realized that Carl sat dead. His stomach had gotten cut open like Martin's, and it looked like some of his organs had been removed. He hadn't had time to check Martin in the bathtub, but when he did check him over, it seemed likely that he would find the same thing.

The bishop had harvested their organs.

"Was he …?" the cleaner asked when Arthur got back into the car. He didn't finish the question.

"Yeah," Arthur said. "He was a friend, too."

"Man, I'm sorry."

Arthur brushed away the concern, focusing on the task at hand. "You said you work for the local PD? Want to make some extra money?"

The guy looked like he hated the idea, but he didn't object. "What did you have in mind?"

"We need to get my friends brought to a safe place and ready to ship."

"Where?"

"Home. They can't go through the system. Some people will come to pick them up in a couple of days and get them out of the country. Do you know somewhere we can keep them until then?"

"The morgue," the guy said. "No autopsies scheduled right now, and the mortician has gone on vacation. The freezer is empty. I can stick your friends in there with some phony paperwork for a couple of days, and no one will think twice."

"All right," Arthur said. "Let's get to it, then."

Chapter 15

A few hours after Arthur got Martin and Carl to the morgue, he finally got a chance to stop running around and relax. Late at night now, it still rained but not quite as much as it had earlier in the day.

He'd just gotten back to the hotel and rented a room for the night. He had spent the better part of the day cleaning up the blood from both of the Hunters and making it look like they had simply checked out earlier this morning without saying anything.

Part of him wanted to go after Bishop Glasser right now, but that made for a bad idea. He could barely think straight, he felt so tired, and he needed to get a real night's sleep before he went up against the bishop.

He didn't have a lot of time to spare because now the bishop would know he was on to him and that he had halted his plan to murder Aram's family. Right now, though, Arthur felt too tired to care.

No sooner had he lain down on his bed to get some shut-eye than his phone rang.

He grabbed it from the nightstand. "Hello?"

"It's me," Frieda said. "Any news?"

"You tell me. I spent the entire day cleaning the blood of my friends off walls and out of carpets. Any word on your end?"

"I spoke to the Vatican, and they said they'll look in to Bishop Glasser. They've heard rumors about him in the past, but so far, nothing substantial. Certainly nothing to justify *this*."

"We will find out the truth tomorrow. I plan on paying him a visit."

"Don't kill him, Arthur," she said.

He made a grunting sound in response.

"I'm serious. He's a bishop, and that gives us a line we can't cross."

"It's a line *he* crossed when he murdered my family."

"Allegedly. We don't know all the details, and we never will if you kill him. I shan't ask you to stay away from him, but I beg you to handle this the right way. If things go south, the Church will never forgive us."

Arthur didn't respond for a long moment. His mind wandered back to when he'd stood in the street, looking down at the dying man. He'd dropped him off at the hospital but didn't know if he'd lived or not.

At that moment, Arthur had thought of himself as a monster.

Sure, he could chock up a lot of the feelings to his overwhelming exhaustion and take it with a grain of salt, but part of him knew it as the truth.

Maybe he was just a murderer.

Maybe the time had arrived to fix that.

"Arthur? You there?"

"Yeah," he said. "I won't kill him. You have my word. I'm done killing."

The words flowed right by Frieda, and he knew she didn't take his proclamation seriously. Why should she? Given his job and duty, and especially considering his history, it seemed a ridiculous assertion to make.

But he meant it. With all of his heart, he decided then and there that he had done with killing. For the Council, the Church, or anybody.

"I have a crew on the way to collect Martin and Carl. They should get there tomorrow morning."

"Good. I'll grab the bishop in the morning before he can get out of town, and then I'll turn him over to the Church."

"When you get him," Frieda said. "Don't turn him over. Not right away, at least."

"What?"

"He makes for our only leverage. We need evidence, something we can bring to the Church to justify our worth."

"What do you mean?"

Frieda hesitated before she said, "Glasser brought over half of our annual operating budget. Without him ..."

"We're broke," Arthur said. "Won't the Church pick up the slack?"

"Not likely. At least not for a few years and not unless we can prove to them that they need us. If we bring the bishop down ourselves, that will go a long way toward proving that to them. Either way, it will take a long time for us to court another benefactor like him."

"So, what happens now?"

She laughed. "Now ... we all get to fly coach for a while."

He chuckled. "The horror."

"You're avoiding her, aren't you?"

The question caught him off-guard. "Who?"

"Abigail. You feel like if you love Abigail as much as you used to love your daughter, that you're betraying Becca, don't you?"

He wanted to object to that idea, but the words caught in his throat. Frieda had it right, even if he couldn't admit it to himself.

Becca had been his everything. The light of his life, and his little angel. She had gotten stolen from him in the most horrible way possible.

When he'd first found Abigail with that cult in West Virginia, it made perfect sense to take her in and protect her. She had given him a reason to go on living and a purpose.

But he'd begun to feel that maybe he hadn't honored Becca's memory the way he should. He worried that spending time with Abigail would dishonor his memory of his real daughter.

He felt terrified that he would forget her. Like, maybe, he had just found a suitable replacement.

"She wants to see you. I think I have the Council convinced to let you adopt her, and the vote happens in a month."

"What? So soon?"

He had fought for permission to adopt her for months, but the idea that it might actually happen felt overwhelming.

"You have to deal with this, Arthur. No more running."

"I'm not running."

"Mmhmm," she said. "Sure."

He sighed, shaking his head. "Okay. I'll come back to Germany as soon as I get the bishop. Goodbye."

"Auf wiedersehen, Arthur," Frieda said.

They hung up, and he dropped the phone onto the bed next to him.

Frieda always got it right about things like this, especially where he was concerned, and this time made no exception. He hadn't consciously avoided Abigail, but that missed the point. She needed him, and he wasn't there for her.

But how could he be? He felt like just a broken man unsure about what part he should play in the world. How could he take care of her when he couldn't even take care of himself?

Right now, he felt too exhausted to deal with any of it: Abigail, Niccolo, Frieda, the dying man. It all piled on and became too much, and he needed a good night's sleep before he could begin to unravel it and make it make sense.

With that encouraging thought, he leaned his head back on the pillow and fell asleep in only seconds.

✳✳✳

What a hell of a sleep.

He didn't often have nightmares, but this proved an exception. Crazy and vivid, they seemed to center around what had happened to him in West Virginia when he assaulted the cult.

He had nearly died and spent the better part of a month in a local hospital recovering.

Because he hadn't set an alarm, it had grown bright out when he finally staggered away from the bed. He kicked himself for sleeping so long, but he did feel refreshed and ready to go.

Emotions he'd felt so strongly the previous night had faded into the background once again. His feelings about his daughter and Abigail and whether or not he was a monster. They remained there but suppressed and easier to deal with.

One thing that hadn't faded, though, was his new conviction that he would never kill another person.

He spent twenty minutes getting showered, shaved, and dressed. It felt incredibly refreshing, and he felt tremendously better once he'd gotten clean and put on a fresh outfit. The morning looked sunny, too, which made it all the more pleasant. He had a feeling that this would turn into a good day.

Only a short while later, he checked out of the hotel room and got back on the road in his little rental car. The bishop lived outside Everett to the West, and Arthur took his time driving through the city on his way.

He'd drawn close now; so very close to confronting the person who'd gotten his family killed. He wanted nothing more than to ask the bishop why he'd done it. Had it been worth it?

He got lost in his thoughts, driving through the center of town, and then he spotted something that pulled him back to reality. Father Reynolds, the local priest he'd met with Niccolo at Rose's home, strode down the sidewalk, up ahead of his car.

He watched as Jackson turned and headed into an apartment building on the right. Arthur frowned, not sure what had set his mind into motion. Something, he felt, seemed wrong, and it only took a moment to realize what.

Someone followed the priest.

✳✳✳

A few moments after Father Reynolds went into the building, another man walked in after him. He had stood waiting, keeping his distance, and it became clear to Arthur that Jackson was his target.

The guy didn't just follow him for kicks; he moved with purpose, hand stuffed inside his pocket and, no doubt, fingering either a gun or knife.

No, he had other things in mind.

The stalker wore jeans and a red flannel t-shirt to blend in with the passersby on the sidewalk. Arthur could tell that he didn't look well-trained at subterfuge. Probably just a regular guy sent here to deal with the young priest.

It brought a distraction, Arthur knew, and remained none of his business. Still, the priest would end up in trouble without his help. He pulled to a stop next to the curb, and with a sigh, he opened the door and stepped out of the car. With not a lot of spare time to waste, he still didn't want to let the priest get hurt.

Or worse.

Arthur followed the two men into the apartment building. When he made it inside, he didn't see anyone on the ground floor, but he could hear footsteps heading up the stairwell to his right. He moved to pursue, climbing the switchback stairs carefully and trying to get a bead on the guy in the flannel shirt.

He rounded the steps to the fourth floor. The guy stood in the doorway leading out to the central hallway. He peered around the corner, not paying attention to the stairwell at all.

The man had drawn a gun, a nine-millimeter, and held it ready while he watched the hallway. Arthur moved up the steps quietly, closing the distance. Finally, the guy heard something when Arthur reached only a couple of steps away, but by then it was too late.

The stalker spun, raising his pistol, but Arthur proved quicker. He caught the guy's wrist and jerked it at an odd angle, slamming his hand and gun against the doorframe. The weapon fell to the floor, landing at their feet.

Then Arthur punched the stalker in the throat, collapsing his airway. The guy tried to fight back, but got caught off-balance and off-guard from the sudden lack of oxygen. He threw a few wild punches, which Arthur blocked and avoided with ease. Arthur twisted under a particularly wild blow, caught the stalker around the neck with his arm, and tightened his grip until the guy passed out.

Once Arthur felt certain that the man had fallen unconscious but remained alive, he set him against the wall, retrieved the pistol from the floor, and slipped it into his waistband.

Just in time, too. A door opened. Arthur stepped around the corner just as Father Jackson Reynolds came out of his apartment. Arthur didn't want the priest to see the unconscious stalker just yet in case he freaked out and caused a scene.

Better to explain to him somewhere in private that he had just avoided getting murdered.

The priest had a bag slung over his shoulder and paused

when he spotted Arthur. He wore a worried expression.

"Oh. Hello, again."

"Hi." Arthur nodded.

"Were you ... uh ... following me?"

Arthur lied, "Yes. I'd hoped I could talk to you in private for a moment."

Jackson moved toward the elevator, keeping his eyes on Arthur. Unsettled, he tried to find a way out of the situation. Arthur didn't give him the chance, and instead, walked toward him with his hands in front of him in a non-threatening manner.

"About what?"

"A lot, actually. Just not here. Where is Father Paladina?"

"Back at the church."

"Alone?"

"No, with a few of my parishioners. Why do you ask?"

Arthur ignored the priest's question, "Why do you have the bag? Going somewhere?"

Jackson pursed his lips. "If it's all the same to you, I'd rather just get back to my church. Niccolo is waiting for me. If you don't need anything specific ...?"

"You don't trust me," Arthur said. "And that's perfectly fine. Right now, though, we have bigger problems to deal with."

"Like what?"

"Let me give you a ride back to your church, and I'll explain everything."

Jackson appeared unconvinced. "I think I'll pass. It's a nice day, and I don't mind the walk."

"I insist."

"No, really, I don't ..."

Arthur pulled up his shirt to show the pistol grip tucked there. Jackson's eyes widened, and his wary look morphed to one of fear. Arthur didn't like threatening him, and he sure as hell wouldn't shoot him, but this was neither the time nor the place to explain everything.

"All I want to do is talk."

Jackson hesitated, and then nodded. "Okay."

He guided the young priest back out to where he'd parked his car, and they both climbed in. Jackson put his bag in the back and sat with his hands folded in his lap. He seemed calm, given the circumstances, and Arthur felt impressed.

He got into the driver's seat and started the car. They lay only a couple of blocks away from Saint Joseph's Cathedral.

"I'm not sure what Niccolo told you," Arthur said, "but I swear I don't bite."

"The gun creates a slight contradiction to that," Jackson said.

"Fair enough, but I won't shoot you. Consider it a prop piece."

"And what, all of this is theater?"

"Something like that."

"Niccolo told me little about you, but I know you two have history there. What happened?"

"A lot of things," Arthur said. "He met me at a bad place in my life, and his impression got skewed. But he's not wrong, and I have a lot to atone—"

"Why are the lights off?" Jackson said, alarmed. He sat looking out of the window at his church, and he grew tense. "The lights shouldn't be off."

Arthur frowned. "Do you think maybe the power went off from the rain?"

"No, that's not common with so little—"

From somewhere inside the church, something crashed to the floor, followed by a shout.

"What was that?" In shock, Jackson reached for the door handle.

Arthur caught his arm, stopping him. "Wait here."

"Something's going on inside my church. Niccolo and Tim could be in danger."

"I know," Arthur said. "This is what I do. Let me take care of it. I'll come right back to get you when it is safe."

Jackson pursed his lips, resting back in the seat, and then nodded. "All right."

Arthur slid the nine-millimeter free and handed it to the priest. "If anyone you don't know comes after you, use this."

Arthur climbed out of the car before Jackson could respond, slamming the door shut behind him. Maybe the priest would just use the opportunity to contact the police or find help, but he didn't have time to worry about that just now. He would have to deal with that problem if it came to pass.

He hurried into the church.

✳✳✳

The main area of Saint Joseph's Cathedral loomed dark and silent when he pushed his way inside. Arthur held the front door open for a long moment, letting light filter in and making a mental map of the area.

Pews and tools lay scattered around, and one of the benches lay on its side in the center of the room. Arthur picked a path across the floor, let go of the door, and moved quietly across the room.

Gradually, his eyes adjusted to the lack of light, but for the moment, he focused purely on sound, listening to what happened around him.

"Vile abomination!"

The words came from up ahead and sounded muffled, as though coming from behind a thick door. Or, maybe, from down below. Arthur moved toward the sound, weaving around the pews to a backroom of the church. He found himself in what looked like an office space, though it lay in complete disarray with papers scattered everywhere.

"You don't belong here. By the power of Christ, I compel you. In the name of the Father, the Son, and the Holy Spirit."

Niccolo's voice, wavering and afraid. Arthur saw an open doorway and staircase off to his right, leading down into darkness. He crept to it and peered in, gun held ready.

"You compel me?" another man asked. Arthur didn't recognize his voice, but it came from the basement as well.

"You do not belong here. Return from whence you came. Through the power of Christ, I demand that you leave this place."

This time, Niccolo's voice sounded stronger, full of confidence. Arthur moved onto the staircase, walking as quietly as he could down the stairs. His eyes had adjusted, and he could see two forms standing at the bottom of the staircase, maybe fifteen feet below him. One of the people crouched, trapped, in a corner just to the right of the stairs.

A moment passed, and Arthur could hear Niccolo's breathing. It belied his confidence, and he took in short and ragged gasps. The other person, though, barely seemed to breathe at all. Arthur moved closer, staying on the far side of the staircase and circling.

"Silly priest. Don't you know you have no power here?"

Then came a sizzling sound. Niccolo let out a gasp of terror, and the other man laughed, taking a step closer to the priest. Something small and metallic clanged to the floor.

Without a sound, Arthur kept moving down the stairs. Only a few steps away now, and his vision had almost adjusted to the darkness. He wanted to make sure that the assailant stood alone before stepping in, and he couldn't hear anyone else in the basement around them.

"How does it feel?" the man asked. "How does it feel to know you are truly alone? How does it feel to know your God has abandoned you?"

A grunting sound came when the guy reached up to choke Paladina. Long enough, Arthur decided. He didn't know if anyone else might have come here or not, but the time to act had arrived.

He stepped in close, punching down with the metal grip of his pistol into the man's shoulder. Bone and cartilage crunched under the attack, and the arm fell to the man's side, limp.

He tried to turn to face Arthur but never got the chance. Arthur bashed him in the side of the temple with the gun, and he blacked out, falling like a sack to the ground between Arthur and Paladina.

Arthur looked past him. The priest stood there, bug-eyed and terrified.

He couldn't help himself from glancing down at the body and then back up at Paladina. Niccolo looked confused and terrified while he stared at Arthur, and Paladina couldn't suppress a small and bitter chuckle.

"*Now* do you believe me?"

Chapter 16

Niccolo felt lifeless and dazed when Arthur led him out of Saint Joseph's Cathedral and into the morning air. It seemed as though he had stumbled out of a nightmare and back into reality and that every ounce of energy had drained from his body all at once, leaving him a wasted and useless mass.

When they stepped out into the sunlight, he winced. Then his eyes started readjusting. The glare felt painful, and the information difficult to process. He barely noticed anything around him and ran on autopilot. Arthur led him like an invalid toward a gray rental car parked in front of the church.

"Are you all right?" Father Jackson Reynolds asked, climbing out of the passenger side of the car with a concerned expression on his face. "What happened? Where is Tim?"

Niccolo didn't have a good answer to any of his questions, so he just shook his head. He certainly was not all right, and he didn't know if he ever would be again. Arthur helped him climb into the backseat of the vehicle. Jackson climbed out and stood beside the passenger door.

"We need to get moving," Arthur said to Jackson. "I'll explain everything."

"Explain what? What's going on?"

"Please, just trust me."

"Trust you? How could I do that? You need to tell me, *right now*, what is going on with my church and where Tim and his son have gotten to. Otherwise, I'll not go anywhere—"

"Just get in," Niccolo said, looking up at Jackson. "Please."

Jackson seemed as if about to object, but changed his mind. Something in Niccolo's face had convinced him that this made neither the time nor the place. Instead, Jackson climbed back into the rental, and they drove away.

Niccolo didn't even ask where they headed. He couldn't bring himself to focus on anything apart from how close he had come to getting killed by Tim, or whatever controlled him, back in the church. His mind had scattered. The world had flipped on its head. All of a sudden, nothing made sense. Everything he had believed, every truth he held dear about the world he lived in, all of it had now come into question.

Nothing made sense.

They drove for twenty minutes or so before Arthur pulled off the main road, following a dirt path into the woods outside the city. It looked like an old access road, not often used.

He took them out of sight of the highway, and then stopped the car. However, he just sat there, staring out the front window with a thoughtful expression.

"Was he ...?" Niccolo said, after the silence became uncomfortable. He couldn't finish the thought, however.

"Possessed," Arthur said. "Yes. He was."

"What are you talking about?" Jackson turned in his seat to look from Arthur to Niccolo. "What do you mean 'possessed'? Who?"

Jackson gave Father Paladina a direct look.

Niccolo had no idea how to explain, but found himself speaking anyway, "After you left, something happened."

"What?"

"Tim ... changed. I don't know what happened to him or if his son is okay, but he ... the lights went out and I ..."

He had no idea how to explain. The insects, the bugs, the body of Tim's son. Tim taunting him and coming down the stairs. None of it made sense, and it all seemed so horrible. Just thinking about it made him feel like something crawled across his skin, and he let out a shudder.

"Arthur saved my life. Tim tried to kill me."

"Not possible." Jackson shook his head. "Tim isn't capable of doing something like that. He wouldn't hurt a fly."

"Tim might not," Arthur said. "But Tim didn't pull the strings inside his body anymore. He's gotten possessed."

A long moment passed in silence. Jackson stared at Niccolo as though expecting him to burst out laughing at any moment and tell him it was all a joke. But, for Niccolo, it proved all too real.

"It's true," Niccolo said, finally. "All of it. Someone sent Tim to kill me."

"Someone tried to kill you, as well," Arthur said to Jackson. The news surprised Niccolo, and he looked up. "What?"

Arthur held up a pistol. "A man wearing a flannel shirt. He carried this. I saw him following you, and if I hadn't intervened, you would be dead."

Jackson stared at Arthur. "Who the hell are you?"

"A Hunter," Niccolo answered with a sigh. He rubbed his face. "He works for the Church."

"Why didn't you tell me before?"

"You aren't allowed to know," Niccolo said. "No one is. He works off-books. A cult and demon Hunter."

Jackson struggled to process the information. "I didn't even think those existed."

"We do," Arthur said. "But not a lot of us."

Jackson turned to Niccolo. "So, what you said earlier at Rose's house ...?"

Niccolo started to speak, but the words caught in his throat. His standard explanation that Arthur was a cold-blooded killer felt hollow now. He had thought that Arthur killed cultists, people who had stumbled off the wrong path and into dangerous territory.

It had never seemed plausible that Arthur might face real demons.

Niccolo had never believed in demons. At least, not the kind that possessed people and seized control. Certainly not the kind he had witnessed firsthand, back in the church, trying to kill him.

Which meant that everything he'd thought he knew about Arthur was wrong.

"It wasn't true," Niccolo said, finally. He turned to Arthur, "I suppose I owe you an apology. I thought you just a cold-blooded murderer. I never imagined ..."

"No apology necessary," Arthur said. "You got it right about me. I have much to atone for, and I think, now, I finally feel ready."

Jackson looked between them. "What are you talking about?"

Arthur looked to Niccolo. "He hasn't got clearance for any of this."

"He deserves to know," Niccolo said.

Arthur hesitated, and then nodded. "Very well."

Arthur took a deep breath, and then he recounted the events that had taken place at the manor in West Virginia. Niccolo had heard the story before, and he knew all of the details, only this time it sounded different. The reality that Arthur had battled actual demons shed everything in a different light.

By the time he finished speaking, Jackson looked completely overwhelmed by everything. He took a long time to process before speaking, "So ... someone betrayed you and got your family killed?"

"Yes," Arthur said.

"And you believe that it happened because of Bishop Glasser?" Niccolo said.

"I don't think it was him. I know it."

"The bishop?" Jackson asked, incredulous.

"Yes," Arthur said. "I believe he lays behind events in the city and has responsibility for the demon possessions. He had two of my friends murdered and tried to kill the family of one of the people for whom I work. The only thing I don't know is why."

"That doesn't make any sense."

"None of this does," Father Paladina said. "But I believe

Arthur.”

“I thought you called Arthur a murderer and liar and said that we shouldn’t trust him.”

“I did,” Niccolo said. “And I got it wrong. I got it wrong about everything, and it nearly got both of us killed. This changes everything.”

✳✳✳

“What happens now?” Jackson asked.

“We need to get to the airport,” Niccolo said. “We have a flight waiting. Nothing has changed.”

“They won’t let you leave,” Arthur said. “You’re both marked now, and they won’t let you leave Everett alive. If you try to go anywhere, they will kill you.”

“Then, you need to help us,” Niccolo said. “You can keep us safe.”

“I have to get to the bishop. If he didn’t know I was on to him yet, then he will when he finds out you haven’t died.”

“If we don’t go now, then we’ll miss our flight,” Niccolo said. “You have to take us there.”

“No,” Arthur said. “You can do whatever you want. I’ll drop you off at a gas station, and you can call a cab to get you to the airport, but I can’t spare the time for the trip. Not yet. I’ll not let the bishop get away.”

Niccolo wanted to object, but it would be a waste. Arthur believed the bishop responsible for the death of his family, and no way could Niccolo talk him out of it.

To be honest, he now believed it might be true. The bishop had acted strangely ever since he’d showed up, and he worried that maybe the bishop had wanted to kill him.

He did know for sure, though, that the safest place for him and Jackson remained with Arthur. The tickets, he could exchange at the airport for a later flight, or maybe fly somewhere else first. It didn’t matter where they went or how long it took to get to the Vatican. They just needed to get out of Everett.

“Fine,” Niccolo said, finally. “We will go with you to deal with the bishop. But, after it is done, you will take us to the airport.”

“Okay,” Arthur said. “But, just so we all get this clear; until we reach the airport, you do exactly what I say, when I say it. Got it?”

“Got it,” Niccolo said.

Arthur turned to Jackson. “You?”

"Got it." Though he looked hesitant, Jackson nodded.

"Good," Arthur said. "Let's go."

Chapter 17

Arthur's adrenaline pumped through his veins as they drove up the long gravel driveway to Bishop Glasser's estate. This was it: the moment he would finally get to ask the person who'd betrayed his family why he'd done it.

Almost immediately, however, he realized that he'd come too late. The estate stood silent and empty. The bishop gone already.

"It feels more ominous now," Niccolo said from the seat behind him. "Even the trees ..."

Arthur glanced through the windows at the forest around them. He hadn't come here before, but he could understand what the priest meant. The trees that ran up along the side of the road looked thin, spindly, and dead. The entire place felt wrong.

"It seems empty," Jackson said, as he pulled the car to a stop.

"We got here too late," Arthur said.

Part of him—and if honest, a fairly large part—regretted his decision to rescue the two priests. Logically, though, he realized that they had nothing to do with it. No doubt the bishop had left last night.

He should have come right away. As soon as he'd rescued Aram's family and before the bishop could flee. Instead, he had spent the time taking care of Carl and Martin and then Niccolo and Jackson.

He grew furious with himself for it. He would still check the building to make sure, but it would prove too late.

"Wait here," Arthur said.

"What if someone comes out after us?" Niccolo asked, in shock.

"Then, scream," Arthur said.

Arthur picked up the pistol from the seat, the one the man had planned to use to kill Jackson. He handed it to Niccolo, and then climbed out of the car.

"If I don't get back in five minutes, drive straight to the airport. Wear normal clothes and try to blend in and don't talk to anyone until you get on a plane and away from here."

He didn't give Niccolo time to respond before he closed the door and drew his revolver. He made his way up to the front door, listening for any sounds of movement. Though doubtful that he would find anyone inside, there remained a chance that some evidence would have gotten left behind about where the bishop had gone.

The door stood unlocked, and he eased it open. It swung open silently, with only a soft swoosh of air. Upon walking into the house, Arthur's heart raced. The place had an effect on him, like an energy, and it elicited outright terror. He couldn't pinpoint why, but it crept through his skin.

Something terrible had happened here.

It only took him a few minutes to sweep the entire building and verify that it stood empty. The bishop had gone, though it looked as if he had left nearly everything behind. Sacrificed and abandoned. The remains of dozens of letters and notebooks littered the fireplace, but they looked too far gone to salvage.

He just had to hope that the bishop had missed something.

Arthur went back out to the waiting priests. "All clear," he said, putting away his revolver. "Help me search the place."

Neither of them objected; although, they didn't seem thrilled at the idea either. They both looked terrified and out of sorts, but he felt unsure how to make them feel any better.

"Let's check the house," he said. "Bishop Glasser fled, and we need to know where."

"What do you mean?" Jackson said. "He's gone? He would need Vatican permission to leave."

"I feel pretty sure he's beyond asking for permission," Arthur said. "He's on the run but is not the kind of person to live without means. Look for any sign of somewhere he might go to hide from the Church. Family, friends, anything."

They split off and set about combing the house, looking for any sign of where the bishop might have headed. Arthur took the upstairs and went through the man's offices, and the other two worked downstairs and combed through the rest of the house.

They searched for over two hours; first, going through all the obvious documents that hadn't gotten burned, and then working their way around the room and looking for any secret compartments or false bottoms to the drawers on the man's desk.

Arthur found a safe nestled behind a painting, though once he had cracked it open, he grew depressed to find that it held nothing of value. The bishop had emptied the safe already.

His luck turned for the better, however, when he found a secret compartment nestled into one of the walls. Inside, he found a stack of letters addressed to the bishop, and also a switch. The letters were from a woman named Desiree Portman. He tucked them into his pocket for later. He flipped the switch, and the wall shifted, revealing a secret passage leading into a fully enclosed room.

It looked like a torture chamber.

Dried blood decorated the walls and floor, and a table sat at the center with straps for wrists and ankles. Various sharp and blunt instruments lay on the tables, giving it the impression of a workshop. The floor slanted inward to a drain, and an opening overhead held a fan that pushed air into the room. The walls, made of brick and concrete, gave the room a heavy and enclosed air. One of the walls had a chain and neck brace hanging from it.

On one of the tables, Arthur found an industrial electric food dryer, the kind he'd seen people use to make beef jerky or dried fruits and vegetables. It was turned on, and inside, he found the harvested organs of maybe ten people.

Some of them would have belonged to Carl and Martin.

As he stood there, looking at the room, he heard movement behind him. He turned, drawing his pistol. The two priests came into the room. Their expressions shifted to horror, though, when they surveyed everything around them.

"Dear God," Jackson muttered.

Niccolo looked as if on the verge of throwing up. Arthur put his gun away and walked over, gently guiding the two priests out of the room.

"You don't need to see this," he said.

"No." Jackson shook his arm free. "I think I do. I might have known these people, and I'm supposed to look out for them. To think ... he did this right under my nose."

"It isn't your fault."

"I might not have killed them, but I didn't do anything to help them, either."

"Why?" Niccolo asked. "Why would he do this?"

"The torture?"

"And harvesting organs."

"It's used in rituals," Arthur said. "To bring demons into the world. Powerful demons. The weaker ones don't prove as hard to bring forth, but the stronger ones usually require some sort of offering to coax up here."

"That's horrifying."

Arthur nodded but didn't respond. Instead, he took the moment to guide both priests out of the room and shut the door.

"We can deal with this later. Right now, we *need* to know where the bishop went. We can't allow him to get away with this."

"We didn't find anything to point to where he might go," Jackson said. "That's why we came looking for you."

"What about you?" Niccolo asked Arthur. "Did you find anything?"

He shook his head. "No. The bishop hid his tracks well."

"No leads?"

"One." Arthur held up the letters. "But it seems a flimsy one. It looks like he had a secret affair that went on for years."

Niccolo frowned. "Then there remains a chance that she will know where he went."

"The most recent letter has a date from over a year ago, but yes, that's what I hope. The letters all got sent from Maine, so I'll head there next."

"Maine?"

"Yes. I'll track her down and see if she knows anything. With any luck, I'll find him there and stop him."

"What happens now?" Jackson asked. "What about us? What about the people who got possessed?"

"I will take you both to the airport and drop you off, and then I'll come back and deal with it."

"Deal with it?" Niccolo asked. "How do you mean?"

"I won't kill everyone, if that's what you mean to ask," Arthur said. "I'm done with killing."

"Okay," Niccolo said. "That sounds like a suitable plan. When we get to the Vatican, I shall report everything and have help sent to—"

"No," Jackson shook his head. "We can't leave."

Arthur frowned. "There are people here trying to kill both of you. It's too dangerous for you to stay in Everett."

"Maybe, but these are *my* people," Jackson said. "My friends and parishioners. I got tasked with looking out for and protecting them, and I will *not* leave them here while we run back to the Vatican."

Niccolo took a steadying breath and turned to face Arthur. "He's right. We can't leave."

"What?"

"I am a trained exorcist, and these people need help."

"It's too dangerous."

"Do you know how to exorcise a demon?"

Arthur frowned. He had a bit of experience and had learned a lot of the rituals, but he'd never sent one back to hell. The most he'd managed to do was piss them off. "No."

"Then, you *need* me."

Arthur looked between them for a second. "Neither of you come prepared to face something like this. It holds more danger than you could ever imagine. You aren't trained."

"No," Niccolo said. "But you are."

"I'm not a babysitter."

"You won't have to take care of us," Niccolo said, holding up the pistol Arthur had given him earlier. "I've used one of these before.”

“Really?”

“At a shooting range, but I know what I’m doing. We can help you deal with this.”

“And we won’t take ‘no’ for an answer,” Jackson added.

Arthur sighed, rubbing his face. “Fine. I can’t force you to do anything, and I could use the help.”

“Where do we start?”

“When did you first get called out here?” Arthur asked. “First reports that something was going on.”

“A few weeks,” Niccolo said. He turned to Jackson, “That sound about right?”

“Yeah, that’s when Rose started acting weird.”

“So, if this just began a few weeks ago, then he might have just gotten started.”

“Started with what?”

“Building an army. Most of the demons here are probably lesser demons, since the stronger ones take more time and resources to call in. That’s why he harvested the organs. We need to find the demons and send them back one-by-one.”

“How do we do that?”

“No clue,” Arthur said. “Normally, when I get brought in to deal with something like this, the demons have already been identified. I just go in and ... deal with it. We don’t have a way to identify targets, however.”

Niccolo hesitated, glancing over at Jackson. “Actually,” he said. “I think we do.”

✳✳✳

“What do you mean?” Jackson asked.

Niccolo turned to face the young priest. “You said earlier, at the baseball game, that you could sense something wrong with certain people in town. As if you could *feel* the demons inside people.”

Jackson shook his head. “That was just a feeling I had.”

“I’ve read about other people who could do something similar,” Niccolo said. “They call it channeling.”

“Channeling?”

“Essentially a gift where you can sense and interact with things normal people can’t see.”

“Why didn’t you say anything before?”

“I didn’t see any way it could be true,” Niccolo said. “With

Tim, did you sense anything odd about him?"

"Yes. And his wife."

"And the waitress," Niccolo said. "At the diner. Patty, I think her name was."

Jackson hesitated, and then nodded. "And about six more people in town."

Niccolo turned back to Arthur, "There you have it. We have the ability to track down everyone affected by this and stop it."

Arthur had heard about such abilities before. It remained a carefully guarded secret within the Church. He hadn't believed it possible—and, certainly, had never had the ability to tell a possessed from a normal person without some outwardly visible clues—but if what Niccolo had told him held any truth ...

That would make Jackson an incredibly valuable person.

In the short-term, though, it would make his job considerably easier.

"All right," Arthur said. "That gives us an edge. We just need to track them down and free them one at a time."

Chapter 18

They drove through the city of Everett slowly and in complete silence. It grew dark out, though only around two in the afternoon, and looked about to storm soon. The mood in the car felt somber.

"Where are all the people?" Jackson asked, finally, speaking aloud the question they all wondered.

Neither Niccolo nor Arthur had a good answer for him. The streets looked empty, and many places that should have appeared bustling remained completely unoccupied.

They stopped at Patty's Diner, and it had a closed sign on the door.

"You said one of them worked here?" Arthur stepped up to the windows and peered inside. It looked empty and dark and as if it had closed in a hurry.

"Yes, Patty," Jackson said. "I noticed her acting strange."

"Does she usually close up like this?"

"No. I've never seen the place shut during the day. That is … strange."

That didn't give exactly the word Niccolo would have used to describe it. A threatening feeling lingered in the air, like something about the city was wrong, and it seemed they didn't make for the only ones feeling it. The streets stood empty and quiet. Many of the townsfolk had hidden away from the oncoming storm, sure, but it came down to more than that.

"What do we do now?" Jackson asked.

Niccolo didn't have a good answer. "Who else should we look for?" Niccolo turned his attention toward Arthur.

"I don't know," Arthur said. "Who do we have next on the list?"

The next two stops they made turned out complete duds as well. In one, they found the mother of an infant baby missing and the door open, but the baby lay safe inside her bedroom, sleeping. Jackson collected up the baby in shocked silence, and they took her to Amanda Lockett's home to watch her.

He didn't explain to her what was going on, and to Amanda's credit, she didn't ask. She had children of her own and didn't seem to worry about the idea of adding one more infant into the mix.

They left from there, out of ideas of where to go next. They decided to go back to Saint Joseph's Cathedral to regroup and think. When they got to the church, they found it ransacked and the walls covered in occult symbols written in paint.

Just seeing the symbols felt painful for Niccolo. He had

studied them in his education at the Vatican, but he'd never seen them outside of symposiums. This belonged to something different, and it unsettled him deeply.

∗∗∗

The church stood empty and quiet when they arrived, but Arthur had expected that. They found neither Tim nor his son, nor anyone else, for that matter.

Pews lay smashed and expensive pottery and vases destroyed. Jackson surveyed the place stoically, but Arthur could tell seeing it in that condition hurt. Niccolo wandered around for a few minutes, looking at the occult writings on the wall, and then headed back toward the office and basement where Arthur had found him. Arthur followed, keeping a cautious distance.

Niccolo found his Rosary in the basement, but the metal had melted and fused together when it had touched the demon's forehead. The cross seemed barely identifiable anymore, and the links had torn and frayed. Arthur watched him slide it into his pocket without a word, though he wore the look of a man who had just lost a limb.

By the time they made it back to the car, all three of them felt the full weight of how bad things had become. However many demons had come to the town, they no longer tried to disguise themselves now that the bishop had gone. They had become like junkyard dogs off their chains—willing to wreak havoc, which made them considerably more dangerous.

"Did a holiday get declared that I don't know about?" Jackson shook his head. "This just feels … wrong."

"Was Patty the first demon you felt?" Arthur asked.

"No," Jackson said. "Why?"

"This doesn't look like normal behavior for demons. They don't usually give up their cover unless either something went wrong or they've reached their endgame."

"You think this is their endgame?"

"Nope. I think the opposite. Something went wrong, most likely when the bishop fled town. Who was the first demon?"

"The first?" Jackson asked. "What do you mean?"

"When you started to feel that people acted strange in town, who triggered that feeling?"

"Rose Gallagher."

"The woman whose house I met you at?"

"Yes. She triggered my contact with the bishop and Vatican.

I worried that she might have become possessed, and then everything went downhill from there."

"Did she feel any different?"

Jackson thought about it for a moment. "Stronger, but I found it hard to tell. Sometimes, the presence seemed stronger, but other times, barely there at all."

"It could have masked itself," Arthur said. "If it knew what you could do, then it probably tried to hide itself from you."

"What do you mean?"

"I think that, most probably, it's the only one Leopold summoned directly. She is likely the strongest one as well. She'll help to anchor the rest of them here."

"Anchor?"

"Many demons don't have strength enough to take control of a host on their own. Those ones prove easier to bring in, but they also tend to fizzle out. Like worker bees in a hive, and when things are going good, they remain completely in control, but when they don't receive directions, they devolve and fall apart. The first demon that Leopold summoned would have provided a sort of foundation for the rest like a general for his army."

"Army?"

Arthur hesitated, and then said, "I think he brought in a fairly large group of demons before we got here."

"Why?"

"I don't know," Arthur said. "I also don't know *how* he did it. Bringing in one demon is a difficult task. Bringing in a dozen should be impossible. I wish I knew what his endgame is, but I don't. All I know is that whatever he planned, it was way bigger than just Everett."

"Thank God we stopped him, then," Jackson said.

"We haven't stopped him yet," Niccolo said.

Arthur agreed, and it just made the fact that the bishop had gotten away that much worse.

Niccolo turned back to Arthur. "So, if we get rid of that demon, it would be like chopping the head off the snake?"

Arthur nodded. "Maybe not, but worth a shot. Let's go see Rose."

✳✳✳

By the time they arrived at Rose's home in the suburbs, the weather had taken a turn for the worse. The clouds gathered thick enough to block out most of the sunlight. It hadn't started raining yet, but it wouldn't take long before the skies opened up.

Richmond Street and the surrounding neighborhood appeared empty and quiet when they approached. Rose's house looked uninviting and closed up from the outside, and Arthur worried that maybe she would have gone as well.

He would manage to hunt her down, of course, but it would take time. Days, maybe, and he needed that time to spend tracking down the bishop.

He parked the car in front of the house and climbed out. The other two followed him, but they didn't approach straight away. Arthur gave them a moment to gather their courage. Even if the demon had gone, it seemed that the time for disguise had come and gone. What they would find inside, doubtless, would prove terrible.

"I can't believe I got it right," Jackson whispered after a moment. "Rose really did have a demon possession. Demons are real."

"Yes, they are." Arthur glanced over at Niccolo. The priest looked terrified as if about to face his death.

Arthur could hardly blame him, considering how dangerous this situation had become. Honestly, if the two priests had any idea how dangerous this situation could actually get, they would run away screaming.

"Will you be all right?" Arthur asked.

Niccolo blinked and let out a shuddering breath. "No. I won't be all right. I can't do this."

"Yes, you can," Arthur said. "You've had training. You know the rituals. You know the process and what you have to say. You can handle this."

Niccolo didn't respond and looked anything but convinced. Arthur felt bad for him, but he didn't have many options right now. He knew how to perform an exorcism and had even assisted on a few over the years, but he didn't have permission to perform one on his own. Only the Church could sanction that, and the only ones who could approve them were exorcists.

Luckily, that meant Niccolo had the authority to sanction and perform this exorcism.

"It won't unfold anything like you expect," Arthur said. "When we get in there, you'll see things you've never even dreamt of. Ignore it, and focus only on the task at hand."

"I know."

"The real world is different than what you learned at the Vatican. You've never seen a real demon before face-to-face, have you?"

Niccolo shook his head. "Never."

"If you don't think you can do this, then we should not walk through that door," Arthur said. "This is your last chance to back out, and if you agree to do this, then there is no turning back. Do you understand?"

"Yes."

"I don't think you do," Arthur said. "This will turn out *nothing* like you expect."

"If we leave now, then what happens?"

"People die," Arthur said.

"That's why we have to do this."

"You're missing the point," Arthur said. "If you attempt to do this and fail, then your fate will be much worse than death."

✳✳✳

The words had an effect on Niccolo, and he swallowed painfully as he thought over what Arthur had said.

"I know," Niccolo said, finally. "We're still doing this."

"Very well."

Slowly, they walked up toward the door to Rose's little home. Arthur felt a tingling of nerves and worry at what would lay inside, but mostly because of his companions. He had faced situations like this before—though he didn't quite know what to expect where the bishop was concerned—but the other two hadn't. He felt unsure what he would do if they panicked and had a breakdown.

"How are you so relaxed?" Niccolo asked suddenly.

"What?"

"How can you stay so calm?" Niccolo said. "We're walking into a woman's home to face a demon possessing her, and that no doubt wants to kill us, and it feels terrifying. How can you stay so calm in the face of that?"

Arthur shrugged. "Yes, it's terrifying, but I've learned how to control my fear and use it for my advantage. I've faced dozens of situations like this before. Each one as terrifying as the last, but after a while, you learn how to look past the fear and evaluate everything for what it is."

"Any quick tips to help us not feel so scared?"

"Quick tips?" Arthur frowned. "No. It doesn't work like that. In this business, nothing comes quickly."

He reached up to knock on the door but hesitated with his fist a few inches away.

"Except death," he added.

Then he knocked, pounding his fist against the frame. Nothing happened, and no movement came from inside the house. The three of them stood on the front steps, glancing at each other and waiting for someone else to act.

"Do you think she's gone?" Niccolo asked.

"A possibility," Arthur said. "Leopold might have taken her with him, but we won't know for sure until we check."

Arthur reached into his pocket and pulled out a small folded cloth. Inside nestled little angular tools that Niccolo didn't recognize. Arthur slid one free, knelt, and stuck it into the lock on the door.

"You can pick locks?" Niccolo asked.

Arthur looked up at him. "I can do a lot of things."

He slid the tool around for a moment, twisted it, and then turned the door handle. It opened a crack; just enough to see in. Arthur stood, put his tools away, and then turned to face the priests.

"Whatever we face in there," he said, "it isn't Rose. You need to know that because the demon will try to manipulate you if it senses any weakness."

"We know," Jackson said.

"No, you don't know," Arthur said. "But you're about to find out."

He pushed open the door.

✳✳✳

The house looked a mess and in complete disarray when the three of them went inside. It stank of rotten and fetid flesh, and the only sound they could hear came from a wheezing noise from further inside the house, and also the chime of an old grandfather clock as it ticked away time.

Niccolo grew horrified as they all stepped inside. The woman's living room had an otherworldly feel to it like the air around them had something wrong. *Inhuman* was the best way he could find to describe it. It took his eyes a minute to adjust, and two yellow orbs in the darkness became the first things he saw.

Not orbs, he realized, eyes.

They watched him in the darkness. Slowly, Rose's face came into focus. She looked wretched and broken with pockmarks and scars covering her face. Seated on the floor, she had her legs twisted at an odd angle. It looked like she had fallen sometime in the last few days and broken her hip and had been unable to crawl anywhere. She looked grotesque and horrible.

If she seemed so to Niccolo, however, it would prove far worse for Jackson who knew her. From the look on Jackson's face, the young priest might break down at any moment. Guilt and shame dominated his features.

"Hello again, Priest," she said. Her voice came out wheezing and thick as if she had mucus at the back of her throat. "Good to see you."

"Rose ... I ..." Jackson said. Niccolo felt for him. He had no idea what to say either. She looked horrid like she'd been through hell.

Probably, she had. Worse, they had come here only yesterday to visit her, and then had simply left. The guilt of that, knowing that all of this had happened after they'd abandoned her to the demon, tore at the priest.

The demon had hidden here all along, biding its time and waiting for them to leave so that it would have complete control over Rose. Now that it had no more reason to hide, and they knew it had come here, it would ravage Rose until she died, if only for the fun of it.

They had abandoned her.

"It looks horrible," Jackson said, taking a half step back. "The demon. God ... it ..."

"What? Cat got your tongue?" the demon asked. The voice hardened. "You've come too late. We've done already."

"Done with what?" Arthur asked.

Rose's head shot to the side, eyes narrowing as she surveyed Arthur.

"Hunter," she said. "I thought I smelled something disgusting here."

"What was Bishop Glasser doing here in Everett?" Arthur asked.

"What does it matter?" the demon said. "That isn't the real question you want to ask anyway, is it? Go ahead, ask me what you want to know. I might even give you a real answer."

Niccolo glanced over at Arthur, who stood frowning. He looked calm and stoic, but a slight tremble in his hand gave away his true demeanor. To see him like that worried Niccolo. He knew Arthur's reputation, knew what he had faced in the past.

If Arthur felt afraid of this demon, what chance did Niccolo and Jackson have?

"Do either of you have a Bible?" Arthur asked, turning toward the priests instead of speaking to the demon. "We need to get started. The demon can't move the body any longer, but it remains dangerous."

"I have one," Jackson said, pulling a small tome out of his robes. "Abridged."

"It will work. Most of what we need, we won't find in there anyway. Niccolo knows everything he needs by memory."

"Ask me, Arthur," the demon said, leaning forward on the floor. Bones ground, and it sounded like nails on a chalkboard. The demon either didn't notice or didn't care. "Ask me about your family. Ask me why they got murdered. Ask me if Bishop Glasser did it himself, and if he enjoyed doing it. Ask me."

Arthur refused even to look at the demon, but the expression on his face spoke volumes.

"Don't listen to it," Niccolo said, softly. "The demon wants to hurt you."

Arthur nodded. "We will need holy water. You know what to do. And salt. Bring any salt you can find in the kitchen."

Jackson headed into the kitchen to retrieve the items and speak his benediction. Niccolo watched him go, and it took him a long moment to realize that Arthur stood staring at him.

"Are you ready for this?"

"What?"

"Once we start exorcising this demon, we *cannot* stop. If we falter for even a few seconds, we risk losing Rose and so much more."

"Losing Rose," the demon said, cackling. "She's gone."

"My rosary got destroyed," Niccolo said, shaking his head. Now that he stood in the room and faced the demon, his self-confidence had dropped to almost nothing. The idea that he could do this seemed like a wishful thought now, not even close to reality.

What in God's name had made him think he could become an exorcist?

"I know," Arthur said.

"I have no stole, no sacraments, and no rites. I have *nothing* I would need to exorcise a demon."

"You know the rites," Arthur said. "You don't need a text to read them."

Niccolo *had* memorized the rites of exorcism and recounted the words thousands of times alone in his apartment, but just now, they wouldn't come to him. They floated around in his muddled mind, and he panicked.

"Relax," Arthur said, gently. "The words are there, and they will come when you need them. Don't worry about that. We have salt, holy water, and faith, and that offers enough. The rest only gives a crutch anyway."

Niccolo took a steadying breath and nodded. "All right."

"Guys," Jackson called from the kitchen. "Get in here."

The two exchanged a glance, and then hurried past Rose to the kitchen. Jackson had a bowl on the counter with a small cross floating in it, a salt shaker next to it, and a Bible on the other side. He stood at the small window overtop the sink, looking outside.

The sky continued to darken, and drizzle fell, but more than that had caught the priest's attention. Two men stood out on the lawn, one carrying a baseball bat and the other a shovel. They stared at the house, unmoving.

"What are they doing?" Niccolo asked.

"I don't know," Arthur said.

"Waiting." Jackson peered out through the window. "They're both possessed."

"More demons?" Niccolo asked, incredulous.

"Yes, but nothing like Rose," Jackson said. "These look faint as if barely in control."

"In control enough," Arthur said.

He went over to the table and grabbed the salt shaker. Then he popped the top off and sprinkled some in front of the doorway, forming a thin line.

"Was this all the salt?"

"All I could find. I found it buried in the cupboards. If she had more, she disposed of it."

"We'll have to make do."

Arthur headed back out to the living room. He grabbed the bowl on the way, and then set it down on the coffee table. Niccolo grabbed the bible and cross and followed.

He pulled the curtains aside, letting light into the room from outside. The demon let out a hiss, followed by laughter.

Another five people stood on the lawn out front, two women and three men. Tim and his wife stood there, Tim carrying an axe, and his wife had a pick. Their expressions looked empty and vacant and unfocused.

"What do we do now?" Niccolo asked.

"The same as before," Arthur said. "Nothing has changed, the only difference is that now we have less time."

He slid a gun out of his pants and popped out the clip, counting the rounds.

"No killing people," Niccolo said.

"I don't plan on killing anyone." Arthur slid the clip back into place and chambered a round. "But I sure as hell won't let them kill any of us. I know where to aim so as not to do critical damage.

You need to start right now and expel this demon."

"What do I do?" Jackson asked.

"Exactly what Niccolo says. You provide his greatest weapon. Just add your faith to his."

"I'm sitting right here," the demon said, rocking in the chair. "You think your faith gives you enough? I'll rip your throat out and drink the blood."

Niccolo did his best to ignore her, focusing instead on preparing for the ritual. He had walked through hundreds of these at the Vatican. He knew the steps, the rituals, the critical moments.

But all in theory. This would prove something utterly different.

He looked at Arthur. "What will *you* do?"

"Keep you alive," Arthur said, heading toward the door. "Don't screw this up."

Then he headed outside. A moment came while the door stood open where they could hear the rain pattering heavily against the pavement outside, and then it muted once more.

Niccolo stood there, listening to the rain against the window and focusing on his breathing. After a moment, he realized that Jackson stood staring at him.

"What do we do?"

Niccolo didn't have a good answer. He had trained his entire life for this moment, and he felt like it wasn't enough. It couldn't possibly ever be enough. He turned to face Rose, sitting in the chair and staring at him with her cold, yellow eyes.

"We begin."

Chapter 19

The cold raindrops chilled Arthur's skin as soon as he stepped outside Rose's house. The possessed people stood in the front yard, staring at him, unmoving and unblinking as the rain ran down their faces.

He had his revolver, but only as a last resort and one he hoped he wouldn't need. He had to hope that Niccolo would handle the demon inside quickly and that they would manage to make it out of here with their lives.

A few feet away from the possessed, he stopped walking and took a steadying breath.

"One chance, Hunter," the woman standing in the middle of the group said. Her voice sounded loud in the rain, though her face barely moved when she spoke. She held a pick and seemed to stare over his shoulder rather than at him. "Walk away now, and we will let you live."

"Not a chance," Arthur said.

He edged to his left, flanking the group to see how they would react. None of them moved: they just kept staring forward at the house.

They were barely in control of the bodies, he realized. Their control seemed tenuous, and the hosts fought back. That meant that whatever anchored them here didn't have much strength now that Bishop Glasser had gone.

Once the demon inside Rose got exorcised, then the hosts would manage to overpower the demons and kick them out of their bodies.

That brought the good news. The bad news came in that Arthur had to tread with care. The people possessed might not have died, and any damage he did to them now would prove permanent. If he killed any of them, he would have killed the innocent hosts, too.

What he needed to do was buy Niccolo and Jackson time to exorcise the demon inside Rose. The problem came from Niccolo not having experience and no preparation for this situation, and facing down a demon made for a serious proposition that proved difficult in the best of circumstances. Arthur didn't have a lot of faith that he would succeed, at least not quickly.

The woman with the pick turned to face him, eyes focusing on him for just a moment before going back to the glazed look.

"Kill him."

✳✳✳

"You know what you're doing, right?"

Niccolo didn't answer Jackson's question; partly because he didn't want to cause Jackson any extra concern, but mostly because he didn't want to say the words out loud and admit that this would make a first for him in more ways than one.

Instead, he focused on preparing himself mentally for the events about to happen. He focused, first, on his breathing, getting his body under control. His heart pumped rapidly, but he didn't have time to worry about that. Next, he focused on his environment and the demon in front of him. He reached into his pocket and felt the cool metal of his rosary. It had congealed, but the shape of the cross remained there. From it, he drew strength.

However, it wouldn't do him any good here. Resigned, he let it fall back into his pocket and turned his mind to the task at hand. He needed to begin.

"Hand me the cross," he said.

"Here you go." Jackson picked it up from the coffee table and handed it to him.

Niccolo held it up before him, studying it and willing it to become an extension of him. It gave a representation of his faith; something he could use to embody his beliefs. Through it came the promise that he did not stand alone in this struggle. He held it to his lips and kissed it.

Niccolo picked up the Bible and turned to Apostle Matthew. He handed the book to Jackson.

"Chapter six, verses nine through thirteen."

"The Lord's Prayer?"

"Keep reciting it, and don't stop until this has finished."

"I can do it in Latin if you prefer."

"The words and your heart matter; the language you say them in doesn't. Recite it cleanly and as loudly as you can until we get done."

Jackson nodded and flipped to the requested passage. He trailed his finger down, nodded, and then began reciting. Niccolo listened to him speak, the words echoing in the small room. Jackson spoke clearly with a strong voice, though the words had little effect on Rose or the demon.

But that was okay: Jackson's words weren't for the demon but for Jackson and Niccolo. Just hearing them gave him strength;

a familiar litany that encouraged and solidified his resolve that God stood with him. The sound of the words spoken aloud gave him confidence, and the prayers and incantations came back to him.

"In the Name of the Father, and of the Son, and of the Holy Ghost. Amen."

Niccolo closed his eyes and called upon the more important verses he had memorized during his education as an exorcist. The incantations that they had drilled into his mind over and over through constant repetition until he could recite them perfectly in his dreams.

He spoke those prayers, first in English, raising his voice above Jackson's prayer:

"In the Name of Jesus Christ, our God and Lord, strengthened by the intercession of the Immaculate Virgin Mary, Mother of God, of Blessed Michael the Archangel, of the Blessed Apostles Peter and Paul and all the Saints. And powerful in the holy authority of our ministry, we confidently undertake to repulse the attacks and deceits of the devil. God arises; His enemies are scattered, and those who hate Him flee before Him. As smoke is driven away, so are they driven; as wax melts before the fire, so the wicked perish at the presence of God."

His faith welled up inside his chest, swelling forth. He switched to Latin and continued chanting. These words came from the Rituale Romanum and the rites of exorcism. With his eyes closed, he focused only on the chant and the power it gave him at that moment. He had spoken them a thousand times before, but something seemed different this time.

The verses had power and meaning he had never known existed before now. Demons were real, and not just something he said he believed in because he was supposed to, and it felt like experiencing the prayer for the first time.

He had made it through the ritual before taking a breath, and then he just stood there. The room around him had gone, and he felt that he stood alone with the demon. He faced it, his enemy. The enemy of Heaven and of Jesus and of God. He would send it away because it didn't belong here.

Through the grace of God, he would banish it.

His heart slowed, the panic subsided, and he gained control over his body. Finally, he opened his eyes.

The demon sat there on the floor in front of him, the same as before, but its entire demeanor had changed. It still looked arrogant and angry, yet another emotion showed on its face now as well:

Fear.

Jackson stood staring at Niccolo and whispering the Lord's Prayer, yet remained focused on Niccolo. He wore a shocked look on his face.

Niccolo stared back at him for a moment, and then he nodded. Arthur had told him true; he had everything he needed to exorcise this demon. Resolved, he picked up the bowl of holy water and held it under his arm, dipping his fingers into it.

The rosary, the garb, the implements that exorcists wore ... none of them mattered. Faith and intent mattered. The words focused those things, directing them like a weapon at the demon. The realization for Niccolo came clearly and powerfully and filled him with confidence.

The demon didn't stand a chance.

He flung his fingers forward, splashing water on Rose's face.

"You have no power here, Demon," he said. "Out."

The droplets burned where they touched, and the demon hissed. It tried to move away from the priest, but the body had failed too fast. It couldn't get away. Niccolo dipped his fingers again and flung more droplets onto the demon.

"You are not wanted here. Christ has power here, not you. You do not belong and must leave."

He flung more water, and the demon hissed again. It lifted an arm to block to water, but Niccolo circled the chair. It tried to crawl away, but its legs failed it, and it couldn't move more than a few inches across the carpet.

Niccolo set to chanting again, the same litany he had finished only moments before, only this time, he didn't just recite it from memory. This time, he spoke the words directly to the demon, addressing it personally. He could hardly believe that he'd feared he would forget them.

How could he forget? They'd become a part of him, and he a part of them.

This time, the impact the Rituale Romanum had on the demon proved greater. He spoke, calling the demon forth and challenging it with his faith. Clearly and with unmatched vigor, he spoke.

Jackson stayed next to him, chanting the Lord's Prayer loudly once more, also in Latin. Their voices echoed in the small room, bouncing off one another and filling it as a symphony. The demon cowered on the floor, pathetic and broken, hissing at them. Niccolo kept circling the demon, splashing it with droplets of water.

He couldn't believe it: they exorcised it. They expelled the demon from Rose, sending it away from her body and back to hell. He could sense the tide turning and the demon weakening and knew he achieved the desired effect. The chant separated it from the body, preparing to send it home. Only a few more moments—

All of a sudden, a huge crashing sounded against the back door. It caught Niccolo off-guard, and he faltered, stumbling over the litany. It brought a momentary distraction, but enough, though, for him to lose his place in the chant. He fell silent. A moment later, Jackson did, too.

The room went deathly still.

Immediately, the courage and strength flowed out of him, leaving him feeling alone and empty. It seemed as if all the light had gotten sucked out of the room and nothing remained.

Another huge crash came, loud enough that he knew the back door was about to break. The people in the backyard had come to stop him, and they came armed and ready for murder.

His faith could protect him from the demon, but it gave nothing against their weapons.

Rose looked like a pathetic and broken lump now, with hair matted to her face and skin red and chafed where the water had hit her.

She made a coughing sound, and then Niccolo realized she sat laughing. It built slowly, maniacal and terrible, punctuated by wet breathing noises.

"What now, Priest?" she asked in a weak voice. "What will you do now? Your time is up."

Chapter 20

The demons came at Arthur in one big group and outnumbered him five to one. They seemed disorganized, however, and it struck him as unlikely that any of them had received serious training on how to fight.

The only advantage lay in that they didn't care about what happened to the hosts, and Arthur did. He would have to take care and pull punches to make sure he didn't hurt anyone, and that made his job considerably more difficult.

He had heard chanting and prayers spilling from inside the house, loud enough to make it through the rain. It had stopped, though, a few seconds ago. What had happened?

Maybe Niccolo had exorcised the demon, and he'd believed wrongly that it would end it. More likely, though, something else had happened, and Niccolo still had to attempt to deal with his fear.

Arthur kept his distance, letting the demons come to him. The first man came in with an axe, swinging it wildly at his head as if trying to split a log. Arthur sidestepped the attack with ease, moving in close and grabbing the wooden handle with his right hand.

He pushed the axe away from his body, rotating close to his attacker, and then kicked out. He aimed for the man's stomach, hitting him a few inches above the groin. The man stumbled back, losing his grip on the axe, and Arthur yanked it loose.

Then he spun it around so that the flat backside of the axe faced forward and swung it down, clobbering the man in the forehead. He held back on the impact, though, not wanting to do any permanent damage if he didn't have to.

The hit made a loud cracking sound when it landed, and the man fell to the ground like a sack of potatoes. Arthur didn't get a chance to make sure the guy was okay, however, because the other demons came at him now, too.

Arthur spun, ducking a swipe from a pick and using the axe handle to block a swing from a man wielding a metal rake. He kept backpedaling across the slick grass, putting distance between himself and the attackers.

They kept coming, though still in a haphazard and disorganized fashion. Arthur dodged and parried, moving backward and circling so that they couldn't group up and surround him. He found an opening and used the axe to trip up the woman with the pick. Another strike to the side of her head with the butt of the axe and she went silent as well. Blood ran down her forehead, but he felt fairly certain he hadn't hit her too hard.

Three demons left instead of five. More waited on the other side that he would need to deal with, and even though he was effective, it still took too long. The house remained silent, though, which didn't give a good sign.

The three demons still circled him. Arthur held up the axe, holding his stance, but they didn't approach. He didn't want to go against them because it would force him to give up his advantage.

"Come on," he said. "What are you waiting for?"

They didn't answer. Instead, as one, they turned toward Rose's home and sprinted for the front of the house. He knew what they'd gone after.

Niccolo.

The defenseless priest.

It looked like they recognized Arthur as just a waste of time and planned to end this a different way. Arthur glanced around and saw more possessed people running up the roads, and some of them came armed with rifles and handguns.

"Uh-oh," Arthur said, sprinting after them.

✳✳✳

"Keep them back," Niccolo shouted, closing his eyes and trying to regain his focus.

He tried to remember where he'd reached in the prayer before the distraction, but it proved nearly impossible to remember which line he'd gotten to. When the words flowed in order, they made perfect sense and held together with glue, but trying to pick one out of the middle became an impossible task.

He would need to start over with his incantation, which would cost them a lot of extra time. Time they didn't have to spare with an angry mob of possessed civilians bearing down on them.

"With what?" Jackson asked.

"I don't know," Niccolo shouted back. "Think of something!"

Another huge thud came at the back door, and this time, wood snapped and assailants tore their way into the kitchen.

This time, though, a deafening thud also sounded at the front door, much closer and louder. It seemed as if one of the demons stood out front beating on it with a baseball bat.

The sound and proximity startled Niccolo, and the bowl slipped from his grasp. The plastic fell to the floor and bounced around, spilling what remained of the holy water into the carpet.

Rose cackled. "Giving up, Priest? But we just started to have fun."

Niccolo's heart raced again, and panic settled in. All his confidence evaporated, washed away by the onslaught. Where had Arthur gotten to? Did he live, or had he got killed?

Were they all about to get killed?

"What do we do?" Jackson grabbed his arm and shook him. He stood there wild-eyed and terrified, and Niccolo doubted he looked much better.

"I don't know," he said. "They're coming from both sides."

"We need to—"

The front bay window smashed open from a hit with a golf club. The glass shattered and flew into the room, and a few shards clipped Niccolo painfully on his exposed skin.

Blood ran down his face, just under his eye. One of the possessed attackers climbed through the front window, ignoring the broken glass and cutting himself on the shards.

Everything had gone wrong. They had lost. It had finished, and they couldn't possibly complete the exorcism. His focus zeroed in on the man climbing through the window, carrying a golf club with murder in his eyes.

"Father Paladina," Jackson shouted. He spun, clutching the Bible to his chest, and he had his eyes wide open. "What do we do?"

Through it all, Rose just kept on cackling.

Suddenly, the man with the golf club went flying forward. He fell face first into the table in front of the couch and rolled sideways onto the floor.

Arthur came scrambling in behind him. He had wrapped his coat around his arms to protect against the glass and came in at speed but carefully.

He slid in, sure and focused in spite of everything. With not a hint of fear on his face, he drew his revolver and stood between Niccolo and the assailants.

Niccolo pleaded, "Don't kill them. They're innocent."

"I won't," Arthur said. "Not unless I have to. More are on the way, and we need to get out of here."

Niccolo heard the words, but they didn't process correctly in his mind. He couldn't think straight. Everything seemed muddied, and he realized he was about to die. It came as a sudden insight for him, but one of which he felt certain.

He was about to die.

But, if God planned that for him, then that made it all right.

The thought came unbidden, almost as if not his own

thought, and it carried with it strength and conviction. He had known when becoming a priest and exorcist that he might get called upon for a situation that could cost him his life in service of the Lord. He had always prayed that if that ever happened, he could face his death well.

It surprised him, though, to realize that as soon as he accepted his death, all fear went away. It felt surreal, and he embraced the confidence.

"I can't give up."

"We have already."

"I can do this."

"We've lost," Arthur said. "If we don't leave now, we won't get another chance."

If Niccolo left, he would have abandoned his faith. God had put him here and given him the tools to face down this demon, and if it became his duty to die, then so be it.

"I know," he said. "You two should go, but I can't leave. I won't."

Just saying the words gave him courage, and he calmed. A serene peace washed over him, and everything moved more slowly around him. The world had gone into slow motion.

"What?"

"You *must* go," he said. "Both of you. But I can't."

"You'll die if you stay," Arthur said.

"Then, I will die."

Niccolo turned to Rose, picking up his cross and focusing only on the demon in front of him. He pushed all other thoughts from his mind, isolating and separating it all. Too many came to face them all, but that didn't matter. He could only do what he could do, and that bade him exorcise the demon inside Rose.

Arthur and Jackson stood behind him, and the rest of the people continued to force their way into the room, but he blocked it all out. Would Arthur and Jackson leave? It didn't matter anyway. He blocked out everything except for the demon sitting on the floor in front of him.

"Hello, Rose."

✱✱✱

When he realized that Niccolo wouldn't leave the house willingly, Arthur growled in frustration. To get him out of here, he would need to drag him.

Which would prove nearly impossible with the swarm of

people trying to stop them. Dozens of them came, and they all attempted to get to Niccolo. The situation devolved at speed and had gone from dangerous to suicidal.

Yet, there Niccolo stood in the center of the room, staring at the old woman as though nothing else happened in the vicinity. The young priest stood chanting, exorcising the demon once again. Not loud this time, barely audible, yet still Arthur could hear every word.

So could the demon. Conviction and certainty weighted Niccolo's voice.

"Hasn't he heard the saying 'live to fight another day'?" Arthur mumbled under his breath.

Yet he couldn't suppress his respect for the priest. In the last few days, Niccolo had changed a lot, and for the better, in Arthur's estimation.

Arthur turned toward the front window. Another woman tried to crawl her way inside. He stepped over to the table, grabbed the errant golf club from the floor, and then used it to shove her outside. She fell backward into the bushes, and Arthur grabbed a corner of the couch.

"Help me!" he shouted to Jackson.

Jackson, though in a daze, snapped out of it when Arthur shouted at him. He rushed over, grabbed the other side of the couch, and together, they pushed it into place to block the window.

When Arthur turned back, he saw another man come around the corner from the kitchen. He ran straight toward Father Paladina with a raised pitchfork. Arthur raised his pistol, took aim, and fired at the man's kneecap.

The bullet hit, and the man fell with a scream, clutching at his knee.

"You shot him," Jackson said in shock.

"He'll get over it."

Golf club in hand, Arthur stalked over to the other doorway and took up position behind Niccolo, ready to hold everything at bay as long as he could.

✳✳✳

At first, it felt like a fire in the pit of Niccolo's stomach; gradually, it spread through his entire body. He chanted out the words of the Rituale Romanum. And though he didn't think about the words at all, they simply flowed out of his mouth. He opened himself up as a vessel, letting the faith take hold. All the while, he prayed to become an instrument, and it felt as though he stepped outside his body and stood watching everything happen rather than participating.

Gradually, his voice increased in volume and intensity, though not his intention for it to do so. The demon clutched at the chair next to it, trying to crawl away and making hissing and gasping sounds.

Then Niccolo remembered something from his last trip here. The doll, the one that had moved around. Demons used physical objects to strengthen their hold on their hosts, and he realized that the one-eyed doll had become such an object.

After turning, he rushed through the house to the room where he had seen it. Arthur shouted at him to stop, but he ignored the man. He rounded the corner and saw the myriad dolls on their shelves.

The one he searched for, with its red hair and missing eye, lay on the floor. The paint had faded, and its dress had torn. It still smiled, but now the grin looked sardonic and twisted.

He picked it up from the floor and rushed back out to the living room. "The salt!" he shouted. "Where is it?"

Jackson turned to him, dazed. Blood ran down his face, and he looked about to fall down, but he pointed toward the floor where the salt had fallen.

Niccolo dashed over to it. He dropped the doll and shook salt onto it. Where it touched the doll, it sizzled, and the gasping noises Rose made intensified. When he looked back at the old woman, all her confidence had gone. The demon grew furious and terrified, realizing what Niccolo was about to do.

"I will kill the woman," the demon said. "I will take her with me when I go."

Niccolo ignored the demon. "I need a lighter," he said, turning toward Arthur. "A lighter!"

Arthur stood facing off against a burly man wielding a shovel. Without turning to look at Niccolo, he slid a hand into his pocket, drew forth a lighter, and tossed it toward him.

Deftly, Niccolo caught it, falling back into the rites of exorcism. He knelt next to the doll, flicking the lighter to bring a flame to life, and then held it to her hair.

It combusted quickly and forced him to back away as it burned. In only seconds, the doll became a raging ball of fire on the floor, and then it had gone. It left behind only a pile of ash and dust.

With renewed focus, Niccolo turned his attention to the demon. It now looked terrified as it tried to crawl away. His words poured forth like a heavenly song, opening up inside him. No longer himself, he'd become just a vessel, locked in a battle of wills against this demon. It didn't stand a chance.

God stood on his side.

His voice reached a crescendo. The battle raged behind him, bringing shouting, gunfire, and screaming and yelling, but he blocked it all out.

At some point, Niccolo deviated from the rites in the Rituale Romanum, though he had barely any consciousness of doing so. He spoke other chants and verses. Words poured forth, entreating the demon, challenging it, and pressuring it. The intensity built until it reached a crescendo. Rose screamed.

"I will kill her!"

Niccolo closed his eyes, focusing all his energy into one final push. One moment of clarity came, through which he could reach out and touch the demon. He could show it God's love and forgiveness and prove to it with finality that it did not belong here.

"I will kill this vessel if you do not stop!"

"No," Niccolo said, opening his eyes and smiling. "You won't."

He reached forward, touched the old woman on the forehead, and with his finger, made the sign of the cross on her forehead.

Everything went quiet.

It happened instantly. He had expected a dramatic shout or scream like in the movies, but it proved the exact opposite.

Heavy breathing reached him, and he turned around to see Arthur and Jackson standing behind him. Arthur looked ragged and beat up, holding a golf club. Around him lay several unconscious people. Jackson appeared exhausted and barely able to keep his feet as he leaned against a couch, holding it up against a window.

The rest of the attackers all lay on the floor, out cold. Many of them looked like they hadn't even made it into the fray yet, and still, they lay unconscious. It had ended.

Everything had finished.

Arthur burst out laughing.

"Not bad, Priest," he said. "Not bad at all."

Epilogue

Arthur didn't plan on sticking around in Everett for long after things had calmed down and the exorcism had finished. He didn't want to linger in Rose's home when the authorities showed up. That never turned out as a good place to end up in his line of work.

Niccolo had done it, and that was impressive as hell. Usually, a priest in his situation would apprentice with a real exorcist for years before taking on one alone. This one had also happened under extreme duress. He didn't know many people who could stay calm in the face of something like this.

He couldn't stick around to congratulate him. The people of Everett would stay safe—though it would take months for things to return to normal—and the time had come for him to move on. He stayed long enough to help patch up the civilians he'd wounded in the fight. Arthur had half expected for Niccolo to chastise him for hurting some of them as badly as he had, but Niccolo didn't say a word.

He felt more relieved than he'd expected when they verified that all of them would live. Even the one who'd come through the window and cut himself badly, and the one he'd shot in the knee would be fine after a few months. Even Rose would survive, though with a broken hip; an incredible feat considering how long the demon had lived inside her.

Without the demon in Rose or Bishop Glasser here to anchor them, they had all lost their grip on the host. Arthur had no illusions about what had happened, though. Bishop Glasser left Rose here because the demon had remained too weak to travel with him, and all of this had brought a distraction to give him time to hide his trail. Though proud that they had saved the people of Everett, Arthur knew it would cost him quite a bit.

What he didn't know, however, was how the bishop had managed to summon so many demons in the first place. He had something, an artifact maybe, that was beyond anything Arthur had ever faced before. To bring in so many demons, even weak ones, like this was unthinkable, and he couldn't leave something so powerful in the hands of the bishop.

About an hour after everything had ended, he prepared to leave. He felt bad for the poor priests trying to explain what went down out here. The Church would send people to help cover everything up and create stories for why the people couldn't account for several days of their lives, and things would go back to normal.

The townsfolk would fill in the details, making up situations just to have some explanation of why they'd awoken injured at Rose's house. No matter how outlandish, if they believed the tales they told themselves, then nothing else mattered. Few of them would ever think "demon," and none of them would say it out loud.

Arthur had grown used to seeing this defense mechanism, and after a couple of stories in the newspapers, and a few weeks, the entire situation would become a distant memory for most of the people who had come here with their axes and bats.

Arthur stood packing up to leave when Niccolo and Jackson came out to see him. He had hoped to slip out before they noticed, but they seemed to have guessed his intention.

"What will you do now?" Niccolo asked.

"Find Bishop Glasser," Arthur said. "I don't know what he planned to do out here or what his end game was."

"What do you mean? It's over."

"No," Arthur said. "Whatever the bishop planned, it has only just begun. I need to stop him."

Niccolo hesitated, staring at Arthur for a long moment. "I'll come with you."

"No, you won't. You'll only slow me down." Arthur shook his head.

"Like hell I will," Niccolo said. "The bishop did this to these people. We all trusted him, and he betrayed that trust."

"That doesn't mean you're prepared for something like *this*."

"I'll talk to the Vatican and force you to take me along if I need to."

Arthur frowned. He realized Niccolo's words pointed mostly to a threat, but the fact that Niccolo had threatened at all and felt willing to put himself in danger reinforced the idea he'd had earlier.

Niccolo had changed a lot.

For the better.

"Fine," he said. "But do me a favor and stay quiet about it. We don't need to get the Church involved in any of this just yet. Take some time here, fix this with Jackson, and get your affairs in order, and then meet me in one week in Colorado."

"Colorado?" Niccolo asked.

"Yes," Arthur said. "I'll give you directions."

"Then what?"

Arthur climbed into the passenger seat and closed the door.

"Then," he said. "We'll go hunt down Bishop Glasser."

About the Author

Lincoln Cole is a Columbus-based author who enjoys traveling and has visited many different parts of the world, including Australia and Cambodia, but always returns home to his pugamonster, Luther, and wife. His love for writing was kindled at an early age through the works of Isaac Asimov and Stephen King, and he enjoys telling stories to anyone who will listen.